Abraham, Cyril
The Onedin Line. Complete and unabridged. Leicester, Ulverscroft.
v.
Large print ed.
Contents.- v.1. The shipmaster. - v.2. The iron ships. - v.3. The high seas. v.4. The trade winds.

I. Title. II. Title: The shipmaster. III. Title: The iron ships. IV. Title: The high seas. V. Title: The trade winds.

THE ONEDIN LINE
The Shipmaster

This saga of the Onedin family begins in Britain in 1860, a booming land of wealth and industrial skill, but the heyday of the great windjammers and clippers is waning. Steam and steel, and the men who can use them, are changing the faces of the seaports. James Onedin is a single-minded opportunist, he worships his ships, the schooner *Charlotte Rhodes* and the towering *Pampero*. He schemes and gambles with them to lay the foundations of the shipping empire he dreams of — the Onedin Line.

This Large Print Edition
is published by kind permission of
W. H. ALLEN & CO. LTD.
London
and
THE NEW AMERICAN
LIBRARY, INC.
New York

CYRIL ABRAHAM

THE ONEDIN LINE
The Shipmaster

Complete and Unabridged

ULVERSCROFT
Leicester

First published in Great Britain in 1972
by Allan Wingate (Publishers) Ltd., London

First Large Print Edition
published October 1978

DEDICATION
TO JOAN

Abraham, Cyril
The Onedin Line, the shipmaster. — Large print ed.
(Ulverscroft large print series: general fiction)
I. Title
823'.9'1F PR6051.B70

ISBN 0-7089-0219-7

Published by
F. A. Thorpe (Publishing) Ltd.
Anstey, Leicestershire
Printed in England

1

ELIZABETH ONEDIN sat dreaming in the Ladies Only compartment of a second class carriage of the Liverpool & Manchester Railway Company, Limited.

The Ladies Only compartment was an innovation somewhat frowned upon by the clergy, who could smell the sulphurous breath of the Tempter in the Company's pronouncements that on most lines certain carriages would be devoted exclusively to the use of female travellers and should, therefore, prove a source of comfort and convenience to wives and mothers visiting their loved ones.

Elizabeth, neither wife nor mother, appreciated the convenience but rather doubted the claims for comfort. Not for the first time she wished she had brought a cushion to soften the rigours of the compartment's wooden seats. And not for the first time she mentally damned brother Robert for so curtly bringing to an end her short annual visit to Auntie Lal and Uncle

Will Perkins. Auntie Lal was as fat as a barrel of lard and her brood of pasty-faced children seemed to take after her, while Uncle Will was as thin as a lathe with a balding tortoise head and slippery hands. But in spite of being a lay preacher and therefore given to solemnity he was not above looking after the creature comforts, even to the extent of the recent installation of a patent iron bath.

Elizabeth sighed at the memory of such luxury and then began to regret not having taken the advice of more seasoned travellers and sat with her back to the engine as she had on her outward, Liverpool to Manchester, journey. At Lime Street station a solicitous porter had found her a corner seat and, dazed perhaps by her pert prettiness, had quite forgotten to demand his quite illegal tip. At first she had quite enjoyed the sight of Liverpool, with its smoke and noise and dirt, receding into the distance, and as the endless patterns of fields fled past she longed to crane her neck and watch the future rushing toward her.

Now she had her wish. For the return journey she had chosen a corner seat facing the engine and for a few minutes had the luxury of a compartment entirely to herself. Thus it was little more than a minor irritation when a group of vinegar-faced ladies joined the train at the last moment to sit beady-eyed and disapproving of the ribboned straw hat perched impishly upon braided flaxen hair.

It was only after the train had left the outskirts of Manchester behind that Elizabeth became aware of a concerted sniffing from her travelling companions. Puzzled, she sucked in one or two experimental breaths but recognised nothing beyond the stale air of the compartment combined with the faint odour of moth balls. Realisation came when, turning her head, she met the united basilisk stares of the quartette opposite. She dipped her head and inhaled surreptitiously. Her nostrils twitched at the aromatic mixture of Eau-de-Cologne and Essence of Roses. Of course — her perfume. Delicate, but enough to bring the gaunt harridan opposite to purposeful feet. Ostentatiously, as though motivated by the combined wills of her companions, she seized the strap and lowered the window a foot.

Elizabeth's rising anger was immediately cooled by the ensuing gale which almost lifted her hat from her head and filled the carriage with smoke and smuts. Eyes smarting and stinging she clamped her lips together and the long Onedin nose pinched with suppressed rage.

She had not long to await revenge. In a moment or two, first one, then another of the ladies began to cough and splutter. The harridan once again came to her feet, snorted triumph, and yanked the window shut. Elizabeth just as promptly opened it again and then sat, obstinate and defiant, suffering a martyrdom of choking fumes, hot ash and gritty coal dust, but sustained by the snuffling and wheezing of the defeated vinegar-faces.

Mercifully the line changed direction before all were suffocated. The smoke plumed away to roll in nimbus clouds across meadow and pasture where toy cattle scampered for the safety of distant hedgerows and toy labourers raised tiny doll-hands in greeting. A fresh clean breeze blew into the compartment carrying with it the roar of the wheels and the distant panting of the pot-bellied engine ahead.

Elizabeth settled back, closed her eyes, and lost herself in her favourite reverie.

Daniel.

Daniel and Mrs. Fogarty.

Mr. and Mrs. Daniel Fogarty.

First she tried out all the combinations and permutations she could imagine. Then she conjured up Daniel's bearded face, the straight-looking, slightly puzzled brown eyes. "Monkey eyes," she often called him. "Brown monkey-eyes." The notion always seemed to amuse him and his face would crinkle into a grin of delight. He was a shy man, unused to feminine company. Sometimes she would deliberately set out to embarrass him for the pleasure of watching him shuffling and cawing in perplexity. At other times she would taunt him spitefully, waiting eagerly for the face to darken with anger and the jaw muscles tighten. There was something about the sheer muscular power of men that both exhilarated and frightened her; a dangerous contained energy that brought a prickle of strange excitement.

They were to be married. To-be-married-to-be-married-to-be-married, chattered the wheels. Promises had been exchanged and it was clearly understood that the moment Daniel was promoted to the top hat and frock coat of a ship's captain, the banns would be read.

She invariably started her reveries with the thought: "We are married. Daniel is away at sea. So, I . . ." Had she been given to introspection she might have thought it odd that Daniel Fogarty figured so remotely in these daydreams.

But it was a fine rich dream. A dream of a house with an endless number of rooms, each magically furnished and refurnished, over and over again.

"Daniel is away at sea. So, I . . ." She had just rung for tea. The tea service was of porcelain and silver. The parlour-maid neat, well-mannered and correctly obsequious. Outside the wind would be howling and the rain lashing at the window panes. But inside all would be still and quiet. Here, in her favourite dream-room, the fire would blaze redly, and the rich flock wallpaper and plum-coloured velvet curtains and rose patterned carpet and plush upholstered chairs would enfold her in their warm benison and keep her safe for ever and ever.

"Daniel is away at sea. So, I . . ." Instantly it is a calm summer's morning and the room magically transformed to delicate pinks and satins. She has drawn back the curtains and there, across the Mersey estuary, with sails as sharp as quills, is Daniel's homeward-returning ship. A rich man's treasure chest filled with good things.

The wailing banshee whistle of the train announced its imminent arrival at Lime Street station, and wrenched her all too soon back to harsh reality and the memory of the buff-coloured telegraph with its stark pencilled message:

"Return immediately. Father dying. Robert."

2

ELIZABETH'S shilling hansom threaded its way through the bustle of dock road traffic. Overhead ships' jib-booms thrust across the width of the road, almost touching the buildings opposite. A forest of masts stood against the skyline as far as the eye could see. Elizabeth contented herself with staring ahead at the rump of the plodding horse with what she conceived to be ladylike indifference to the bawling humanity about her. Surreptitiously she was counting her coppers. Four pennies, a sixpence, and a silver threepenny bit. One shilling and a penny. So be it. The man must be satisfied with a penny tip.

The hansom passed Salthouse dock, turned left into the narrow thoroughfare of Cotton Hey, and stopped outside the shop with its weatherbeaten signboard bearing the legend: "S. Onedin & Sons. Ship Chandlers."

Elizabeth stepped down from the cab,

spilled her money into the outstretched hand of the cabby, gave him her most brilliant smile, picked up her valise and hurried into the shop before the fool could recover his wits.

The shop was small and dark, the stock meagre. The all-too-familiar sour-sweet odours of tarred hemp, canvas, and linseed oil reminded her bitterly that this was home.

Robert looked up at the "ting" of the shop door bell, glowered across at Elizabeth, then returned his full attention to the customer he was serving. She was an Irisher by the look of her, wearing the long black knitted shawl and single gold earring that was the mark of her kind. Her man would wear the other. It seemed to be some sort of plight between them. As though, thought Elizabeth, four filthy, hollow-eyed, spindle-shanked brats clutching the drab's skirts were not plight enough already. She hated serving the creatures, forever whining and pleading for credit and not above thieving anything they could lay their hands upon. Robert, she knew, for all his shopkeeper's civility also despised the wretches and only longed for the day when the shop would be open to a better class of customer.

Elizabeth lifted her skirts and, keeping her distance as though in mortal dread of contamination, raised the counter flap and made her way to the back parlour.

Robert finished serving the woman with a pennyworth of ship's bread, a ha'porth of dried hamburg beef, and a scraping of lard, may it please your honour. He bowed her to the door, thanked her for her custom, and bade her a polite good-afternoon. Really, he thought as he closed the door behind her, the city seemed to be infested with riff-raff lately. He recollected a fine outspoken article in the *Liverpool Mercury* only that very morning: "The wild Milesian holding out his hat is the sorest evil this country has to contend with." Robert heartily endorsed the sentiment. In his considered opinion giving money to beggars merely aggravated the mischief. The *Liverpool Mercury* continued in its fine outspoken way to draw the attention of all honest hard-working Saxon citizens to the fact that, in this year of 1860, no less than £20,750–6–4 had been expended in outdoor relief on 50,000 Irish paupers. A situation not to be borne, etc.

Thinking of money reminded Robert that Elizabeth owed him sixpence for the telegraph he had been forced to send and that she had had the effrontery to drive from the station in a hansom cab, no less. Her extravagances passed his comprehension. He would deal with the little minx immediately.

A curtain concealed the door leading from the shop to the parlour. Robert twitched it aside and bawled a peremptory command for Elizabeth to come to the shop instantly.

His answer was an immediate and imperative knocking from the floor above.

He flushed in sudden embarrassment at his forgetfulness and his bovine features composed themselves into an expression of lugubrious piety. In the bedroom above his father lay dying. Lowering his voice to a sepulchral whisper he hissed:

"Elizabeth!"

Elizabeth, pausing on the landing at the head of the narrow stairway, heard his call. But, in no mood to listen to brother Robert and his everlasting complaints, she eased open the bedroom door and slipped inside like a bright-coloured shadow.

Inside the bedroom, Robert's wife, Sarah, was standing at the bedside, her fingers lacing and interlacing with anxiety. Elizabeth tip-toed forward and looked down at the shattered hulk of her father. His face had something of the look and colour of crumpled canvas. From time to time his eyelids fluttered open, but the eyes betrayed him, the mind now no more than a cocoon of faded memories, his breath a shallow whisper that seemed to rustle about the quiet room as though searching for one last tenuous hold upon the very walls themselves.

Elizabeth jumped, startled, as in one corner of the room a shadow moved in shadow. Coughed drily.

The Reverend Mr. Samuels glided forward, practised condolences shaping behind his lips. He glanced at Elizabeth's bright plumage with pinched disfavour before laying a comforting hand upon Sarah's shoulder and eyeing her swollen belly with the approval of a man who has already fathered ten.

"The Lord giveth, Mrs. Onedin, and

the Lord taketh away. His Will be done."

"Amen," responded Sarah, dutifully.

But a thousand thoughts were racing and tumbling through her mind. It was typical, simply typical, of Elizabeth to intrude at such a moment.

Sarah had long visualised the scene. Ever since, in fact, her father-in-law had been taken with the first seizure.

At his last moments she alone would be at his bedside. Elizabeth, whose very presence would drive the Angel of Death himself to distraction, would have been packed off somewhere, anywhere. Robert would be taking care of the shop below; and James would be away at sea. The presence of the Reverend Mr. Samuels was an unhoped-for bounty. A man of the Cloth, he could bear true Witness to those last touching moments when, in Sarah's mind's eye, the old man would reach out and take her hand. With his dying breath he would beg forgiveness for his past harshness toward her and Robert. For he had been such a miser, mean as ditch-water, counting every penny and treating dear Robert as dirt and both as slaves. And then, with his very, very last breath, he would summon enough strength to bequeath the shop to Robert. It was no more than common justice. Robert was the elder brother. The shop was his of right. It was theirs. Theirs! They had worked so hard. No one, no one should take it from them now! But there stood Elizabeth, reeking of perfume, dressed like a Thing from the streets and her great blue eyes filled with crocodile tears. Elizabeth had always been his favourite. Spoiled from birth. Temperamental. Wayward and selfish with no thought for anyone's wishes but her own. Oh, things would change once they had the shop. She would work for her bread and butter — Robert would see to that.

But if the old man should rally, however momentarily, and see Elizabeth? Sarah's heart froze at the thought. To be robbed of their birthright at this last moment? Oh, dear God, she thought, why, oh why doesn't he die?

Sarah realised that she had been holding her breath and that the Reverend Mr. Samuels' fingers had tightened upon her shoulder. Suddenly the room seemed to have acquired a strange stillness, a quietude, a seeming absence of sound. Dust motes hung in the hot August sunlight. Then the room swam into the green of a dream as Mr. Samuels' soft white fingers closed upon the tassel of the roller blind and gently drew down the shade.

"Let us pray," he intoned, "for the soul of the dear departed."

At that moment Robert was sweeping the pavement outside the shop. Not from any consideration of the sensibilities of passers-by but out of regard for the floor of the shop. Horse-droppings, rotting in the road and scattered on the paving, were more often than not carried into the premises and, trodden into the block flooring, were the very devil to remove. Elizabeth, he knew, hated the business of scrubbing out and usually skimped the work. Well, very shortly things would change. Elizabeth would learn to put her back into it or whistle a different tune.

A couple of barefoot ragamuffins trotted around the corner screeching at the top of their lungs. The elder of the two stopped suddenly and pointed upward. He shushed his companion with exaggerated reverence.

"Shut yer arse, Willie. There's a deader in there."

The pair turned and, round-eyed, tiptoed back to the roaring living world of the dock road.

Robert also looked up. The blank blind window stared down into the street. A sense of relief flooded through him.

"It's over," he thought. "It's over. The shop is mine."

He set his features into an expression of stern stoicism as, out of the corner of his eye, he caught a glimpse of his neighbour, Mr. Simpson, the butcher, approaching.

Mr. Simpson removed his hat and stood by Robert's side.

"A sad day, Mr. Onedin," he enunciated with funereal solemnity. "A sad day."

"Aye," agreed Robert. "A sad day for us all. But we were prepared, Mr. Simpson. We were prepared."

"A long illness, patiently borne," quoted Mr. Simpson. He nodded his head sagaciously. "He did not suffer, I trust?"

"He kept his faculties to the end," replied Robert ambiguously.

Mr. Simpson was fond of a good quotation.

"In the midst of life?"

"Ah," said Robert wisely. "Ah."

Mr. Simpson tried again.

"We shall not see his like again."

Robert nodded heartfelt agreement.

"True, Mr. Simpson. True."

"You'll give him a good send-off, then?" queried Mr. Simpson, angling for an invitation.

"You may be sure we'll do the best we can," responded Robert, thinking of the cost.

They stood side by side for a few moments. Two portentous men surveying their world. A gust of wind picked up a piece of tattered newspaper and playfully buffeted it along the street. Mr. Simpson sniffed the air.

"Wind's shifting, Mr. Onedin."

Robert nodded agreement.

"It'll bring rain, Mr. Simpson. Mark my words. It'll bring rain."

"And lay the dust," pronounced Mr. Simpson. "There's always a mercy in the hand of Providence."

Robert wagged his head with the wisdom of long experience.

"Bad for trade, Mr. Simpson. Bad for trade."

The butcher nodded non-committal assent and decided that his own business had been neglected long enough.

"He was a good man, your father. None better," he pronounced, by way of dismissing the subject, and strolled back to his shop.

Robert sucked in a breath and commenced to put up the heavy wooden shutters. It was inconvenient, very inconvenient, but the shop must be closed for a decent period of mourning. Certainly until the day after the funeral. At least it would give him time to take stock. Put one or two innovations of his own into practice. There was the signboard, for example. The very first thing he would have it repainted.

"Robert Onedin. Ship Chandler," he thought.

He slipped the iron bar into its slots, mulling over the wording. "Ship Chandler & Provision Merchant," perhaps? Yes, Provision Merchant held a ring of promise.

His father had been such a stick-in-the-mud, resentful of change, suspicious of progress. "Robert," he was wont to say, "was breeched too early and thinks he can teach an old dog new tricks." Old Samuel Onedin had held rigid views. "A place for everything, and everything in its place." "The cobbler should stick to his last, and the tradesman to his trade." Samuel Onedin's trade had been that of candle-maker. He was a candler; and thus he pronounced "Chandler" until his dying day.

Robert remembered those early days with bitterness. His father boiling the hot wax and he and young James moulding candles far into the night until the skin was burned from their fingertips; and Elizabeth squawling in the corner. Later she was taught to make tapers but, child though she was, soon rebelled. Face set in obstinate lines she made the tapers too short or too long and sometimes even twisted them into wild shapes of loops and coils. Their father was a harsh man and beat her savagely. But her screeches and shrieks had not been of fear but of the mad rage of the helpless. The following day every taper in the shop was found to have been rolled or hammered flat. For this she had been beaten again and then shut up in the attic on a diet of bread and water. She had responded by smashing the attic window and screaming the house down until a gang of roughs had congregated in the street outside and, convinced that a child was being murdered, threatened to burn down the shop and Onedin in it.

Robert grinned at the memory. Elizabeth always did have a talent for getting her own way. James, now, James was a different kettle of fish. James had always seemed quietly obedient to his father's wishes. He worked in the shop, ran errands, sat late at night to his task of candle-making — an obedient boy, two years Robert's junior, who worked with a sort of desperate quietness, regularly turning out his quota of candles and not a word of complaint. On James's thirteenth birthday he had appeared with a bundle consisting of clean shirt and stockings and calmly announced his intention of shipping as a boy aboard a westbound emigrant packet flying the red and gold Callon flag. Their father had started to remonstrate but James's hard pebble-eyes had stared him down. "Look elsewhere for your cheap labour, candler," he had said, and turned his back on the shop once and for all.

And now, ruminated Robert, James was a shipmaster and no doubt the apple of Callon's eye.

He made the padlock fast and looked along the street.

Mr. Jenkins, who owned the stables four doors away, was already scattering handfuls of straw upon the cobbles to deaden the horses' hooves. Robert made a mental note: Mr. Jenkins must also be asked to attend the funeral. He would speak to Sarah on the matter. But they really must try to keep the list of mourners as low as decently possible. Dying was such an expensive business. He had already chosen the coffin. Cheap, but of polished oak and with brass handles. Nothing tawdry about it. There would be four mutes, the undertaker and the undertaker's assistant. A two-horse hearse should be sufficient. There was something ostentatious about four great black horses pulling no more than the weight of a man. Two, perhaps three carriages. Robert decided he would be very firm about it. Then there was the matter of catering afterwards. Baked ham was an imperative. He would pick one up from the wholesaler and Sarah could boil it overnight and finish it off in the oven. Tea was no problem, there was a quarter chest of best Congou in the shop. Sarah could brew it weak and add a pinch or two of washing soda for body. Yes, he could safely leave that side of things to Sarah. She was a good wife. A wife any man could be proud of. Robert was imbued with a sense of well-being and complacency. On the day they first met she had been nothing but a skinny barefoot slip of a thing driving pigs to market. Who would have credited that today that same lost-looking waif would be wife to a man in his own way of business? Yes, he decided, that sign-board must come down. He would have a new one put up in its stead: "Robert Onedin. Ship Chandler & Provision Merchant."

Head busy with schemes of progress Robert entered the shop, pulled down the blind and barred and bolted the door behind him.

A puff of wind skirmished along the street again, skittishly lifting Mr. Jenkins's new-laid straw before just as quickly expiring with a faint sigh of regret as though the effort had been too great.

That same fitful wind had teased out a thin line of cloud far to the south and west. The cloud caught the eye of the masthead lookout of the brig *Maisie Rose*. Hailing the deck, he pointed to the starboard quarter.

James Onedin screwed his eyes against the sun's brassy glare and stared in the direction of the seaman's pointing arm.

"Where away?" he bawled.

The lookout depressed his arm.

"Sou' and west. Low down on the horizon."

James considered.

Liverpool lay ahead. But for the past three days the wind, blowing steadily from south and east straight down the funnel of the Mersey, had kept the *Maisie Rose* beating to windward. A distant cloud might herald a shift in wind. If so, it created a series of fresh problems. How best to take advantage? James looked at the rest of the ships scattered across the estuary, wheeling and clawing like a flock of gulls against an invisible cliff face. And the tide was on the turn. It would be ebbing shortly. No ship could hope to make headway against the Mersey river in full spate.

An outward bound clipper flying the red and yellow Callon pennant stormed down river. Braced sharp on the starboard tack, royals and staysails fast, white foam spewing from her bows, she dipped her houseflag in acknowledgment of the *Maisie Rose* and ran up a hoist of signal flags.

James squinted through his telescope and read off the signal: "Owner's code: Awaiting cargo. Advise steam tug."

This voyage had proved troublesome enough already and James was double damned if he would suffer the final indignity of being towed into port by some stinking sidewinder of a tug.

As Mr. Baines, the mate, bent on the answering pennant James swung himself into the shrouds and ran aloft hand over hand.

Sixty feet above sea level James's view of the horizon increased from four to nine miles. Fifteen feet above him perched the lookout. He pointed again and James scanned the horizon south and west. Sure enough there was a line of white cloud almost touching the rim of the sea. Taking the spyglass from his belt, James focused then searched further west, out toward Ireland. Something shone white and gold, reflecting back the sunlight. James steadied against the slow roll of the ship, focused with more care. The blob resolved itself into the anvil shape of cumulus cloud trailing its coat of rain. He exhaled a breath of satisfaction and snapped the telescope shut. The wind would come first, then the rain.

For a moment or two he indulged himself in the luxury of solitude. A segment of the world, his world, lay mapped before him.

The wrinkled surface of Liverpool Bay broke here and there about the sand spits of the Great Burbo Banks and the bubbling shallows of East Hoyle. The stubby thumb of the Wirral Peninsula jabbed at the narrow throat of the Mersey. On the other side lay the port of Liverpool. Even in mid-August a pall of coal-smoke overhung the city and stretched wind-plucked tenuous arms down river. Steam ferries fumed across the river, their churning paddles giving a curious illusion of black insects running across the water.

James had the odd sensation that he had

only to stretch out an arm and the entire world would be within his grasp.

A disputatious gull, screaming maniacally, settled at the end of the yard, bringing him out of his dream and back to the immediacy of the present.

His problem was one of mathematics and geometry. The geometry was to meet the incoming wind at precisely the correct point and then turn and run in like a surf rider gathering speed. The mathematics involved calculating the next turn of the tide so that the *Maisie Rose* would have wind and sea behind her. A strong sou'-wester would hold back the ebb, then the flooding tide should carry the ship safely over the sand spits and straight up the throat of the Mersey before the rest of the scattered flock of shipmasters could gather their wits.

His brain busy with calculations, he clambered down to the deck and stood beside the mate.

"Bring her around and wear ship, Mr. Baines, if you please," he said.

Baines may have been surprised but he never questioned an order.

"Ready about," he bawled. "Liven

yourselves, you pox-ridden longshoremen. Jump to it. Move!"

As the helmsman spun the wheel and put the helm up, Baines was among the crew, kicking, cursing, cuffing.

Too exhausted for resentment the hands hauled in the spanker sheets, braced the yards, the foretopmen and maintopmen straggling along the deck to clamber tiredly aloft.

The ship spun on her heels and reached for the open sea.

3

THE funeral took place at three o'clock on Thursday afternoon beneath lowering skies and a drum-beating downpour of rain which, despite the sheltering umbrellas, soaked the mourners to the skin and depressed their spirits to a uniform quality of abysmal misery.

Robert and Sarah, squelching unhappily behind the coffin on its seemingly interminable journey from the lych gate to the chapel, clung to each other like two survivors from a shipwreck. Behind them Elizabeth hissed her displeasure and clutched the more tightly to Uncle Will Perkins's supporting arm. Uncle Will Perkins, a stern moralist, froze at the unmistakable feminine pressure and firmly put aside sinful thoughts. His head bent as though from a hinge, he walked with the rigidity of an automaton and accepted the rivulets of water trickling down his spine as both a benison and a warning from the

Almighty. Cousin Wilberforce Onedin, forty years a bachelor, escorted Aunt Annie Wagstaffe who, hobbling with the aid of a silver-topped ebony cane, reminisced at length of past funerals and gave off an odour of lavender and peppermint humbugs.

Behind them straggled the lesser lights. Neighbouring shopkeepers, including Mr. Simpson and Mr. Jenkins each wishing he had sent a wreath and a card by way of condolence instead of risking pneumonia by traipsing behind the coffin of a man whose lifetime seemed to have been spent in quarrelling with his fellows. Mr. Simpson sneezed violently and Mr. Jenkins bugled into his handkerchief. "Like father, like son," he thought, gazing through rain-stung eyes at Robert's hunched back. "Every ounce as mean as his father," and Mr. Jenkins's hopes of hot spiced rum toddy after the funeral took a melancholic turn for the worse.

The bell ceased clanging its monotonous dirge as they thankfully entered the chapel. Trooping down the centre aisle and shuffling in order of precedence along the first two pews, they lowered themselves to their knees in attitudes of prayer. The Reverend Mr. Samuels divested himself of cloak and gloves and passed them to the verger before mounting the steps to the pulpit.

Aunt Annie Wagstaffe stealthily fished for another mint humbug. Cousin Wilberforce Onedin whooped and hawked, looked about him hopelessly for a spittoon and finding none erupted into his handkerchief. Uncle Will Perkins inflated his nonconformist nostrils to their fullest extent and sniffed for the slightest suspicion of the telltale reek of incense. Mr. Simpson chopped off a sneeze in mid-flight and almost exploded as a consequence, and Mr. Jenkins concluded that surely the least that could be expected from Robert would be a nine-shilling cask of ale.

The Reverend Mr. Samuels shivered in the chapel's dank air, listened to the rain rattling upon the roof tiles and chose as his text: "What profit hath he that hath laboured for the wind?" Ecclesiastes. Ch. 5, v. 16. He considered the text particularly apt for a seafaring community and especially so when addressed to a congregation of tradesmen whose livelihoods depended upon the Godsent winds of the sea. He began by extolling the virtues of thrift as practised by the deceased, praised his industry, and assured the sorrowing family that their father would be welcomed into everlasting life.

He continued with the parable of the good seed and the bad seed, stressed the importance of good husbandry, urged them to praise a beneficent Providence for its manifold blessings, reminded them that to every purpose there is a time and judgement, and warned them to beware of the idolatrous practices of the Ritualists and Tractarians.

Uncle Will Perkins folded his arms and nodded stern approval, while outside the sun at last broke through the towering banks of thundercloud and the rain turned golden and ran down the roof like silk.

The mourners trooped along to the open grave with its mound of raw red clay and the slate headstone bearing the inscription:

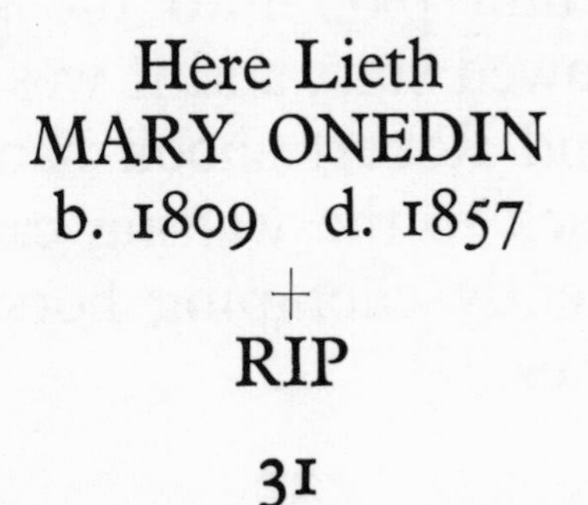

As Samuel Onedin was lowered to join his wife and Mr. Samuels intoned "In the midst of life we are in death," Sarah wept copiously, Robert stared stonily at his boots and Uncle Will Perkins's lips moved in silent repetition to count and test every word like a man suspicious of spurious currency, and Elizabeth raised her eyes to look directly into the bearded face and pale blue eyes of a tall young man who seemed to have arrived from nowhere to stand at her side. He carried a tarred stove-pipe top hat and wore a black frock coat and a high collar that seemed to be in danger of choking him.

She mouthed "James!" and the apparition grinned and winked before resolving its features into a grimace of staid solemnity.

"Ashes to ashes, dust to dust," droned the Reverend Mr. Samuels, and Robert, scooping up a handful of wet clay, dropped it with a dull plop into the grave. The others followed suit; and it was over.

James and Robert shook hands and led the way back to the waiting carriages and the impatiently chomping horses nodding black plumes.

"We berthed two hours ago," said James. "I heard the news and came straight away." He handed Sarah and Elizabeth into the carriage. "When did it happen?"

Robert climbed in and sat beside his brother.

"Three days ago," said Sarah, and dabbed at her nose with a black linen handkerchief.

"It was a seizure," said Robert.

"A stroke," corrected Sarah. "The third. It took him in the night. We were with him until the end. It is a great pity," she added, "that both sons could not have been present. I am sure it would have brought great comfort to him."

James grinned his crooked grin. "I'm afraid even I could not sail a ship into the wind, even to oblige Father. And in the event I daresay my presence would have hastened rather than hindered his departure."

Sarah looked shocked. "James! Your own father!"

James sniffed. "He was a cantankerous old devil, there's no gainsaying it." He turned to Robert. "Did he leave much?"

Robert had the grace to look embarrassed and allowed Sarah to answer for him.

"Just the shop," said Sarah, speaking more sharply than she intended. One never knew with James which way the cat would jump.

"To Robert," added Elizabeth, maliciously. "And a word of advice for you."

"In which case," said James, "he seems to have left little of value to anyone."

"He said," said Elizabeth, "that a man who walks a twisty lane will travel far, but arrive at the same destination at the end."

James sniffed disparagement. "There spoke a man with little sense of direction." He addressed himself to Robert again. "Without Father to hold you back you should be able to expand the business, Robert."

Robert shifted uneasily, the old familiar resentment returning. It was easy for James to hand out advice, it didn't cost him anything. So Robert spoke rather curtly.

"One step at a time, James. One step at a time. I'm well satisfied with things as they are."

James eyed his brother with exasperation. The fool could never see beyond his nose.

"You shouldn't be," he said. "They are building ships two hundred and more feet in length and clad in iron . . ."

"It's monstrous and flying in the face of providence," snapped Sarah, taking Robert's part. "Iron," she pronounced with the air of one making an unassailable point, "was never made to float."

James wasn't listening. His eyes seemed to be looking into a distant future.

"Sixty hands to crew them and every man jack to be fed. Acres of sailcloth. Miles of cordage. Now is your chance, Robert. Take it."

Robert shook his head. "The Owners could never be persuaded to buy from a little man like me. Nor could I afford fancy kickbacks to ships' captains."

"On the west coast of America there is a place called Sacramento where they pay as much as twenty gold pieces for a cask of flour. Think of the profit, Robert," he urged. "Think of the profit."

"Think of the losses," replied Robert. "The ship that carries the flour must round the Horn; and on that passage losses are heavy. You should know that as well as any, James." He spoke heatedly. James snorted his contempt.

"Weak ships and weak men. Give me a ship — one well-found ship — and I'll make your fortune, Robert."

Robert was growing angry. James spoke as though ships and merchandise could be conjured from the air.

"There is a sight more to business than just plain buying and selling," he said, putting — he hoped — an end to the conversation. "You may take my word for it."

James swallowed his irritation. He held out one open hand.

"I buy." He held out the other. "I sell. Wherein lies the profit?"

Robert pointed. "In between, of course."

James shook his head firmly, brought both cupped hands together.

"No, Robert. The profit lies with the man who possesses. The Owner makes the profit. Not the employee, however well paid."

"Aye," said Robert sourly. "And stands to lose most."

James's exasperation was growing. He

spoke as though his mouth was filled with grit.

"The man who has nothing, loses nothing; and lies in a poor man's grave to prove it."

Sarah was shocked. "Really, James! To speak so of your own father!"

Elizabeth's eyes held a hint of mockery. "Will you be the better for lying in a rich man's grave, James?"

James looked down his long nose and sniffed disdainfully.

"Aye. For I'll have earned it."

The carriage creaked and bounced across the worn cobbles fronting the Goree Piazzas. Gulls, remote and baleful, white familiars vented by the wind, wheeled and screamed their demoniac cries. James lowered the window and poked out his head.

"Stop here, coachman," he called, opened the carriage door and hopped down into the street. "I have business to attend to," he announced, and as the driver flicked his whip and clucked at the horse, he turned on his heel and walked purposefully past ale houses and spirit vaults, chandlers and corn merchants, to a pillared portal stained with soot. A polished brass plate set in the wall announced that these were the premises of:

CALLON & COMPANY
Shippers
Shipping Brokers
Shipping Agents

A Disaster Beggar sat with his back against the wall, exhibiting scars and mutilations proclaimed, by a placard hung about his neck, to be the result of shipwreck. James ignored the rattling tin cup just as he ignored the street musician standing barelegged and bareheaded in the gutter, scraping at a fiddle. Two doxies clamoured and spat over possession of a moon-faced drunken seaman, and a runner herded a family of frightened emigrants toward the doorway of a festering lodging house. The familiarity of the scene did not even impinge upon James's consciousness as he took the whitened stone steps two at a time, received a salute of recognition from the one-armed porter, and climbed two flights of stairs to the shipowner's head office.

4

AGNEW, Callon's chief clerk, left his dais and scurried down to shake James by the hand. The rows of clerks, seated at long counters, bent their heads more industriously over their ledgers, scratching and scraping, copying bills of lading, cargo manifests, contracts of affreightment, charter party documents, dock warrants and warehouse-keepers' certificates; the thousand and one contracts and notes and letters and bits and pieces of paper necessary before a ship could set sail, or having sailed, return to port and discharge its cargo.

Agnew was a bowed greybeard of wire-framed spectacles and an unrivalled knowledge of the business of every shipowner in the port of Liverpool. Obsequious to his betters, a tyrant to his inferiors, he controlled the office with the steely discipline of a man-of-war.

"Mr. Callon will see you immediately,

Captain Onedin. This way, if you please, sir."

James grunted acknowledgment and followed Agnew up the short flight of stairs to the small landing outside Callon's inner sanctum. Agnew tapped politely and ushered James inside.

Mr. Callon came to his feet, dismissed Agnew with a nod and motioned James to a chair.

James's employer was a broad-shouldered, broad-faced man. At 58, thirty years James's senior, he wore a suit of heavy serviceable broadcloth and a gold Albert looped across a distended paunch. He had blackened teeth, a spatulate nose and angry black eyes like two currants in a bun, the whole face being framed by gingery mutton-chop whiskers. He set a bottle and a glass before James.

"Ye'll take a glass of Jamaica, Cap'n Onedin."

It was a command as much as an invitation and James, who detested rum, thought it politic not to refuse. He poured and formally wished his employer good health.

Callon had returned to his chair behind

the massive desk. He sniffed acknowledgment and scowled at the ship's papers before him.

"You were overdue, Captain?"

James nodded. This, he knew, was but a preliminary skirmish. The worst was yet to come.

"We left Lisbon eighteen days ago," he said. "It hasn't been a passage to boast about. Head winds all the way and we were kept beating to windward off the Bar for the past three days."

Callon grunted. It was an old story. The wind that blew a ship into port was not likely to blow it out again. He made a pretence of inspecting the ship's papers once more.

"Full cargo, I see?"

James was tired. He had had no sleep for the past seventy-two hours and precious little before that. Nor did he care for cat-and-mouse games; particularly when he was cast in the rôle of the mouse. He therefore answered shortly and with an edge of irritability.

"Wine. Hides. Sheepskins. And a thousand cases of Seville oranges. But we are sprung forrard, I'm afraid, sir. We've been manning the pumps since five days out."

Callon glared. "Sprung forrard! Ye've been driving her too hard, man!"

The charge was unjust and both knew it.

"In your service, sir," James reminded him, coldly.

"May heaven preserve me from such service," snapped Callon. "More damned expense. An Owner's hand is never out of his pocket, these days."

"She's riddled with worm below the waterline." James spoke stiffly, bottling his anger with an effort. "I drew the matter to your attention in my last report, sir."

"And yet, knowing this, you drove her hard?" Callon raised anguished eyes imploring heaven to bear witness.

"You required a fast passage," said James flatly. He was tiring of the game. Callon had taken a calculated risk, gambling on fair winds and an easy passage. The gamble hadn't paid off. Ranting and raging could not alter the fact one iota.

Callon thumped the desk. "Confound you, sir. Of what benefit is a fast passage if you return with a ship half filled with water and a ruined cargo? I tell you now, Captain Onedin, that a like repetition will cost you dear. There is no room in my service for incompetents." He huffed, fished out his watch, scowled at the dial as though defying it to mislead him and snapped it shut. James stifled a yawn by taking a careful sip of the rum. He could not for the life of him understand how any man in his right mind could acquire a taste for the stuff. Its cloying sweetness sickened him. Callon's face, he noticed, was mottled with rage. The man was a fool, he thought. God, if only he had a ship of his own. Just one ship. He'd show Callon and his kind a trick or two. He became aware that Callon was talking in a more conciliatory tone.

"One day," he was saying. "One day we'll have you master of a western ocean packet, eh? Suit ye better than the Portuguee wine trade, I warrant, eh, eh?"

James was totally unmoved. Callon's pie-in-the-sky promises were as well known as his roaring and bellowing. A firm believer in the whip and the carrot, he would first berate some unfortunate subordinate, either reducing him to a nerve-strung wreck or tempting the more intransigent into fighting a losing battle; then, having assessed the victim's value to the company, would hold out the promise of riches to come. There was but one response: a suitable expression of gratitude, an admission of sin, and a promise to prove worthy of Mr. Callon's faith and trust.

James ignored the bait by saying, "Senhor Braganza sends his compliments, sir, and begs to remind you that his contract will be due for renewal in seven weeks' time."

"I had not forgotten." Callon smiled as affably as he could. "I shall have Agnew write directly. We must take good care of the Seenyor, eh? That Portuguee wine shipper is our bread and butter."

James agreed politely. There was enough truth in the statement to make sense. Callon & Company had six ships on the Lisbon run. Two brigs and four topsail schooners; and the trade was increasing. James had a strong respect for his employer's business ability. First, by means of the wine trade, he had obtained a foothold in Lisbon. Then his ships crept along the Portuguese and Spanish coast picking up cargoes wherever obtainable — and heaven help the master who returned with a ship not loaded to the gunwales. Now Callon was increasing the tonnage of his fleet, replacing the schooners with the larger and faster brigs. But although the wine trade — and the growing ancillaries — were undoubtedly the firm's bread-and-butter, the cake, as James well knew, was earned on the western ocean emigrant trade. Even though the newfangled, steam-assisted sailing ships made the crossing in half the time and at ten times the comfort, the rates were higher — £8–16–0 by steamer as against £3–10–0 by sailing ship. The poor had no choice and could be packed like herrings. The boom days of the mid-fifties were over but there were still fat profits to be made from ships outward bound with a cargo of scabrous humanity and back again with cotton and linseed oil. There seemed to be no end to the rain of gold that poured into the counting houses of shipowners like Callon & Company. This was a time of expansion and James felt again the sense of urgency that was never far from him lately. *The man who possesses is the man who makes the profits.* The words rang through the corridors of his mind like distant echoing bells.

Callon had leaned back in his chair and was lighting a cigar with the self-satisfied air of a man who has brought a difficult interview to a successful conclusion.

"I am afraid there'll be no bonus money for you this voyage, Onedin." He smiled hypocritically. "I am giving you the *Starling* while the *Maisie Rose* is being refitted. You sail in seven days' time."

The interview was at an end.

"Thank you, sir," said James, rising to his feet.

Callon shook hands. "Agnew will attend to you on your way out."

James nodded and left the office, closing the door quietly behind him.

Agnew was waiting, neat little piles of sovereigns and silver before him.

"Twenty-two pounds, twelve shillings and sixpence. If you will sign here, Captain Onedin, sir?"

James counted carefully, swept the money into his leather money pouch, and scribbled his signature on the proffered receipt. He calculated swiftly. This should bring his total savings to one hundred and seventy-five pounds. At this rate he would be long in the tooth and grey in the beard before he could afford a ship of his own. He bade good-day to Agnew and walked away from the desk. A couple of posters beside the door caught his eye. One extolled the virtues of shipping by Callon & Company, the other read:

—TO BE SOLD—
by
AUCTION

The SCHOONER
CHARLOTTE
RHODES
—of—
220 tons BURTHEN
Built at a COST of
£2,800
To Carry 570 TONS
DEADWEIGHT

Requires No Ballast
Sails Fast in Light Winds

—To be AUCTIONED—
On Behalf of
CAPTAIN J. WEBSTER
Of 12, Sailmakers Row
—at—
Duke's Yards on August 28th 1860

He tore the notice from the wall and tucked it under his arm. Agnew waited until the door closed behind James, eyed the blank space, and then hurried across to impart his news to Callon.

5

THE living-room behind the shop had been given the status of parlour and as a consequence seemed to suffer from a loss of confidence in its own identity. A tall Welsh dresser leaned uneasily against one wall as though it had arrived unexpectedly and was unsure of the length of its stay. From time to time mysterious rumblings would set its fringe of crockery to jigging a tinkling ghostly dance, and puffs of soot would tumble down the chimney to spark the embers into flickering fireflies of light. The gas jets burned with spears of yellow flame and added their heat to that of the August night. A cloth of dark green rep covered the baking table and a centrepiece of artificial flowers added a tawdry air to the remainder of the furnishings: two awkward armchairs and a horsehair sofa garnished with thread-bare magenta velvet, a rush-seated rocking chair that emitted plaintive squeaks of dismay at human contact, and a scattering of plush-upholstered chairs with backs as straight as ramrods, upon one of which sat Uncle Will Perkins, his waxen face gleaming with pallid beads of perspiration, his hands dangling between his knees and slithering one over the other like pale white eels.

The men were grouped in a corner. Cousin Wilberforce's wan consumptive features were highlighted by two burning spots on each cheek and occasionally he would heave himself upright as though jerked on strings to shatter the drone of conversation with an earsplitting cough, afterwards furtively expectorating into one of his many handkerchiefs. Mr. Simpson overflowed his chair like some strange black treacle mannikin petrified into immobility. He was waiting for Robert to finish his peroration in order to introduce his favourite topic — the iniquitous rate of taxation which, at 9d in the pound, was — in Mr. Simpson's strongly held and often expressed view — well on the way to ruining the country.

Mr. Jenkins was well contented. Robert had done them proud. Two quarts of quite good ale, a hot rum toddy to ward off the flux, and a glass of Malaga to toast the deceased; all rested pleasantly in Mr. Jenkins's stomach and left him with a sense of general good fellowship to the world at large.

Aunt Annie Wagstaffe had long since been hoisted into a cab and, reeking of rum and mint humbugs, been packed off to her lair at Litherland from whence she only emerged at tidings of birth, marriage, or death.

Robert, leaning against the overmantle, a cigar in one hand, a glass of Malaga in the other, was holding forth on trading prospects for the future. There was no doubt, in his considered opinion, that England was embarking upon an era of prosperity. Gladstone, in his considered opinion, knew what he was about. Mr. Gladstone was, in Robert's considered opinion, the best Chancellor of the Exchequer this country had ever had, and Mr. Cobden's free-trade policy showed which way the wind was blowing. To which avowal Mr. Simpson, a Protectionist to the core, honked disapproval.

Elizabeth and Sarah had cleared the table of the funeral meats, scones and seed cake and now sat side by side upon the sofa, each wrapped in her own private world of dreamy thoughts.

Sarah thought of the child growing inside her. They would call it Samuel and it would be the luckiest baby ever born to have Robert for a father and to eventually inherit a flourishing business.

Elizabeth brooded uneasily. After marriage women became swollen and had babies. If she married Daniel would she become as monstrously misshapen as Sarah? The idea was unthinkable. She had carefully and obliquely canvassed the Reverend Mr. Samuels' opinion which did little to enlighten her. He had quoted scripture: "Children are an heritage of the Lord; and the fruit of the womb is His reward." He had also pronounced that it was God's decree that women should bring forth children in pain and anguish; an asseveration which did little to comfort her. She decided that she would pray regularly to God not to send her a baby until she and Daniel had been married for a long, long time. She pushed the thoughts into the lumber room of her mind, firmly closed the door upon them and, Robert's voice beating like surf upon her ears, settled down to her favourite reverie. "We are married. Daniel is away at sea. So I . . ." But somehow this time the dream eluded her and the memory of Daniel intruded more and more. She remembered how once, on the way to Divine Service, she had stumbled and Daniel had put out a supporting arm and his hand had closed upon her breast, squeezed so gently, and her heart had churned its way into her throat and her mouth burned dry in an instant. She recaptured the sensation and her heart fluttered again; it had been a strange experience; agreeable; exciting; but oddly frightening. She planned on Daniel's return to manoeuvre him into a repetition of the incident. As the house refused to return to her dreams she concentrated on what she would wear for the occasion. A dress of fine lawn, cut low to show. . . . She gulped and flushed crimson at the thought and raised her eyes to meet Uncle Will Perkins's fishy stare. Uncle Will Perkins noticed the blush, hurriedly averted his eyes and prayed fervently for release from lusts of the flesh.

Robert, sensing that his discourse was heading toward the dangerous shoals and shallows of political discussion, abruptly altered course in mid-stream and trimmed the sails of his conversation to the prevailing winds of general approval. It was his considered opinion, he stated firmly, refilling their glasses, that the labouring classes were their own worst enemies. As no one seemed disposed to challenge this observation he added heatedly — and didn't care a tuppenny who heard him say it — that drink was their downfall. If the poor would only practise the virtues of thrift and frugality and spend their wages with honest tradesmen, instead of squandering their substance in ale houses and gin palaces with the result that they were continually whining for credit then, in Robert's considered opinion, the country as a whole would be the better for it: money was made to circulate and who the more likely to turn principle into practice? Sound plain-dealing shopkeepers such as themselves, or rapacious publicans who waxed fat on the misery of those unfortunate indigent starvelings?

"Emigrants is the worst," pronounced Mr. Simpson. "Droves of 'em." He waved a hand expansively, encompassing the entire city of Liverpool. "Scottishers and Irishers."

"Irishers is the worst of all," interjected Mr. Jenkins knowledgeably.

"To them that hath it shall be given. From them that hath not it shall be taken away," quoted Uncle Will Perkins, and lapsed into his former attitude of doleful introspection.

"Exactly," said Robert, warmly. "I couldn't have put it neater myself. 'From them that hath not it shall be taken away.' Scripture," he explained to his audience. "The emigrant class do not all arrive empty-handed. Many have a pound or two saved toward their passage. But hardly a one sets foot in my shop." My shop. The words had slipped out and not so much as an eyebrow raised in contradiction. Robert was suddenly imbued with a pride of ownership that inflated his chest like a balloon. He realised that for the first time in his life he was speaking to his fellow merchants as an equal. No longer was he interrupted or ignored; now they listened to him with the polite respect due to a compeer. The shop was his! To do with as he chose! No more explaining, hoping, apologising, begging, pleading. He was free at last! And with the realisation came an urge to be rid of their silly vacuous faces and rush into the shop to count, to touch, to fondle every article of trade, every commodity, as though only by actual contact could he finally establish the reality of possession. He owned it! And not only the shop, but the very building itself — the bricks and mortar, the leaking roof, the creaking stairs, every room and every stick of furniture and no one to gainsay him.

He became aware that their faces were turned toward him, waiting for him to continue the argument, long familiar to them all. The emigrants had a little money but long before it could find its way into the tills of local shopkeepers the poor wretches were mercilessly exploited and robbed by lodging-house keepers and so-called commission agents with their gangs of bully-boys. Robert opened his mouth and closed it again, struck with a sudden brilliance of thought: tomorrow — the very first thing tomorrow — he would approach one of the commission agents and offer to pay him his five per cent in return for steering the emigrants to his shop. He could easily recover the cost by simply adding five, or even six per cent to the price of goods.

He was saved from prevarication by Elizabeth who, yawning indelicately, inquired, "Where on earth can James be?"

6

JAMES was returning home. There was an air of despondency about the slump of his shoulders and the hang of his head. He was tired, dog-tired, and his brain no longer seemed able to function with any sort of clarity. He walked unseeingly with a loose shambling gait, his gaze fixed in mindless curiosity upon his feet which, darting alternately into view like two sleek black fish endlessly overtaking one another, had the effect of numbing his mind into a strange unthinking placidity. It was only when he bumped into a lamplighter shouldering his long bamboo pole with its curved hook and glowing wick that he realised that he was hungry and thirsty and had not eaten since breakfast.

A creaking signboard stained with the winds of the sea announced the presence of "The Whaleboat Inn". James pushed open the door and stepped inside. The atmosphere was close and stifling and thick with the reek of tobacco smoke. Negroes, Lascars and Chinamen rubbed shoulders with Scandinavian, German, American and English seamen. Dockland harlots squawked and shrieked like so many brightly-coloured parakeets. A group in the middle of the floor, led by a ship's shantyman, were singing the plaintive fore-bitter "The Widow Malone" while a one-legged ancient spun dexterously upon his wooden leg in time with the tune. The shantyman had a powerful and melodious voice which rang across the room:

> "So lovely the Widow Malone,
> Ohone!
> So lovely the Widow Malone.
> From the Captain down
> To the scum of the town,
> Everyone's . . ."

Roared the sailors:

> "Everyone's courting the Widow Malone.
> Ohone!
> Everyone's courting the Widow Malone."

James skirted the group, made his way past the long deal table to a railed-off area reserved for the quality customers. He sat at a small table, ordered a brandy and hot water, a pot of best ale and a portion of beefsteak pie with potatoes and cabbage. Waiting for the order to be filled he lit one of his favourite long thin black cigars, stretched out his legs and mulled over the day's events.

He had left Callon's office burning with anger and indignation, the poster tucked beneath his arm, and immediately stepped out smartly for Duke's Yards. They lay by Wapping Basin and his first sight of the *Charlotte Rhodes* sank all his hopes and confirmed his worst fears.

Her keel must have been sitting on the mud for she leaned helplessly against the granite wall of the quay as though the effort of pulling herself upright had been too much. She had a forlorn and lost look about her and bird droppings had limed her decks and masts until the ship seemed to be in a state of petrifaction. Her decks were a squalid mess of offal, rubbish, and an agglomeration of broken boxes, old rope and rotting canvas. She was a sorry sight and, to James's seaman's eye, little more than a rotting hulk ready for the breaker's yard.

He walked away and then looked back.

The *Charlotte Rhodes* had fine lines, there was no doubt about it. The cutwater was designed to slice through water like a knife and the sea must have run sweetly beneath her counter.

James paused and then walked slowly back.

He stood for a long time, hands clasped behind him, head thrust forward, the long Onedin nose pinching and whitening with the effort of concentration. His gaze wandered slowly, slowly over the ship and in his mind's eye he visualised her as she once was, as she might be. Rerigged. The slack shrouds tautened and the rotting ratlines renewed. New bowsprit and topmasts. For a ship of her size she must have been designed to carry a mass of canvas. Big fore-and-afters. Gaff rigged on the mizzen. Jibsails booming and square topsails bellying in the wind. James unrolled the auction poster and read it again: "Sails fast in light winds". By God she would. Such a ship would give the *Maisie Rose* a run for its money. The spark of an idea flickered in James's mind, then died again. First, the reality.

A rusted iron ladder was set in the quayside. He clambered down and stepped on to the canted deck slippery with slime.

A tatterdemalion figure emerged from a dark recess at the break of the poop. One eye was sightless, the other glared spitefully at the intruder. The apparition wore a ragbag collection of evil-smelling clothes. An appalling limp made him move crabwise across the deck. James turned his blue pebble-eyes upon the wreck.

"You'll be the shipkeeper," he said.

The man craned his head and cupped a hand to one ear. James could now see that one side of the man's face had been smashed to pulp. From the sightless eye down to what had once been a chin the flesh was ridged and puckered, and the jawbone seemed to have disappeared into his mouth. James felt neither compassion nor aversion. He had seen many such. The shipkeeper was probably a seaman who had fallen from aloft and lived to tell the tale. Somehow he had found himself a temporary sinecure as watchman aboard the ship. Understandably he would be resentful of intruders.

James took a shilling from his pocket and held it out. He spoke clearly and distinctly, giving the man a chance to lip-read. "Your keys, if you please, shipkeeper."

The shipkeeper took the shilling, rummaged beneath his patchwork garments, and produced a bunch of keys held together by a short length of signal halyard. James took the keys and noticed that the halyard had been neatly spliced into a loop and finished with an American whipping. The man had probably taken his tumble aboard a Yankee blood-boat. The one eye still glowered its hatred, but the hand holding the shilling knuckled a forelock deferentially. Sounds came from the side of the twisted mouth, a husky wobbling burble which James liberally translated as "Thankee, Cap'n, sir," but for all he knew, or cared, could equally have been a curse. He nodded dismissal and set off on his tour of inspection.

James unlocked the padlock fixed to one of the iron battens holding the threadbare hatchcovers in position. He knocked out half a dozen wedges, peeled back the single tarpaulin and heaved one of the hatch-boards to one side. A stench, rank and foetid as though from the Pit, rose from the hold and sent him back coughing and choking. He threw off a couple more hatch-boards and went in search of a lantern.

He made his way forrard to the fo'c'sle head where the ship's stores would normally be kept. On his way he stamped hard on the deck planking. Once or twice he paused to scrape away the filth with his knife. The seams were open, but that was a small matter, they could easily be recaulked. The planks were of oak and seemed sound enough.

Beneath the fo'c'sle head another padlock held a temporary wooden door in place. James fished for a key and, lifting down the door, poked his head inside.

The smell, although damp and stale, held a familiar odour: the rich sweet smell of tarred hemp, the warm sickly fumes of fish oil mingled with the sharp pungency of paint and varnish. James stepped inside and struck a match. Something squeaked and scuttered across his feet. Half a dozen pairs of red eyes were pin-pointed in the darkness and then with a dry scurrying they were gone. Cobwebs strayed across his face. He struck a second match and saw a ship's lantern hanging from a beam. He shook the lamp and oil slopped in the container. The wick spluttered at first but soon burned with a steady yellow luminence.

The forepeak was a triangular cavern of curved sides with its apex at the ship's stem. Once lime-washed, it was now encrusted with a scabrous powder, mottled and stained and glittering with salt crystals. Holding the lamp high James ducked his head and stepped further inside.

Hanks of tarred rope and spunyarn hung from the deckhead and a cask of colza oil had seeped its contents across the deck. Blocks and tackles dangled like the pendulums of strange antediluvian clocks and fat hawsers of coir lurked beside lesser coils of manilla and hemp. Baulks of canvas were stowed against the ship-side. James moved across and fingered the sailcloth. It was mildewed, the fabric rotting. He grunted irritably; waste always angered him. Then fishing out his knife again he set to methodically poking, scraping and prodding at the ship's timbers.

Thirty minutes later he was thoughtful and satisfied. Every plank, every rib, every beam was as sound as a bell. Whoever built the *Charlotte Rhodes* certainly knew his business. He closed his clasp knife and, still carrying the lantern, stepped out on to deck again, blinking in the late afternoon sunshine. He made his way back to the hold and a flurry of pigeons clapped their wings and bolted into the sky.

Clambering down the ladder he stepped into two feet of water.

The air was foul and sour and as cold as the tomb. He waded out and pustules of evil-smelling bubbles broke the surface in his wake. A few pieces of timber and the swollen bodies of dead rats bobbed on the surface. James turned up the wick of the lantern and stared around him. The hold stretched in cavernous darkness. The opening in the hatch above emptied hot August sunlight down a golden shaft. He moved away from it into the greater darkness, toward the after bulkhead and the massive trunk of the mainmast. Above his head thin points and blades of light filtered from the open seams of the deck above. The mast was of Norwegian pine.

Now rooted in the keel, it rose from the flooded hold to reach for the sky sixty feet above.

James slopped his way across to the shipside and patiently set about his methodical tour of inspection.

An hour later he clambered out, cold and wet and with a throbbing headache from the effects of foul air. He replaced the hatchboards and made the tarpaulin snug and fast. Then he lit a cigar and sat on the hatch and, while the slanting sun dried his clothes, teased his brain into adding and subtracting — like profit and loss columns — the results of his afternoon's work. The ship was built of teak and elm on oak frames and certainly above the waterline as sound as the day she was built. The flooded hold worried him. There was a downtown pump forrard and another aft and for a shilling or two he could have a couple of dockside longshoremen pump her dry. But if the hull were as sound as he suspected that would serve to tip off any prospective buyer with as sharp a nose as himself. No, he would leave her as she was; with luck that should depress her price. The owner, he thought, must be the world's prize idiot to even consider auctioning a ship in such condition. And why the devil had he allowed her to deteriorate so? He shook his head. The world, he well knew, was full of madmen; he thanked the Almighty that he was not one of them.

James spent the rest of the evening prowling over the ship. He rummaged through the seaman's fo'c'sle beneath the forepeak and the master's quarters and tiny chart-room under the poop. Finally he unhitched a nearby painter's punt and poled himself around the seaward side of the ship. She was sheathed with "yellow metal", an alloy of copper and zinc which was reputed to resist the corrosive action of salt water better than pure copper.

He returned the punt to the quayside, clambered out, and made up his mind there and then that he would put in a bid. Money was the problem. There were bound to be others who realised the ship's potential. It was by no means unusual for shipmasters with a few pounds to spare to invest in a secondhand schooner, put wife and family aboard, and sail for the profitable trading grounds of India and the Far East. And such men had a sharp eye for a bargain. James doubted that his paltry £175 would take him far along that road. And then there would be the further financial problem of refitting.

James walked away lost in thought and the one-eyed shipkeeper watched him go, his solitary orb a red glare reflecting the light of the setting sun.

The tobacco smoke stung his eyes and the noise in the "Whaleboat Inn" seemed to pound inside his skull. James sighed and pushed away his empty plate. The problem admitted of no solution. He left the table, shouldered his way through the crowd of seamen and their hangers-on. Tired and mud-bespattered he wended his way back to the shop.

Robert unlocked and unbarred the door to stare at his brother in disapproval for the lateness of the hour and perplexity at James's grimy appearance. Robert's surly expression reminded James fleetingly of their father. Too exhausted to answer the inevitable rain of questions he bade Robert a curt "Good-night" and took himself off to the tiny attic which served as his bedroom when ashore.

He stripped off his clothes and sluiced himself down from a pitcher of cold water. Then he pulled a clean nightshirt over his head, tumbled into bed, blew out the candle and slept like a log.

7

THE morning sun made a watery pattern on the low ceiling. James awoke, focused his eyes. The pattern wavered and shifted. His mind and body, long attuned to the slow roll and pitch of a ship at sea, felt a momentary unease at the strange stillness. Sounds, filtering through to his consciousness, had the unreality of a dream.

It was always the same that first morning ashore. He required a period of adjustment. He liked to lie awake for those first few luxurious minutes, singling out and identifying each individual street noise. The lumbering creak and harness jingle of a passing cart. The clop of hooves. A sudden whinny and neigh from a stumbling horse. The mutter of voices rising and falling like broken surf and the ring of hob-nailed boots upon the cobblestones outside. A street away a hoarse-voiced muffin man called his wares, and down below Robert withdrew the shop door bolts, bade someone a cheerful "Good-morning", and clattered down the wooden shutters. He knew the time without looking at his watch. It would be six o'clock precisely. The neighbours claimed that the town hall clock was set by Onedin's shop. It had been his father's habit and James had no doubt that Robert, as usual, would follow where others led.

He stretched and yawned "Come in" to Elizabeth's tap at the door.

Elizabeth carried his breakfast tray. She gave him a hostile smile and bade him "Good morning" in the tone of one who has been up and about and finished half a day's work while some people lay abed until the sun was cracking the pavements.

James hated breakfast in bed but took the tray and thanked her politely. He knew the reason for this seeming consideration for his comfort. He was an intruder, an alien presence who periodically disturbed their routine. There was breakfast to be prepared, then the pots and pans to be washed and scoured. The iron grate must be blackleaded and the brass fire-irons rubbed and polished. Then there was the shop floor to be scrubbed and the step whitened.

Elizabeth's fair hair hung down, there was a smut at the side of her nose and a grimy streak across her forehead. Her sleeves were rolled to the elbow and she wore an apron of coarse sacking. James suppressed a grin. From the mutinous look on her face it was evident that Robert had lost little time in exerting his authority. One of their father's favourite aphorisms was that Elizabeth had been born late into the world and would be one of the last to leave it. She was certainly a born procrastinator and James's heart sank as he realised that she had every intention of settling herself for a gossip.

Elizabeth perched on the edge of the bed and as he wolfed down three slices of cheap belly bacon, a fried egg and a thick slice of white bread dipped in bacon fat, he tried to close his ears to her chatter and concentrate on the problem of acquiring the *Charlotte Rhodes*.

The root of the problem was money, and money was a commodity in short supply. "To be sold on behalf of Captain Webster" — whoever the devil he might be. One thing for certain sure, the man was a fool. No one but a raving idiot could allow a ship to deteriorate so. Webster. The name plucked at a distant chord of memory. Robert would know. Robert knew all the waterfront gossip. One hundred and seventy-five pounds. The figures scratched at his mind and he became aware again of Elizabeth's prattling. Something about when she was married to Daniel Fogarty she would have a house full of servants and a carriage and pair, no less. Didn't the flibberty-gibbet realise that even promoted to ship's captain the man would be poorly enough paid by Callon? If his own one hundred and seventy-five pounds in saving were anything to go by. One hundred and seventy-five pounds. How best to put it to work? A straight offer would be flatly refused — but as a down payment with a promise of a steady income to follow? This Webster might conceivably nibble at the bait. Webster, Webster, Webster? Where the devil had he heard that name before?

James finished his breakfast and pushed the tray to one side. The window curtains stirred and a sea air, sharp and fresh, invaded the room.

Elizabeth bibble-babbled on as though

her tongue was hinged at the root. He noticed with mild surprise that her features were slowly crimsoning and her eyes lowered demurely. She pimped and preened and he caught the name Frazer. "Young Mr. Frazer," she was saying. "Such a dandy. I declare that I cannot so much as step into the street without finding him bowing and scraping and raising his hat and bidding me a 'Fair good-morning, Miss Elizabeth' and 'May I have the honour of escorting you, Miss Elizabeth?' or 'Permit me to pay my respects, Miss Elizabeth'. He's such an importunate fellow as never was." Elizabeth giggled.

Frazer. James knew that name well enough. Frazers were shipbuilders of repute and the old man as tough as the timbers from which he built his ships. James recollected where he had last seen the name. Cut into the tonnage beam of the *Charlotte Rhodes*. She'd be sound enough. Any ship that left Frazer's yards was built to last. Young Frazer? James placed him immediately. A foppish young man of mincing ways and soft educated drawl. It was said that he had tried to persuade his father to invest in building the new-fangled steamships, but old man Frazer had stamped hard on that notion. So the son had been rolling his eyes in Elizabeth's direction, had he? In which case he would be well advised to steer clear of Daniel Fogarty. A mate of a sailing ship was not usually noted for conversational niceties. Fogarty would break young Frazer in half. Perhaps Robert could be persuaded to lend him the balance of the purchase price? Knowing Robert it was a forlorn hope, but worth the trial.

Robert's voice, querulously demanding to know if Elizabeth was prepared to stir herself today, or must he carry the entire burden of the shop on his own shoulders, rang through the house, broke against the door and put an end to Elizabeth's wagging tongue and hopes of evading the morning's drudgery.

She picked up the breakfast tray and scurried from the room. James could hear her voice and Sarah's raised in shrill magpie bickering and the deeper boom of Robert's interceding.

James rolled out of bed deciding that he had wasted time enough.

Shaved, washed and dressed in his best shore-going rig, James clattered down the narrow stairs and pushed open the living-room door.

He was in luck. Robert was seated alone at the breakfast table drinking from a mug of steaming tea. He could hear the sound of vigorous scrubbing from the shop and the murmur of Sarah's voice, no doubt talking to a customer.

Robert grunted acknowledgement of James's "Good-morning, brother Robert", and immediately launched into his favourite grumble.

"That sister of ours," he said, as though linking James to some measure of responsibility for the dilatory Elizabeth. "That sister of ours doesn't know she's born. I have never" — he raised imploring eyes to heaven to bear witness — "I have never known such an idlebones in my whole life. And you, James," — unable to meet James's eye, Robert blew accusingly into his tea — "do not help matters by keeping her gossiping half the morning. If I have told her once, I have told her a hundred times, that the shop must be scrubbed out before the first customer sets foot in it. But does she pay attention?" He shook his head. A man thwarted by a wilful child. "She does not."

James shrugged. It was an old tale. Elizabeth regarded herself as the household drudge and naturally resented the fact.

Before Robert could gain a second breath James unfolded the auction poster and laid it on the table in front of his brother.

"What do you think of her?"

Robert read the poster carefully as though sitting for a bar examination and then pronounced his opinion.

"Old Josh Webster's ship. A poor bargain at any price."

James's hopes rose.

"How much?"

Robert sucked noisily at his tea.

"Around five hundred. Less with an ounce of luck. The Websters must be close to penury. The old man has taken to the bottle while that vinegar-faced daughter tries to keep up the fiction that he has the fever. He has." Robert made the gesture of drinking from a bottle. "The Barbados fever."

James nodded. Tippling was a shipmaster's occupational hazard and in the long run more dangerous than the sea itself.

"Daughter, you said?"

Robert stared into his empty tea mug as though looking for secrets, sat back, blew his nose vigorously and turned his watery gaze upon James.

"You must remember her. Regular churchgoer. Sits in the end pew. Two rows from the back. Always dresses in black. Tart as a crab-apple and the wrong side of thirty. She keeps house for the old man."

James considered. "Just the two of them?"

Robert sucked a tea leaf from between his teeth.

"If you mean, is she married?—the answer is, no. Who would have her? Poor as a church mouse and thin as a pin."

James filed the information away. A drunkard with a spinster daughter. A combination that pointed to a dire need for money. He returned to the subject of the ship.

"Asking price should be low?"

Robert yawned, glanced at the mantelshelf clock ticking its way into the future. He nodded bored agreement.

"Bound to be. From what I've heard she's only fit for stripping and turning into a coal hulk."

He was already moving toward the shop. James sucked in a breath and took the plunge.

"Under five hundred pounds, you reckoned? I have one hundred and seventy-five saved. Will you stand the balance, Robert?"

Robert stared at James aghast.

"Lend you the balance? For that wreck? You can't be serious, James."

"Frazer's yards built her and Frazer's build sound ships." He strove to keep the edge of irritability from his voice. Arguing with Robert was like banging your head against a wall of cotton-wool.

"She's not sound now," said Robert with an air of finality.

"I've been over her," said James. "Every inch. From stem to stern."

Robert shook his head. "No."

James glared at the fool.

"Damn it, man, you'll not lose by it. I'll give you a note of hand."

Robert sighed at the nincompoop.
"On what security?"

James watched Robert's face. The suspicion of the miser afraid for his little hoard was written large. Security to Robert meant money chinking into the shop till.

"A partnership," said James, and knew he'd lost before the chandler opened his mouth to stutter, "A partnership? In what? No, don't tell me." He raised a protective hand and flapped at the air between them as though it, too, was tainted with spurious promises. "Don't tell me," he repeated. "You'll put to sea in that leaking bucket, and make our fortunes, no doubt?"

James had the expression of a man who has swallowed bile. He looked at Robert in disgust, unable to trust himself to speak.

Robert snorted and jabbed a forefinger. "You seem to think you know where the money-tree grows. Believe me, fortunes are not so easily made. Even with a well-found ship you would be hard put to earn so much as a crust. The sea routes are spoken for and the Owners have little taste for competition."

"And it would seem," said James, sourly, "that chandlers have even less.

Open your eyes, man. The world of commerce lies at your very shop door — but you are too blind to see it. Three hundred and twenty-five pounds, Robert, and it is ours for the taking."

"I doubt if I could lay my hands on three hundred and twenty-five shillings, much less pounds." He turned away, putting an end to the subject.

"You have the shop and stock."

Robert turned back, quivering with the rage of the weak man pushed too far.

"Shop and stock?" His voice rose to a squeak. "You have the effrontery to demand that I mortgage wife and family against a foolhardy venture doomed to failure before it starts? Your presumption is past belief. Do you imagine for one moment that you can finance a business — any business — simply by holding out your hand like a beggar?" Exasperation put venom into his voice. James stared at him coldly.

"Keep your purse strings tight, candler, you'll have need of your coppers one day." He marched from the room, through the shop and out into the street, Robert's voice bawling after him: "You speak of the world as your oyster, but that shell has long been prised open, I can tell you!"

8

ELIZABETH tipped the pail of dirty water into the gutter and a cloud of bluebottles buzzed with alarm to rise and fall, spin crazily in the sunlight before returning to hum their protest upon a pile of horse droppings. One pair, seemingly mad with fury, whined into the shop to be pursued and swatted to pulp by a Sarah as angry as any bluebottle ever born.

Flies were a curse. From spring to late autumn they waged an unceasing battle against the swarms of intruders, fly swatters never far from their hands and sticky papers hanging from the ceiling. Elizabeth didn't know which she disliked the greater — the persistent enemy or the rolls of fly paper, thick with dead and dying, which sometimes caught in her hair so that she had to stand stock still, her skin crawling with apprehension, until Robert or Sarah released her.

She leaned on the mop handle and noticed that beneath the faint white down on her arms the skin was already turning a golden brown. That was something else she hated about the summer. The sun seemed to seek one out everywhere; it was utterly impossible to keep a ladylike complexion. She stared down again and, yes, there were freckles she was ready to swear; tiny minute freckles! Really, it was not to be borne! She was about to roll down her sleeves only to recollect that the shop step had yet to be whitened — no doubt Robert would be trumpeting his displeasure at any moment. James seemed to have left him with a flea in his ear which meant, if past performances were anything to judge by, that he would shortly be venting his spleen on her. She wished she were married. She would be safe with Daniel. She would marry him tomorrow were he here, but he was such an obstinate fellow. "The moment I have me Master's," he'd say, "and not a day before." Really, there were times when dear Daniel's inflexibility of purpose could be something of a bother. When she showed petulance he would admonish her: "Never take second best. Wait till we're wed, then you'll want for nothing." So she waited, longing to escape from the tyranny of the shop. He was right, of course. The mate of a brig on the Baltic timber trade earned barely enough to keep a dog alive. The perks, such as they were, found their way into the captain's pocket. She sighed. If only Daniel were rich! She would have a lady's maid and boxes of fine dresses and. . . . The thought immediately raised the spectre of Albert Frazer. He was tall and really quite handsome and his manner of dress showed impeccable taste. Such expensive material; and so beautifully cut!

Lately he had taken to stabling a chestnut mare with Mr. Jenkins. A transparent subterfuge, for it was common knowledge that the Frazers lived in style with paddocks and stabling enough for a regiment of cavalry. Mr. Jenkins, that odious man, reeking of beer and tobacco, was naturally delighted with the arrangement and would greet her with many a knowing wink and leer. The mare, she learned, was called Nomad and its great brown eyes seemed puzzled at its change of circumstances like some pampered creature suddenly fallen upon hard times. Nomad's coat was of shimmering silk and her nostrils of the finest velvet. Elizabeth simply could not resist slipping away from the shop from time to time to stroke the long brown nose and entice the inquisitive muzzle with handfuls of carrot and turnip. And more often than not Albert Frazer would appear from nowhere and pass the time of day. He was all politeness and consideration itself and never once did he cause her so much as a moment's embarrassment. Nevertheless in some strange way she felt that a silken net was being woven about her.

Robert's hateful voice broke in upon her musings.

"Do you intend to idle there all day, Miss Lazybones?"

She jumped, startled to find him at her elbow. He was wearing his best suit of broadcloth and his hat was clamped firmly on his head. He glowered at her and blew through his moustache.

"I am going out," he snapped. "Business. Look after the shop."

Elizabeth picked up the pail and scuttled quickly indoors, thankful that Robert had overlooked the yet-to-be-whitened step.

James asked the way of a passer-by and found Sailmakers Row to be a group of old cottages, bent with age, staggering up a short steep hill. They huddled together as though for warmth, blank eyes peering hopelessly at the high brick wall of the gasworks opposite.

Number 12 stood at the top end. It was somewhat different from its fellows in that it had had annual coats of whitewash, and although the paint was cracked and blistered and peeling from the front door the brass knocker had been vigorously polished. James noticed approvingly that the tiny window panes were clean and discreetly covered with lace curtains. He ran a finger around his stiff, unfamiliar collar, drew in a breath and rat-a-tat-tatted politely upon the knocker.

He waited patiently until he heard the snick of a key turning in the lock, the rasp of a bolt being drawn. He doffed his hat the moment the door part-opened. He saw a lean-shanked unattractive spinsterish woman looking out at a sour world through sour eyes.

She eyed James, stiff-necked, ready to slam the door in his face. "Probably thinks I'm a creditor," decided James, and the knowledge gave him renewed confidence. He cleared his throat.

"Miss Webster?"

The black unwavering sparrow-like stare gave nothing away.

"I am." The voice was flat, uncompromising.

James tormented his face into a polite smile.

"My name is Onedin. Captain James Onedin. I apologise for the inconvenience, Miss Webster, but I crave the indulgence of a few moments' conversation with Captain Webster."

Her voice had a harsh snappish quality.

"To what purpose?" she asked. Not a hint of common politeness. She obviously cared little for James Onedin and his affairs.

"A matter of business." He was careful to keep his own voice equally flat, matter-of-fact. But he watched her expression carefully and caught a sudden flicker of something — a haunting fear? — behind her eyes.

She answered quickly, rather too quickly, and made to close the door.

"I am sorry, Captain Onedin, but my father is indisposed."

James decided that his first assumption

was correct. She did take him for a creditor. He spoke quickly.

"It is a matter of some consequence."

"To you? Or to us?"

The door was swinging shut. James unfolded the auction poster and showed it to her. The door hesitated a foot from the jamb, then opened again. She stared at the poster.

James took his opportunity.

"I had hoped to make an offer which might well save the bother of public auction."

At last she displayed interest.

"A private sale?"

James nodded.

She considered.

"Do you represent yourself alone, or others?"

"Myself," replied James. He pressed home his advantage. "But with respect, Miss Webster, my business must lie with your father."

She opened the door fully and stepped to one side.

"Very well, Captain Onedin. If you will step inside I will inquire as to whether my father will receive you."

She ushered him along a short narrow passage and opened the sitting-room door.

"If you will wait here, sir?"

"Thank you," said James.

She paused at the door and the black eyes stared at him bleakly.

"You will not object to the presence of a woman during the course of your discussion."

James blinked. It was not a question. A flat statement of fact. Take it, or leave it.

She drew herself up stiffly, clasped bony hands in front of a dark plain skirt that showed here and there a neat darn.

"My father is a sick man," she said in that same even tone. "I would not have him taken advantage of." Her face was thin, and time had etched lines beside a prim mouth. She waited a moment for the courtesy of an answer — tall, unbending, straight as a dried stick — then, taking her visitor's silence for acquiescence, she bowed her head slightly and was gone, softly closing the door behind her.

James fished out one of his favourite thin black cigars and sniffed the air. The room had the smell of dampness that came from lack of use. He doubted that the father was ever permitted to set foot in this private sanctuary. There was no question about it, that scraggy daughter ruled the roost. He struck a match and lit his cigar. The room seemed to sigh its disapproval. He could find nowhere to put the dead match. A firescreen of Chinese silk work stood before the grate. He peered over the top. It was obvious that the ironwork was regularly blackleaded and the brass fender and fire-irons glowed with the same obsessive cleanliness. He slipped the match into his pocket and slowly took stock of his surroundings.

The room had an air of genteel poverty. A green horsehair sofa and matching chairs with antimacassars placed with precision. He looked more closely and nodded his satisfaction at their threadbare look. On the mantelshelf stood a few ornaments surrounding a gilt ormolu clock with its fingers stopped at a time long forgotten. An ornate gilt frame surrounded the portrait of a severe-looking young woman who stared reprovingly into the room from a remote past. Something about the dark unwinking eyes, narrow features and prim sour mouth pointed to the mother of the sallow-faced spinster.

A companion portrait in an identical oval frame hung at the other side of the fireplace. James found himself peering closely at a plump young man in the full dress uniform of a naval lieutenant, all high stock and golden epaulettes. Beneath the portrait was a long horizontal dust shadow on the faded flock wallpaper. No doubt the once-young lieutenant's dress sword hung there until lately. He laid himself a private wager that it, and a few other bits and pieces, were even now down at the pawnshop. Evil times indeed. The pair must be in dire need of money. He touched the heavy purse in his pocket. Few such could resist the immediacy of gold coin. His hopes rose. The outcome might easily depend upon the extent of their indebtedness to local tradesmen. The hard-faced daughter was going to be the problem. But he would make an offer, a very fair offer. If he could coax them into bargaining he would have that ship before nightfall. Money and terms were negotiable commodities. No more than a little give and take on either side until an accommodation agreeable to both parties was arrived at. There was nothing complicated about finance. All that was required was a clear head and resolution of purpose.

He heard the shuffle of footsteps and a low murmur of voices from the passage outside. When the door opened he was standing in an attitude of polite boredom in front of the empty firegrate.

She performed the introduction as though conferring a favour, shepherded her father to a chair, then stood quietly behind him, still and watchful, a tall image of the woman in the portrait.

Webster had the look of an animated frog. He had a squat body and little frog eyes pouched in a heavy frog face and, to the abstemious James, reeked of rum and brandy. There was a day's growth of white stubble on his face. Alcoholic tremors shook his hands and from time to time the man's entire frame shivered as though he had the ague. He wore an old-fashioned high stock, a plum-coloured waistcoat and his suit was worn thin at the elbows and showed the dribbling signs of food stains. "He must slobber like a baby," thought James and turned his full attention upon the pair.

Webster's red-rimmed eyes glowered malevolence, a weak man's last defence against a hostile world. He licked his lips and gestured toward a plush upholstered chair.

"Take yer ease, man," he growled. "Take yer ease." He looked appealingly at his daughter. "A glass of brandywine for our guest, if you please, Anne."

She hesitated fractionally, then, taking a key from the pocket of her skirt, unlocked a corner cupboard and produced a decanter and two glasses, setting one before James, the other within reach of her father. James shook his head.

"Thank you, no, Miss Webster. I prefer a clear head when discussing business."

She flushed and her dark eyes almost spat anger at him.

"My father is not yet fully recovered from the fever, sir." She poured a half tumbler of the golden liquid and the old man's hands clutched greedily at the glass and carried it to his lips. He swallowed the brandy like a child gulping milk.

"I know the symptoms well," said James gravely.

She looked down her nose at him.

"A fever contracted on the Slave Coast, Captain Onedin." She let it sink in. "In the service of his country." Almost defiantly she poured a second half tumbler. The old man's hand was now steady. He took the glass, rolled the contents slowly, savouring his unexpected good fortune. He belched, dabbed his lips with the flourish of an earlier century, leaned back, crossed one stumpy leg over the other and launched into his favourite grumble.

"Retired me on half pay, they did, my smart Lords of the Admiralty. There is little gratitude in this world, young man, little gratitude. But I beat to wind'ard and outgunned 'em. Bought the *Charlotte Rhodes*. As sound a ship as ever spread canvas. But I'm no penny-pinching trader to spend me days dealing with rogues and scallywags . . ."

She interrupted quickly.

"Father!" She turned her full attention upon James. "We understand, Captain Onedin, that you have it in mind to make an offer for the ship?"

Webster leaned forward all eagerness to impress. "A lovely vessel, sir, a lovely vessel. Worth a fortune in gold. As seaworthy a vessel as you'd find in a year's search. A sharp young feller like yourself would make her pay. I'm too old a dog for new tricks. Built of good British oak in Frazer's yards . . ."

James interrupted the maudlin old fool.

"I must tell you, sir," he said coldly, "that I know all there is to know about the *Charlotte Rhodes*. I spent the better part of yesterday going over that ship from stem to stern, from truck to keel." He looked straight at the dragon. It was obvious that she was the decision-maker in this family. "How much are you asking?"

She drew in a breath. "Six hundred and fifty guineas," she said quickly.

James permitted himself a thin smile. "I should add, in all fairness, Miss Webster, that I have also made diligent inquiries as to your circumstances."

Webster thumped the table.

"Insolent jackanapes!"

"All business," said James calmly, "is a matter of negotiation. Before one can negotiate with certainty it is necessary to fully comprehend the strengths and weaknesses of the other side."

The frog face turned mottled with rage.

"Tradesman's trickery, by God! I'll have none of it. D'ye hear, sir? None of it! Damme, I'd burn the ship first!"

The woman stood still and unmoving, her gaze calm and calculating. She spoke quietly as though not in the least offended.

"I take it you do have an offer in mind?"

"I do," said James. He paused. "One hundred and seventy-five pounds."

Her shoulders sagged, disappointment showing in her face. A little flame of spirit seemed to die within her. The offer was ludicrous. James held up a hand. "One hundred and seventy-five pounds in gold," he said levelly. "And a partnership."

Outside, a patent-medicine man called his wares. A door slammed somewhere and a child's voice rose and fell in a wail of anguish.

She touched her father's shoulder. He looked up and read the decision in her face. He shook his head with the obstinacy of the old. "No," he said. "No."

She frowned and dipped her head in thought. Her teeth gnawed at the long, thin, almost bloodless, lower lip.

"A partnership?" She spoke the words

slowly as though in communion with a deeper inner self.

James saw his opportunity.

"To our mutual benefit, Miss Webster," he said quickly. "A proper form of contract, drawn by lawyers, and under which I would undertake to refit the ship at my own expense." God knows how, he thought, but possession was the key. He'd manage somehow.

She seemed to read his thoughts.

"We should require more than good intent, Captain Onedin."

The old man snarled his rage. "Words," he said. "Words, words, words. Words in the air. Words on paper. It will come to the same in the end. He'd hoist his sails and that's the last we'd see of him or the ship. Money. Money talks the sharpest language. Cash on the barrel, sir. Cash on the barrel. Otherwise . . ." He sat back. "I'll have no part of it."

She held James's gaze and her father's outburst went unheeded. James kept his voice even and steady. He felt that he was charting a course between twin rocks. One mistake and his hopes would founder.

"We would show trading profits. A

steady and growing income to set against a small capital — which, with respect, Miss Webster, your father's 'fever' would suck dry within a year or two."

Webster pounded his fist upon the table.

"Ye young scallawag," he roared. "Ye blackguarding villain! Anne — show the creature the door!"

She sniffed, clamped her lips together and bobbed her head slightly as though nodding agreement with an invisible counsellor. She kept her unwavering stare upon the visitor but her eyes seemed to have an unfocused quality as though her gaze were turned inward to examine some microscopic substance, the quality and texture of which somehow eluded her. Then she moved quietly to the door and held it open.

"If you please, Captain Onedin. My father desires to consider the matter closed."

James came to his feet. The woman had stressed the words "my father". He felt exultant. The implication was obvious. She was prepared to leave the old fool with his decanter while they settled the business together. He bowed stiffly to Webster and walked to the door.

"Take and drown yerself in a bucket!" roared that Ancient Mariner. "In a bucket, sir. In a bucket!"

She closed the door behind James and led the way along the passage, away from the front door, James noticed, and toward the kitchen.

"This way, if you please, Captain Onedin," she said.

She ushered him into the kitchen. An ash fire smouldered in the grate and a much-scrubbed deal table bore a basket of laundry. There were a pair of fireside chairs and two spindle-back dining chairs. A stone sink with wooden draining board and cupboards below a fat wooden towel rail. Brown painted shelves held cheap crockery, pots, pans, mops and jugs. The floor was stone-flagged and uncarpeted and the sandstone walls had been liberally coated with whitewash.

She closed the door and turned to face him.

"Well, sir," she demanded, "are you fool or charlatan?"

The attack took James by surprise.

"Neither, I trust."

"Then the onus of proof is upon you, is

it not?" She walked restlessly about the room, her thin arms folded tightly across her thin chest as though locking herself in thought.

"I assure you," James began, "a deed of contract . . ."

She shook her head impatiently.

"Which would last the lifetime of my father only. And then . . ."

He shrugged. "Safeguards can be built in."

"All of which would rely upon the success of the ship. Ships can founder." She looked at him levelly. "Or be sold."

"I give you my word, Miss Webster, that is not my intent."

"But it might very well be the effect." The corners of her mouth turned down in the rictus of a smile. "Not a very good bargain, sir."

James felt a sense of exasperation welling up within him. Would the damned woman never stop quibbling? He understood her problem; she had taken the bait of a promised steady income, but, naturally, she required some sort of guarantee of security. The devil of it was he had nothing to offer.

She was regarding him thoughtfully.

"You need the ship with some urgency, Captain Onedin?"

"To make a beginning," said James.

"Then your need must be great indeed." Again she gave him that twisted smile; but there was more than irony in her tone; the question had a probing purpose.

James sniffed. "As great as yours, perhaps?"

She nodded as though he were agreeing with her.

"Indeed, yes. I have little taste for penury. One day my father's weakness will assuredly drive him to the grave and I shall be left penniless. At best I shall be constrained to live off the charity of friends; at worst it will mean the poorhouse. I assure you, sir, I have little fancy for either." The dark eyes seemed to search him out. "You do understand the problem?"

"Security?" James drew in a breath, about to continue as persuasively as he knew how. She cut him short.

"In return for the ship," she said in that same flat tone.

James decided upon a piece of plain speaking.

"I will not hide it from you, Miss Webster. I cannot put up surety . . ."

She seemed not to hear him but continued to talk as though she had decided upon a clear course of action and all that remained was to clear up one or two minor details.

"There is my father to be considered. He is a weak and foolish old man, but I will not see him left destitute."

James tried again.

"I do assure you that a partnership agreement would carry safeguards enough."

She shook her head.

"And I assure you, James Onedin, that there is only one form of partnership that would ensure the sort of security I require."

She waited, her sallow cheeks slightly flushed. James looked his incomprehension.

"And the ship," she added, "would not cost you one penny piece."

James stared at her.

"What?"

"As a dowry," she said calmly.

His mouth dropped open and he gaped like a fool.

"There is only one way in which a woman may escape poverty."

"Marriage?" The word stuck in his throat. The woman must have taken leave of her senses. But there was nothing wild about her uncompromising gaze. He had an uneasy feeling that he had met a woman with a will as inflexible as his own. But marriage? She could not possibly be serious.

"I would have," she was saying, as though this outrageous proposal were the most natural in the world, "the protection of your name and a share in your success."

"Or failure," said James, like a man clutching at straws. "Or failure."

She smiled her crooked smile again.

"I think you and failure to be poor bed-fellows, James Onedin."

He noticed uneasily that this was the second time she had used his Christian name. He needed time. Time to think. He took out one of his thin black cigars and examined it as though he had never seen its like before. She lighted a taper from the fire and held it out with a steady hand. He inhaled deeply while his brain raced, accepting and rejecting possibilities. There was a cold core at the centre of his brain, something still and quiet around which, in moments of stress, the winds of emotion would revolve leaving him strangely untouched. It was a sense of calmness, a lodestone buried deep within him that pointed his life toward a distant, sometimes only dimly realised, goal. It didn't fail him now. He looked at her. She must be at least five years his senior. Her hair was dank and pulled back from the high forehead in a severe bun. She was certainly no catch — and no doubt, he thought wryly, well aware of the fact. He would have to accept total responsibility for her as his wife; and then there would be that drunken sot of a father. On the other hand he would have the ship plus his one hundred and seventy-five pounds; with that sum as capital he could re-rig the ship — or Robert could — yes, Robert was always greedy for money — the sight of so much gold could easily persuade the fool. . . . His mind raced on, busy with schemes. The Braganza wine contract. If he could snap that up from beneath Callon's nose? If the price were marriage — what of it? Everyone married sooner or later — he had supposed vaguely that one day he should, if only to provide a son and heir, otherwise there was little point in existence. He had never fully understood his contemporaries' penchant for marrying a pretty face. Feminine comeliness had never affected him. In his experience that type of bloom faded quickly and frequently concealed a stultifying vacuity of mind. This woman, now, had a mind like a steel trap. He had a grudging admiration for the manner in which she had out-manoeuvred him and then seized her one opportunity. She wanted security; he wanted the ship. Very well, so be it. A simple exchange. But he would make one last try to dissuade her. He expelled a long-held breath and a vast cloud of cigar smoke.

"I must, in all fairness, warn you, Miss Webster, that you may very well be exchanging one form of poverty for another. I have but one hundred and seventy-five pounds in the world . . ."

"And ambition." She blew out the taper.

"I have ambition enough for an army of Napoleons," he said. "But it takes more than ambition to feed, clothe, pay creditors."

"I have had my fill of creditors," she said bitterly. She replaced the taper in the jar on the mantelshelf and remained for a moment looking down at the smouldering fire as though searching for secrets. "You would be hard put to find a better housekeeper," she said as though proffering qualifications. Her voice was bitter again. "And a less complaining. I am well trained on that score, at least."

James grunted.

"It is no easy road, and one that I would prefer to travel alone."

She turned and looked at him sharply.

"A minute ago you were speaking of partnership."

He wagged his head.

"I could buy my way out of that kind of partnership, but the one you have in mind is for life."

She sniffed disparagement.

"If you find the price too high then you must look elsewhere for your beginning."

She made him feel uncomfortable. He cleared his throat, ran a finger around his collar.

"It is not that. It is . . . well . . . marriage is something which requires a deal of thought."

She seemed exasperated now.

"And I took you for a man quick to

decision. Very well — we shall say no more about it."

The creature was moving toward the door. He was being dismissed. The discussion was at an end. She really was, he thought, a most remarkable woman. He scratched his head and grinned a lopsided grin.

"You may not find me so great a catch, either, Anne."

He managed her Christian name with an effort. It almost stuck in his throat.

Again he faced that long searching look.

"For better, or for worse?" she asked.

"For richer, or poorer," he responded awkwardly.

She took a step toward him. There was was a softness, a sadness in her face. The dark luminous eyes held a strange glow.

"I therefore plight thee my troth?" Her voice shook a little.

Emotion terrified James. He coughed drily and couched his acceptance bleakly.

"The ship will require cordage, new canvas, timbers caulked."

She smiled her understanding and held out a hand.

"It is a bargain then?"

He took her hand and held it and found that he didn't know what the devil was expected of him. Her hand, he noticed, was as dry as a bundle of sticks. His own was perspiring a little. He realised it was the first time they had touched. He cleared his throat and coughed his dry cough again.

"A bargain," he said and grinned his crooked grin. "I wonder who shall have the better of it?"

9

THE family, seated at the dinner table, greeted his announcement with open-mouthed disbelief. Robert held a forkful of boiled mutton suspended in mid-air.

"You — married? To that — Plain Jane? Good God, man, you never clapped eyes on the creature until today!"

Sarah gaped at James as though he had taken leave of his senses.

"I don't understand," she said. "I don't understand. I don't understand. I don't understand." To James's mounting irritation she kept repeating the senseless phrase over and over again like a child trying to grasp an imperfectly understood lesson.

"There is nothing to understand," he snapped. "It is a marriage of convenience." Their pale faces turned toward him like so many waxen images. He breathed heavily. "There was no other way of obtaining the ship. Robert — I should like a word with you — privately."

Robert dropped his fork with a clatter.

"No — other way — of obtaining the ship?"

"He's mad," said Sarah. "Mad, quite mad." There was a note of hysteria in her voice. Elizabeth giggled. "Oh, James, you fool!" She hiccupped and choked over a piece of meat. James glowered at her.

"I find no humour in the situation," he said stiffly. "It is as valid a reason as any other for contracting an alliance."

Robert spluttered.

"Contracting an alliance! Good God, man, you speak as though you were marrying into property. That Plain Jane is naught but the daughter of a penniless wastrel!"

"A ship," snapped James, "is as much property as any heap of bricks and mortar — and a far more profitable investment. I am content with the bargain. There is no more to be said. Robert — when you have finished gaping, a word with you, if you please." He turned and walked through the connecting doorway to the empty shop, irritated beyond all measure at their imbecilic questions. The decision was his and his alone. He owed explanations to no man. He walked around the closed shop, lighting the gas jets and half-listening to the sounds of their silly women's chatter. At least Anne—if he had taken her measure correctly—would not badger him with pointless infantile gossip. "Anne." He mused over the name and found he could actually think upon it without regurgitating the word as though coughing up a fishbone. "Anne." A sensible name for a sensible woman. Sarah's high-pitched voice floated through to him. "He is mad," she was saying. "Quite, quite mad. He has quite taken leave of his senses." And then Elizabeth's confounded giggle: "And the creature is such a fright as never was."

"And so much his senior." This from Sarah in a hushed whisper as though age were a crime in itself.

Robert appeared in the doorway. He looked at his brother, shook his head and had the grace to appear somewhat shamefaced.

"I would advance you the money, James, but . . ." He shrugged hopelessly.

James grinned at him.

"To save me from a fate worse than

death? No, Robert — but you can do me a better service."

He took three carefully folded sheets of paper from his pocket. Each in the copperplate script of a lawyer's clerk. He passed one to Robert.

"Read that."

Robert took the sheet of paper and read quickly, then looked up at James, puzzled.

"I don't understand."

James sighed. He'd had his fill of fools for one day and therefore spoke impatiently.

"It is simple enough for a schoolboy to understand. No more than a deed of partnership between us."

Robert hurriedly put down the paper and backed away in alarm as though the very words were a snare and delusion set to trap the unwary.

"Oh, no, James," he said, fear in his small round eyes. "Oh, no. We have been through this before. I cannot afford it as well you know. I simply cannot be party to . . ." He trailed off as James slapped the paper with such force that the scale pans jangled at the ends of their brass chains and the top packets of tea from Sarah's carefully built pyramid tumbled to the floor.

His pale blue eyes bored into Robert's brown.

"I now own the ship, you dolt—or shall when I'm wedded," he qualified. "This document makes you equal partner. You take half the profits."

Robert was suspicious.

"Why?" he asked simply.

"As I shall be sailing the ship myself someone must be on hand to look after my interests ashore. It is common prudence that the man must be a partner. And who else could I trust better than my own brother?"

Robert considered, his suspicions by no means allayed.

"And my liabilities while you are away foraging for cargoes?"

James shrugged.

"If the ship goes to the bottom, I go with her. You stand to lose . . ." He spread his hands. "The prospect of a profit."

Robert picked up the paper and read again carefully. He chewed at the ends of his moustache, then his eyes lighted with cunning.

"I know your tricks, James. You think to refit and store the ship at my expense, no doubt. No, James, no. I am too smart a dog to be caught with a meatless bone. I'll have none of it . . ."

He broke off and his eyes widened like windows in the sun as James took his washleather purse from his pocket, loosened the neck and slowly spilled a rain of bright golden coins upon the counter.

"One hundred and fifty pounds in gold, Robert. More than sufficient, wouldn't you say?" and knew he had won when he saw the greed glinting in his brother's eyes. He reached out and fanned the golden hoard across the counter top. "Let us call it an earnest of good faith." He pushed the paper and two copies toward Robert, dipped a pen in the inkwell and held it out. "You sign here . . . and here . . . and here."

Robert took the pen and scrawled his signature. Hardly able to keep his gaze from the fortune lying spread before him, he failed to see the glimmer of triumph in James's eyes.

Men swarmed over the *Charlotte Rhodes* like a horde of leafcutter ants, each with his burden, each fixed of purpose.

The ship stood in the graving dock, kept upright by great baulks of timber shoring her sides. Carpenters' planes rasped and adzes swung and chipped and shaped. Far below the metal workers' hammers beat a fierce tattoo at the copper sheathing. Pitch bubbled in iron cauldrons and sent pungent smoke swirling across the dockside. Men tightened the shrouds, sweating the bottle screws until the iron wire thrummed and sang. Riggers scrambled aloft, sending down new lines, reaving new blocks and sheaves. Painters dipped their brushes in hot tar and covered the shipside in a thick sticky protective coat while pot lads and apprentice boys ran multifarious errands between scraping and sanding and polishing. Hammers chinked upon caulking chisels as the deck carpenters ran oakum into the open seams and the carpenters' mates followed with ladles of boiling pitch.

James stood on the dockside, a sail plan tucked beneath his arm, watching with a critical eye as a brand new fore upper-topsail yard was hoisted into place. He nodded his satisfaction. Work was going apace. With luck the ship should be finished in time and he would be able to set sail immediately after the wedding. The wedding. He sighed at the enormity of the demands likely to be made upon his purse. The banns had been read once and neighbours had fallen over themselves in their eagerness to offer congratulations and fish for invitations. Family only, he had told them surlily, family only. And Sarah and Elizabeth had been in a twitter of excitement ever since and apparently took it as a personal affront that he refused flatly to extend invitations to Uncle Will Perkins and Cousin Wilberforce and the rest of the Onedin tribe. He would have none of it, he told them sternly. It was his wedding and he, no doubt, would be expected to foot the bill. Anne, thank God, had been in wholehearted agreement. All she required was the benefit of clergy and the celebrations could go to pot. A sensible woman, he decided yet again. A remarkably sensible woman.

The remarkably sensible woman appeared at that moment from the ship's tiny galley. Her sleeves were rolled to the elbow, she wore a mob cap to cover her hair and a canvas apron to protect her skirt.

She was begrimed and blackened from the tips of her fingers to the roots of her hair. She paused for a moment to inhale lungfuls of fresh air, then she smeared her forehead again with her forearm, waved cheerfully to him and disappeared once more into the galley. A most remarkable woman, he thought with an odd pride of possession. A remarkable woman.

He returned his attention to his sail plan and was deciding to have another word with the sailmaker to impress upon that harassed man that it was imperative that the cringles of the topsails *must* be double sewn, when he became aware of the soft susurration of skirts and the distinct odour of feminine perfume. He groaned to find Elizabeth standing chirpily at his side. She carried a parasol and had braided her hair and dressed in her fanciful best.

"What the devil do you want?" he demanded irascibly.

She pouted.

"To see how work is progressing. And to seize upon the opportunity of meeting your lady-love." She giggled. "I think you keep her beneath the stairs and only let her out to bay at the moon."

James felt himself shaking with anger.

"Put a guard on your tongue, Miss." His voice held a rasp that brought a flush of shame to her cheeks. She touched James's arm gently and spoke contritely.

"I'm sorry, James. It was a silly, stupid jest." Her large candid blue eyes looked into his, pleading forgiveness as she had done all her life. "Please can I go aboard?" she asked.

"No," said James curtly. "You may not. Ships and docks are not fit places for . . ."

"Why, there she is!" said Elizabeth as Anne reappeared from the galley lugging a heavy pail of rubbish. Elizabeth moved toward the gangway. James gripped her arm.

"If you say one word that gives offence . . ." He left the sentence unfinished.

"I shan't. I promise," said Elizabeth. "In fact I am sure that we shall be firm friends." She scurried across the gangway, her crinoline billowing behind her, and without so much as a glance at the horrifying thirty-foot drop to the granite floor below.

James walked toward the ship's stern

and paused to watch the rudder being tested. Steering chains clenched to either side of the massive wooden rudder were passed under the counter and led to the deck above by way of a pair of hawse pipes. The twin chains ran along either side of the deck to disappear beneath the poop. Here the ends were shackled to the manilla wheelrope which was then passed around the barrel of the steering wheel. A rigger turned the wheel and the rudder swung smoothly from side to side on its greased pintles.

James moved back a pace or two and ran a satisfied eye over the ship's graceful lines. Her sheerline flowed sweetly from bow to taffrail and her stern run would lift before any but the strongest following sea.

He was mentally calculating ballast tonnage, shingle, he thought, at 23 cubic feet to the ton, when a laconic voice broke into his train of thought. He looked over his shoulder to see a dandified young man sauntering toward him.

James gritted his teeth: there seemed no escape from pestiferous visitors. He viewed the newcomer with hostility.

The young man wore spotless linen, a lavender suit and grey top hat. He carried a silver-topped ebony walking stick and flicked at imaginary specks of dust with a pair of soft kid gloves. He had a trim fair moustache and spoke in a soft educated drawl that grated on James's nerves. He supposed he must pay the devil his due and so returned the young fop's greeting with brusque politeness.

"Good-morning, Mr. Frazer." He could hardly keep the contempt from his voice.

If Albert Frazer was aware of it he gave no sign. He smiled affably and presented a finger and thumb to the brim of his hat.

"Just passing," he began, conversationally. "Thought to add m' congratulations on your forthcoming nuptials."

"Thank you," said James curtly.

"Took us all quite by surprise."

Anne walked along the deck toward the master's quarters, aft. She looked toward James. Albert removed his hat and offered a flourishing bow. Anne blinked, stared at the apparition, shrugged her thin shoulders and disappeared below.

Albert replaced his hat. "A splendid

match, I should say. Peas from the same pod, eh?"

James looked at him suspiciously, but the dandy's features were as bland as his voice. He smiled pleasantly at James as though they were lifelong friends.

"I would appreciate an invitation," he murmured.

"To what?" asked James.

"To the wedding, of course."

James snorted. "It is to be no grand affair."

"Quite right," assented Albert. "Far too much pomp these days." His stick traced a pattern in the dust at his feet. "I take it that Miss Elizabeth will grace the occasion with her presence?"

James laughed shortly. "So that's the way the wind blows? You have little hope in that direction. My sister is already promised."

"The ladies are notoriously fickle creatures." Albert stifled a yawn.

"Not Elizabeth. She has a mind of her own. You are wasting your time, Frazer." He almost added "and mine, too", and was only restrained by the thought that his ship was berthed in Frazer's graving dock. He could hardly pitch the young fool off his own property.

Albert leaned back on his stick.

"Thought you might care to put in a word for me," he suggested, casually. "Influence of a brother, y'know?" He beamed amiably upon James.

James stared at him.

"Why the devil should I?"

"Self-interest. You are a sharp chap, Onedin. Very sharp. No offence. Paying you a compliment."

"One I can well do without," snapped James. "Come to the point."

Albert considered a moment, pulling at the lobe of one ear.

"Putting it as delicately as I can — you married into shipping. Mm? Thought you might care to consider the possibility of another alliance? Shipbuilding. We have the yards, y'know." He yawned again. "Just a thought."

James couldn't believe his ears. This, if it was anything at all, was a formal proposal. He actually wanted to marry the girl. The young idiot must be completely besotted.

"Are you serious?" he asked.

"But of course. Wouldn't have broached the matter otherwise."

James looked sharply at him. Beneath the banter he read an inflexibility of purpose. By God, he thought, he means it.

He needed time to think this thing through. The bait of the shipyards so brazenly dangled before him certainly had its attractions. The Frazers were not only rich but a powerful clan in shipping circles. If his sister were married to the son . . . the prospect was dazzling indeed.

Albert waited patiently for his reply. James decided to move with caution. It was early days yet. He must not prove over-eager. He also wondered, not for the first time, what on earth men found so fascinating about Elizabeth. In James's view she was an empty-headed chatterbox and as temperamental as a racehorse.

"Hrrmph." He coughed his dry cough. "You might," he said, "find that my sister holds strong views on the subject."

"I should be more than disappointed if she did not," replied Albert, quite at ease. "But obstacles of their very nature are ours to overcome. Do you not agree?" He stroked his little moustache. "Given a free hand, of course." The implication was obvious.

James grunted.

"My sister is of age and no doubt more than capable of handling her own affairs in her own way. I take it," he added, "that you and she have actually met?"

Albert touched his little moustache again.

"Not formally," he said. "Not formally. Looking forward to the pleasure."

James called to a passing pot boy, gave him brief instructions and a penny to hasten his feet.

"She will be coming ashore immediately," he told Frazer, and turned to busy himself with his sail plans. Albert gazed up at the lofty masts.

"Quite a transformation."

"Mm?" James, having settled one business, now wanted to concentrate on the other without irritating interruptions from gilded amateurs. He felt sure he could add a couple of staysails and a flying jib. And a gaff topsail, perhaps? He really must speak to the sailmaker. He became aware that the nincompoop was still wagging his tongue

"You have her a trifle over-sparred, I fancy," he was saying. "Expecting to make a fast passage, eh?"

"That's my business," said James gruffly.

Albert pointed with his stick toward a group of scavengers — longshoremen who hung around the docks on the off-chance of picking up any odd jobs that might be going; drifting in the background was a pasty-faced clerk wearing a curly-brimmed bowler hat. The frayed celluloid cuffs of his trade protruded from the ends of his too-short jacket.

"It would also seem to be the business of your former employer. Isn't that one of Callon's wretches skulking beside the site office?"

James grunted acknowledgment. "I've seen him. He's a clerk named Drummond. He'll learn little enough from this source."

"Keeping your own counsel, eh?" suggested Albert. "Very wise. Very wise." He let his bored glance wander over the ship. "I think you'll find her best sailing point with the wind a trifle on the quarter."

James grunted sourly. "What ship doesn't?"

Albert smiled. "A steamship, perhaps?"
James snorted.
Albert raised an eyebrow.
"I take it you have little fancy for the floating kettles?"
James hadn't.
"The wind," he said, as though explaining a lesson to a child, "blows free for every man's use. Your steamships are expensive to build and even more expensive to run. They burn costly fuel which in turn takes up valuable cargo space. They catch fire, blow up, turn turtle. I am afraid, Mr. Frazer, I have little time to waste in profitless discussion."
Albert sighed and looked at James with the pitying expression reserved for those who have not yet seen the light.
"Those are the disadvantages. Have you given consideration to their prime advantage?"
"What?" James wished to God he'd put an end to the conversation.
The tip of Albert's walking stick drew a line in the dust.
"The shortest distance between two points is a straight line." He swung his stick to the shoulder, military fashion, and

James realised that the young man was no longer smiling. He spoke in earnest and there was a light of fanaticism in his eyes. James remembered that it was said of Frazer's son that he had a bee in his bonnet about building steamships. He had hawked his crazy designs from one shipping company to the other only to be met with gales of derision. It was fortunate that Albert had the backing of his father's name, otherwise he would soon be looking elsewhere for his bread and butter.

"If," Albert was saying, "you should ever change your opinion, please consider our yards at your disposal. I do have one or two notions which might interest a fellow as sharp as yourself. . . . Ah — here she comes at last." He looked at James anxiously. "You'll not forget your promise?"

Elizabeth walked sedately along the narrow roped gangway and ashore. She had her gaze fixed demurely upon James as though he stood entirely alone in the world and she had no other purpose in life but to obey his every wish.

"Elizabeth," said James, formally, as though quoting from a book of etiquette.

"May I present Mr. Albert Frazer. Mr. Frazer — my sister, Elizabeth."

Elizabeth turned and blushed prettily, fixing her large blue eyes upon Albert as though he had just that moment sprung from the earth. Then she dropped him a graceful curtsey. Elizabeth's dying swan act, the family called it.

Albert, James noticed to his surprise, was also blushing to the roots of his hair. He bowed deeply, his hat held in one hand, the other extended to take Elizabeth's fingertips.

"Miss Onedin, this is indeed a pleasure." He proffered an arm as Elizabeth regained her full height. "May I have the privilege ?"

She rested a hand on his arm. Albert ducked his head in a short bow to James.

"I am indebted to you, Onedin," he said.

James watched the pair walk away, Albert's head bent as though intent upon not missing a word; Elizabeth chattering like a magpie. There was no doubt about it. The world was full of the oddest people. But . . . if Elizabeth played her cards right it might be possible to persuade Frazers to withhold their accounts for a month or two. Then, of course, there was the problem of Daniel Fogarty. Still, no doubt Elizabeth could be relied upon to handle that situation if, and when, it arrived. Elizabeth certainly seemed to have been born with more than her fair share of feminine wiles. Thank God Anne wasn't like that. Now there was a sensible woman. A remarkably sensible woman. In the meantime he really must speak to the sailmaker.

Whistling cheerfully James pointed himself in the direction of the sailmaker's loft and concentrated upon the problem of an additional gaff topsail. Yes, by God, he would order one, and damn the expense.

10

THE wedding took place at St. Bartholomew's church, the Reverend Mr. Samuels officiating.

James was on tenterhooks, convinced the ceremony would never end. The wind was blowing favourably from south and east, it would be slack water in an hour's time and he could sail on the ebb if only that slack-jawed mumbler in the pulpit would come to the point. He stole a glance at Anne at his side. She stood perfectly still, head bowed submissively and swathed from head to toe in her mother's bridal gown. James fidgeted, clamped his lips together and blew a gust of air through his nostrils. As though it was a long-awaited signal the congregation clustered in the pews behind commenced a rapid shuffling of feet, clearing of throats, snuffling of noses. Mr. Simpson burst into a paroxysm of sneezing, Cousin Wilberforce whooped and hawked and Aunt Annie Wagstaffe popped another mint humbug into her mouth.

That was another thing, thought James, bitterly. He had made it perfectly clear from the outset. It was to be no grand affair. Members of the immediate family only. No reception. No fal-de-dals. He had found himself overridden, his wishes ignored, amid such a bustle of to-ing and fro-ing, coming and going, a sending-out of inscribed invitations to a heart-sinking growing list of relations so distant he was barely aware of their existence and neighbours near and far. Even Anne, that sensible woman, seemed to have been caught up in the madness, her fingers busily stitching and sewing, and then that rumpot her father had been packed off to a tailor to be measured for a new suit, no less. Good God, they must think he was made of money! There was a new suit for him also — he had objected strenuously, but the family had screamed at him until his head rang and he gave way yet again — and a new suit for Robert; and Elizabeth and Sarah seemed to spend their days at the dressmaker's and their nights discussing materials. Thank God a man was only married once. Twice would bankrupt a Rajah.

Only a week ago they had had their first quarrel — if such a clash of wills could be particularised as a tiff.

He had announced his intention of sailing immediately after the ceremony. Anne had looked up from her sewing and smiled a strange, shy, vulpine smile.

"Why, James," she had declared, "you are quite the romantic."

James had immediately set her mind at rest on that score. It was not romance, he had explained carefully, but a matter of extreme urgency. He must try to reach Senhor Braganza before Callon had wind of his scheme. Naturally he would sail alone. A 200 ton topsail schooner was no place for a woman.

"A wife's place," she had stated firmly, "is beside her husband."

He had argued. The accommodation would be cramped. The small crew would be dockside sweepings and seamen were not noted for their delicacy of language. She would inevitably be seasick, shipboard food was of notoriously poor quality, and if they ran into bad weather she might very well be soaked to the skin for days on end.

"We shall manage," she had said quietly.

He had tried again. The passage could be dangerous. The ship would carry every shred of canvas it could bear. A mistake could drive her under, or tear the masts out of her.

She had calmly bitten off the thread.

"Then my best place," she had said, "is surely with you. For I assure you I have no more fancy for widowhood than I had for spinsterhood."

He had opened his mouth to protest, but she had cut him short.

"We sink or swim together," she had said. "And that is an end to the matter."

Yes, he thought, only half-aware of Mr. Samuels' droning voice, a most remarkable woman. Remarkable.

A silence fell upon the church. Robert, standing at his side, nudged his arm. He looked down to see his brother holding the thick golden wedding ring toward him. He took it and, carefully following the Reverend Mr. Samuels' instructions, slipped it over her finger. He only made one mistake, from a lifetime's habit saying "Aye, aye," instead of "I will," and then in no time at all it was over.

He brushed aside their congratulations and hurried his bride to the vestry where they signed their names in the book and he waited in a fury of impatience for Mr. Samuels to complete the marriage certificate. Then they plunged out into the open air where a second ordeal awaited.

One of the new-fangled wet-plate photographers halted them on the church porch, marshalled them into a stiffly-posed group, admonished them not to move so much as an eyebrow and disappeared beneath the black canopy of his strange contraption. Mr. Simpson fought to hold back a sneeze and Cousin Wilberforce almost strangled in the effort to choke down a cough. James began to feel that every bone and muscle were clamped in a vice when the photographer's assistant closed his eyes, turned away his head, and dipped a lighted taper into a trough of powder. There was a muffled explosion, a blinding flash and a cloud of smoke. Children screamed delighted fear and a horse bolted with its trap. The photographer emerged triumphant and insisted upon repeating the performance with bride and groom alone, with bride and groom and "*immediate* members of the family only, please". This latter creating an acrimonious dispute between Aunt Annie Wagstaffe, Uncle Will Perkins and Robert.

Then it was finished and all that remained was to run the gauntlet of well-wishers. It was only then that James saw that Mr. Baines, his Mate — whose duty should have kept him aboard ship — was not only there in person but had also assembled the sheepish-looking crew, dressed in guernseys and duck canvas, to stand and halloo at either side of the aisle.

He and Anne ran for the carriage and Anne — following precise instructions — tossed her bouquet toward Elizabeth. It fell short — a sure sign of ill-fortune — only to be scooped up and presented to a glowing Elizabeth by the gallant Mr. Frazer — a sure sign of good fortune.

This vignette James noticed from the corner of his eye as he and his bride, pelted with rice, ran for the waiting carriage.

Anne, white muslin streaming behind her, sallow features flushed either from exertion or happiness, scrambled first into the open carriage bedecked with streamers of ribbon and banks of flowers. James stood stock still and stared aghast. Some fool had removed the horse from between the shafts. Before he could protest the giant Baines was at his elbow propelling him headlong into the carriage. The seamen grabbed the shafts and, urged on by the Mate's stentorian bellowing, set off at a brisk trot for the docks.

The remaining carriages followed more sedately in order of precedence, Sarah, Robert, Elizabeth and Captain Webster — smart as a button in his new suit and licking his lips in anticipation of a fountain of free-flowing liquor — immediately behind.

Robert, to James's surprise, had freely offered to foot half the bill himself, and Albert Frazer — not to be outdone — had promised to supply all refreshments, including a couple of cases of champagne, no less. It was a source of wonder to James how otherwise sensible people could be persuaded to empty their pockets and pour good money straight down the nearest drain in commemoration of events which must barely touch upon their lives.

He turned and looked at Anne sitting

beside him. Her face was flushed and, to his astonishment, tears were streaming down her cheeks.

"What's the matter?" he asked anxiously.

"I'm happy," she said. "So happy." And sobbed the harder.

James gave up. He had taken her for such a sensible woman and yet here she was claiming that she was happy and weeping as though her heart would burst. The whole business was totally incomprehensible. He decided to put the subject entirely from his mind and turned his attention to Mr. Baines jogging cheerfully at the carriage side and exhaling an odour of hot spiced rum over bride and groom alike.

"Are we ready to put to sea?" hissed James.

"All squared away and singled in," answered Baines. "Watchman aboard and a guard on the gangway. We'll be out on the ebb. Sing!" he suddenly roared. "Sing, you pox-ridden lubbers. Begging your pardon, Mrs. Onedin, ma'am."

It was Baines's "Mrs. Onedin" that finally convinced James that he was, not only in fact, but in name also, married.

And, moreover, married to that remarkable sobbing creature at his side. He then realised that she had stopped crying and had changed to bubbling laughter. Really, he thought, a most remarkable woman. Remarkable.

The sailors were singing lustily:

"When I was a chitterling I sailed with the rest,
On a Liverpool packet bound for the West.
We anchored one day in the harbour of Cork,
Intending to put to sea for the port of New York.
Singin' ro-o-o-oll, ro-o-o-oll, roll, bullies, roll!
The Liverpool Judies has got us in tow!
The next I remembered I woke in the morn,
Aboard a three-skys'l yarder bound south round the Horn;
With an old suit of oilskins and two pairs of socks,
And a cauliflower head and a dose of the pox."

He stole a glance at her again. She was gurgling with laughter and beating time with one hand. A most remarkable woman. Most remarkable. James stretched his legs and settled back, relaxing for the first time in weeks.

The carriage dropped them at the foot of the gangway.

The *Charlotte Rhodes* leaned against her mooring lines, her forefoot chuckling in the water. New paint and cordage gleamed in the afternoon sun. The brasswork of the compass binnacle, the skylights, the port-hole rims and the boss of the steering wheel had been polished to a mirror-brightness that struck lancing rays of golden light across the deck. Ropes were belayed and hung in neat coils from the pins of the fife rails. The teakwork had been laboriously sanded and varnished. The capstan was painted white with black insets at the capstan bar sockets. The scuppers were painted the traditional red — a reminder of bloodier days when anything that carried sail was a fighting ship.

The crew had already skipped aboard

across the gap between ship and dockside and Baines was waiting to hand Anne to the deck from the gangway when James realised with sinking heart that there was yet one more ceremony to perform.

The seamen stood shuffling their feet. But although their faces were abashed, their eyes were bright with expectation. James need look no further than the short cask standing upon the main hatch. He inwardly groaned, convinced that the ship would never sail this day. His new father-in-law, he noticed, had wobbled aboard after him, his nose drawn to the cask as a bloodhound to the spoor. The others, tactfully, had remained on the quayside.

Mr. Baines had apparently been elected spokesman. He fished beneath his guernsey and produced two small packages, presenting one to Anne, the other to James.

"With the compl'ments of the crew, ma'am, sir," he said, and stood waiting throughout an interminable silence as James and Anne solemnly unwrapped their gifts. Anne was the quicker for he fumbled like a raw landlubber who had never set eyes upon a knot or hitch before. Anne gasped with delight and held out to him a necklace of minutely carved ivory. James examined it. It was beautifully fashioned. One of the crew at least must have sailed aboard a china bird — the popular name for a tea clipper. He discovered his own present to be skrimshaw work — spouting whales and bobbing longboats carved on walrus tusk. Hmph, he considered, there must also be a whaler among the hands. There was no question about it, Mr. Baines certainly knew how to pick a crew. He ran his eye quickly over the assembly. The whaling man was easy to find — bow-legged, covered in tattooes, a part-shaven pate and a scalp lock — a southern-ocean man who hunted the Big Blue in the Antarctic. The china bird would be the young dandy wearing gold earrings, dungarees of finest duck canvas held in place by a broad belt fancifully studded and holding an ivory-handled sheath knife. James wondered, not for the first time, where the devil Baines found them. Off-scourings of the docks, he had told Anne, but this crew were saltwater men every one.

He made a short speech of thanks because it was expected of him and then invited them to drink a health to his wife and himself. They raised a ragged cheer and crowded around the cask. Baines raised an axe and knocked in the head and they dipped their tin mugs, filled them to the brim and wished mumbled regards to Captain and Missus before swallowing the fiery liquor as though it were soothing syrup. Webster, he noticed, lost no time in dipping his beak with the rest. He nudged Anne and whispered to her to get her father ashore as a distant church clock struck the hour of three.

The old man bid a tearful farewell as though his daughter were bound for the ends of the earth, cast a hopeful glance at the half-empty cask, then rolled ashore to take his place with the others.

Baines hastened the crew to their stations with the promise that they could finish the rum once the ship was under way, the longshoremen dragged the gangway ashore, fitted the capstan bars and commenced to warp the ship out through the open lock gates. A couple of hands hauled in the mooring lines and the rest ran aloft and strung themselves out along the footropes of the fore topsail yards.

As she cleared the lock gates the tide began to ebb. The tops'ls rattled down and the square sails filled and the *Charlotte Rhodes* began to move slowly through the water. Baines ordered the jib run up and the ship's head promptly began to turn. The spanker next, checking her. Then, in mid-river, the big fore-and-afters and the remaining jibs took the wind. The *Charlotte Rhodes* heeled, her forefoot bit into the water, the helmsman felt the tug of the rudder and the play of the wheel and was satisfied.

Anne remained at the taffrail looking shoreward to the diminutive figures waving and hallooing on the sea wall until they disappeared from sight. Then she went below to change out of her wedding dress.

Robert, Sarah, Elizabeth and Albert Frazer watched the ship slip away down river, her sails red and aflame in the sunlight, then they returned to their waiting carriages and the reception.

Callon also watched the *Charlotte Rhodes*' departure from the mullioned window of his private office. Agnew stood at his elbow.

"Well, Agnew?"

"Our Mr. Drummond has just returned from Customs, sir. She has cleared for Lisbon."

Callon mused for a moment.

"The Braganza contract."

Agnew shrugged. "It could be, sir."

"It will be, if I know Onedin," rumbled Callon. "That young whelp is too ambitious by far. Always has been. What ships do we have available, Agnew?"

Agnew tugged at his ear. "There is the *Firefly*, sir. She will be clearing for Philadelphia in forty-eight hours. Full cargo and seven hundred and fifty emigrants."

"I want her out on the next tide." Callon made up his mind quickly. "And send Captain Davis to me."

"Very good, sir," said Agnew. He had been half-expecting it. He had never trusted Onedin from the moment he had set foot in the office. The man had no sense of loyalty. No sense of loyalty at all.

Left to himself Callon sat at his desk, rapt in thought. The *Firefly* was a packet ship, but she had made some smart runs to Australia in the past. Given fair winds she should leave that scow of Onedin's standing. Taking her to Lisbon was no problem, it merely meant adding another couple of days to a voyage which normally took anything from a month to six weeks. Even longer with contrary winds. The fact that he was thereby prolonging the horrors of an emigrant-ship voyage never entered his head. Emigrants were cheap and profitable cargoes. They walked aboard at this end, fed themselves as best they could during the voyage, and those that survived walked ashore at the other end. Yes, Callon decided, he was taking the right course. If Onedin was simply tramping around the Portuguee and Spanish coasts scrounging for cargoes, then no harm would be done. He'd been intending to have a talk with Braganza for some time. He thought he might be able to squeeze the little man for another half per cent freight — he could offer the bait of bigger and faster ships and a regular service. On the other hand, if Onedin was such a fool as to try to snap up that contract — and he wouldn't put it past the rogue for a minute — then he, Callon, by God, would teach the young upstart a trick or two.

Satisfied with his reasoning, Callon sat

back and viewed the future with equanimity.

James clattered down the companionway to their tiny quarters aft. He paused at the foot of the ladder; Anne had lighted the oil lamps which swung slowly on their gimbals throwing moving shadows across the white-painted bulkheads. She was wearing a flannel nightdress and, seated before the mirror, in the act of pinning up her hair. James hesitated. In truth this was a side of marriage he had given little thought to. He had an uncomfortable feeling of embarrassment and tried to hide a sudden urge to run away by sitting on the edge of their bunk and pulling off his boots. He concentrated on the task as though his feet had never known the inside of such strange objects before. Anne stood up and turned to face him. He felt suddenly awkward, gauche. He discovered that inexplicably he had lost the use of his tongue. Anne looked at him and then lowered her head, shy and miserable. To his alarm he saw that her lower lip was beginning to tremble and tears were flooding her eyes. She licked her lips and spoke as though the words were being dragged out of her by an agency over which she had no control.

"Your sister, Elizabeth," she began, and faltered.

"What?"

"She is beautiful," she said, and the tears began to stream down her cheeks.

James "hmphed", walked to the cabin compact and made a business of filling the basin with water. He tried to speak lightly, not fully understanding what was expected of him.

"A bit pinched about the nose," he said. "But some seem to think she has a fair share of prettiness. At least Daniel Fogarty and that fop Frazer seem to find it so . . ." He trailed off.

"I wish I were," she said miserably.

He stared at her. "What?"

"Attractive. But I'm not. I'm plain and ugly and my skin is dry and sallow and . . ." She gulped and looked at him piteously. Her face began to crumple.

James took a step toward her. He reached out his arms and put his hands upon her thin shoulders. He held her at arm's length.

"Anne. Look at me."

She raised her head.

"Anne," he said earnestly, meaning every word. "If men married for beauty alone there would be a power of lonely women in this world."

Apparently he had said the right thing, for that remarkable woman moved toward him, sniffed and smiled through her tears, and rested her head upon his shoulder.

"Do you really believe so?" she asked.

James did.

"You silly pigeon," he said. "You silly pigeon."

11

ROBERT and Sarah viewed Elizabeth's latest flirtation with misgivings and Albert Frazer's intentions with suspicion. For all his studied politeness and mock-gallantry the inescapable fact was that persons in Albert Frazer's station in life did not — indeed were not permitted to — marry so far beneath them.

Sarah tried to warn of the pitfalls that lay in the paths of the innocent. Elizabeth needed no telling. A keen play-goer, she was only too well aware of the inevitable consequences of a lapse from grace. Abandoned by society the unhappy creatures went demented to wander the highways and by-ways eternally lamenting their misfortune, or — more satisfyingly — wasted away of consumption in some bare and frowsty garret, penitent at the last but with none to bring them comfort. Elizabeth's private opinion was that these heroines were an insipid and characterless lot thoroughly deserving of all that fate held in store for them.

Robert was more forthright. He berated, abjured, scolded and roared like a bull, all of which simply served the purpose of hardening Elizabeth's determination to play with fire until her fingers were burnt — the phrase was Sarah's; Robert preferred "putting your head in a noose". "She will bring shame upon us," wailed Sarah. "Not in this house," thundered Robert; and both chanted "Wait until Daniel Fogarty hears of your perfidious behaviour!" "Daniel Fogarty does not yet own me!" stormed Elizabeth and raged from the house to her tryst with Albert.

In truth, she thought later — bored almost out of her mind at a performance of Signor Verdi's *Il Trovatore* — even Daniel could not take exception to Mr. Frazer's behaviour; he was at all times the perfect gentleman — rather too perfect for Elizabeth's tastes — she would have preferred a more passionate declaration. The fact of the matter was that she was becoming a little tired of Albert's attentions. She was of a nature that craved excitement as a flower craves the sun.

Yes, she decided as the hansom jogged its way home, she would settle for Daniel Fogarty. For all his faults, his uncertainty of temper and coarse manners, he at least had the merit of sharing her own predilections for the theatre and music hall. She could not imagine dear Daniel sitting through that incomprehensible caterwauling for more than ten minutes. Her back and neck ached from the effort of sitting bolt upright. She remembered how when she once attempted to speak she had been peremptorily shushed from all sides, and Albert had smiled and put a finger to his lips. When the second interval arrived she could stand it no longer, pleaded a headache and begged Albert to send her home. He had expressed sympathy and offered to accompany her but she had refused firmly: she would not, she said, rather tartly, think for the world of spoiling *his* evening's entertainment.

He had called for her cape and helped her into the cab, as polite and considerate as ever, but she was aware that he knew full well the reason for her displeasure. There would be no more invitations to operas, that was certain sure.

She sighed unhappily and wished she were married. But not to Albert Frazer. The rich seemed to live such dull lives.

Robert hastily unbolted and unbarred the door for her.

"You've been visiting Uncle Will and Aunt Alice. Just returned by the Manchester train," he hissed, then in a loud affable voice: "Elizabeth! We have a little surprise for you."

He ushered her into the living-room beaming like a magician who has produced a rabbit from a hat.

Daniel Fogarty came to his feet as she hesitated in the doorway, blinking in the harsh glare of the gas lights. His bearded face crinkled with delight and he took her in his arms and swung her off her feet in a rib-crushing gorilla-like hug. "Dan . . .!" she started to say, and he kissed her full on the mouth and waltzed her round and round the room.

"What a day!" he trumpeted. "What a day!" He tumbled her breathless on to the horsehair sofa and then stood flushed with triumph by the fireplace while Robert poured wine and Sarah threw her a warning glance and asked meaningly, "And how is Aunt Alice?"

Elizabeth felt a mounting fury with Robert and Sarah. Why the devil must they spoil it all by prevaricating so? Now she found herself, willy-nilly, caught up in the web of their deceit. She had had every intention of telling Daniel about her disastrous evening with Albert Frazer. She would have made light of it and mocked Albert's affectations, and Daniel would have laughed boisterously and hugged her and there would not be the slightest hint of envy or jealousy. Oh, left to herself she could handle Daniel easily enough. But now she was trapped in this stupid lie.

She had to answer Sarah's question. They were all waiting; Daniel out of politeness and obviously bursting to tell his news.

"Very well," said Elizabeth. "She and Uncle Will send their regards." And the little harmless untruth caught her and ensnared her and charted a new course for her life.

Daniel drained his glass.

"What a day!" he repeated. "The things that happen when a man turns his back for a month or two are beyond belief. We berthed today and the first thing I hear is that James — James, of all people — is married. Married! And to that scrag-end of mutton, Anne Webster! And now he owns a ship!" He shook his head as though overcome at the folly of man, and Robert topped up their glasses again. "It's the strangest damn' marriage I ever did hear of! And now the pair of them have gone off voyaging in the *Charlotte Rhodes*. The *Charlotte Rhodes*! By God, it must have cost him a pretty penny to refit her — the last time I saw her she was sitting on the putty and looked only fit for the breaker's yard."

Robert's hand shook, his face paled and he sat down weakly in a chair.

"I daresay," continued Daniel, unconscious of the effect on Robert, "that a voyage or two will take care of the bills. There is no doubt about it, owning your own ship is the quickest way to a fortune."

Robert brightened and mopped his brow.

"Unless," added dear Daniel, cheerfully, "she should sink or pile herself ashore. Salvage can cost a mint of money if you're not insured." He wagged his head wisely. "There are no short cuts to wealth in this world."

Robert slopped more wine into his glass and his eyes rolled in his head like a creature *in extremis.*

Daniel emptied his glass again and held it out to Robert for more. He raised his glass high.

"And now let me give you a toast. To Captain Daniel Fogarty," he announced, looking directly at Elizabeth.

She understood with a tremor of excitement that almost turned her limbs to water. The last obstacle had been removed. They could be married! At last, they could be married. Dear Daniel. Dear, dear Daniel!

"Oh, Daniel," she said. "You've had your promotion!" and ran to his arms and buried her face in his beard and kissed his lips, his cheeks, his eyes; she thought she would never stop kissing him. "Oh, Daniel, Daniel, Daniel," she crowed.

"Congratulations," said Robert, shakily, thinking of the dwindling pile of gold and the mountain of bills.

"Oh, Daniel," said Sarah. "I am so happy for you. For you both," she added firmly, and then winced as the child moved in her belly.

"Is it settled? Really and truly settled?" asked Elizabeth, nuzzling him.

Daniel's habitual caution reasserted itself. "Well, almost," he said. "As good as."

"Oh, no," wailed Elizabeth, releasing him. She felt that she had lived her life on half-promises and unfulfilled pledges, promissory notes that never fell due.

"I had it from Agnew," said Daniel, reassuring her. "Mr. Callon could not give me the news himself for it seems that he has gone haring after James — in the *Firefly*, no less. What the devil," he asked, "has James been up to that he should put Mr. Callon in such a choler? By God," he said, "he's running foul of the wrong man there."

"Mr. Agnew said . . . ?" prompted Elizabeth.

"Mr. Agnew, my dearest, is Mr. Callon's confidential clerk. He has assured me that Mr. Callon intends to give me command of the *Barracuda*. The *Barracuda*!"

The name meant nothing to Elizabeth.

"The *Barracuda*," he explained, "is a barque of eighteen hundred tons and with accommodation for twenty-five first class passengers. She is engaged on the Australian wool trade. Mr. Callon must think well of me to give me such a promotion."

Elizabeth's blood ran cold.

"Australia?" she asked faintly.

Daniel laughed and squeezed the breath from her body.

"I promise not to set foot aboard until we are wed, you goose."

She pouted. "But Australia is so far away."

"Then you shall sail with me and serve your apprenticeship as a bride aboard ship." He laughed boisterously again, and, catching the infection of his humour, she laughed with him.

"And tomorrow," he said, "I am to be measured for a new suit. With four gold bands upon the sleeve. Then we'll have a day out — at the seaside. You can spare her for the day, eh, Robert?"

Robert raised drowned eyes. "What? Oh, yes, yes, to be sure," and lapsed into gloom again.

"When will the banns be read?" asked Sarah, practically.

"The moment Mr. Callon returns. He will wish to impart the news himself. You do understand," he added in lowered voice as though he had just broached a secret of State, "that I rely upon your discretion. Strictest confidence," he added, pushing a finger against his lips, and Elizabeth realised that dear Daniel was in a state of inebriation. He swayed across the room and picked up his hat.

"Must be on my way," he announced, choosing his words with the care of a man speaking a strange language. He smothered a hiccup and bowed to Robert and Sarah. "Thank you for 'spitality. Robert. Mrs. Onedin."

"I'll lock up after you," said Elizabeth, smiling, and escorted him through the shop to the door. He stood swaying gently as though the floor was a deck heaving beneath his feet, and lurched to one side with exaggerated politeness as she withdrew the bolts. She hesitated for a moment and then, putting her arms about his neck, drew his head down and kissed him softly, lingeringly. In spite of the cursed crinoline she felt her body drift into his. She took his hand and guided it to her breast and once again her heart seemed to leap into her throat and her mouth ran dry. She squirmed and pushed into him and felt his answering thrust; her head hung back and her breast seemed to have swollen to twice its size; her mouth had opened and his tongue seemed to be pushing its way down her throat; her head swam dizzily and every breath she had ever taken seemed to be enclosed within her skull. She heard Robert's cough and the clink of glasses in the living-room and they moved apart and stood looking at one another as if they were total strangers. His eyes looked like great brown globes illumined with a strange inner light. She touched his cheek gently. "Dear Daniel," she said softly. "Dear Daniel."

He took her hand and kissed her fingertips. "Tomorrow," he said. "Tomorrow." And then he was gone.

She looked out and watched his progress along the street. He walked sedately at first. Then he suddenly hurled his hat high in the air, gave a hop, skip and a jump and a great whoop of joy before disappearing from sight around the corner.

He was as good as his word and called for her promptly at ten o'clock. They greeted each other shyly, then he took her arm and walked her to the Pier Head.

They crossed to Egremont by steam ferry and stood leaning against the rail by the paddle box and watched the great wheel thrashing the water. He had already visited his tailor, he told her, and ordered a frock coat with black rather than brass buttons — he considered gold braid to be ostentatious enough. "But it is a company rule," he explained, "and I shall have to bear with it." He would also be condemned to wear one of the new cheese-cutter hats. He held his stove-pipe top hat in his hand as security against the breeze. "But only on formal occasions," he said. "Passengers expect their money's worth and don't feel safe unless the Master is instantly recognisable and dressed like a May horse."

"I think you will look more handsome than ever," she said. "You could wear your uniform at our wedding. You would cut quite a figure."

He fingered his hat nervously and shook his head.

"I'd feel a fool," he said, smiling. "You don't want to marry a fool, do you?"

She thought she had never been so happy in her life. And when he conducted her up the companion-way, past the barrier and the notice saying: NO PASSENGERS PERMITTED BEYOND THIS POINT, and introduced her to the ferry-boat Captain — who wore gold braid and a smart little cap, she noticed — to stand upon the railed-in enclosure that ran like a sort of bridge between the two paddle boxes, she thought her heart would burst with pride and excitement. The Captain was a grizzled veteran of handlebar moustache and mutton-chop whiskers and gallantry itself. He showed her how the boat was manoeuvred by striking a plunger bell that directed the engines to go forwards or backwards. He even let her strike the bell herself and immediately one of the great paddle wheels stopped turning and the little ship swung sharply around leaving a great curved creaming wake behind it, and the black smoke belching from the funnel changed direction to pour across the deck below, and she laughed to see the passengers suddenly scampering from one side of the ship to the other to escape the pall of soot and smoke.

It was going to be a fine wonderful day, she knew, and this was only the beginning.

They disembarked at Egremont pier and strolled arm in arm along the Ham-and-Egg Parade as far as New Brighton. They ate freshly peeled shrimps from a stall and drank lemonade and then Daniel insisted they went to a beach photographer's tent where they had their likenesses taken. She sat in a chair and he stood stiffly by her side while the photographer, a man of flashing black eyes, oiled hair and moustache — of Italian extraction, she thought — fussed about and screwed iron clamps to their necks, begged them not to move a muscle, scampered away to crouch beneath the canopy, made a few adjustments, reappeared, held one hand high, removed the lens cap, and counted slowly to thirty. She held her breath until she thought her lungs would burst. Then it was over. The Italian gentleman removed the clamps and scurried away to prepare the plates and Daniel took the opportunity to kiss her again. A nice warm friendly sort of kiss, and then they stood holding hands until the photographer returned to tell them that it was an excellent likeness and would they call back in fifteen minutes?

They wandered along the beach, scuffing at the sand, and looked at New Brighton Lighthouse which, Daniel assured her, had been the saving of many a ship; and went on to tell her hair-raising stories of the wreckers that once haunted this coast — far, far worse than the notorious Cornish wreckers, he swore. Then, the tide being out, they walked as far as the Rock Fort and stared in wonder at the massive sandstone walls and the deep slits of gun emplacements.

"Never fired a shot," he told her. "Never once."

They walked around the fort on the landward side. It was low and squat and almost covered with water at high tide. There was a stillness about it, an atmosphere of brooding power that gave them an odd sense of security. Seabirds wheeled and banked, frantically diving for scraps, and a big outward-bounder, loaded to the gunwales, her sails patched and sides salt-encrusted and travel-stained, rounded the Point and fled to the west in a flurry of spume and a wake of screaming gulls.

They walked back hand-in-hand to the photographer. He was waiting for them, their pictures mounted and framed in ornate imitation silver and wrapped in layers of tissue paper. Daniel paid him and slipped the photographs into his pocket for safe-keeping. They called at a tea shop and had freshly cut sandwiches, sticky cream cakes and a pot of tea. Then it was time to return.

On the ferryboat Daniel had a sudden inspiration.

"We'll go to the theatre," he said. "And supper afterwards, eh?" He looked at her anxiously—as though she could conceivably be offended at such a splendid end to such a perfect day. She hugged him with joy and, caring not a toss for the disapproving stares of their fellow passengers, kissed him delightedly mouth to mouth.

They went to see one of the new Sensation Dramas at the Prince of Wales Theatre and Elizabeth rose in her seat and screamed her apprehension as the hero made his death-defying leap into a sea of blue gauze, and the audience stamped its feet, whistling and roaring its approval and not ceasing the uproar until Jack Lovelorn once again clambered the rigging of the sinking ship and repeated the performance.

She hissed and screeched at the villain and would have torn his black heart out if she could have laid hands on him, and tears splashed down her face at the heroine's heart-rending plea of: "Who — who shall help me? If ever retribution came to woman, it has come to me now!" This, she decided happily, was entertainment on the grand scale and infinitely superior to the feeble bleatings of fat middle-aged sopranos and stout bearded baritones. Really, she thought, that nincompoop Albert doesn't know what he is missing! And she clutched Daniel's arm the tighter as the villain was unmasked for the dastard he was and virtue was once more triumphant and hero and heroine were reunited to live happily ever after.

They walked along Dale Street toward Moorfields, passed a barrel-organist and a plague of ragamuffins surrounding the baked-potato men and trotter sellers; passed bulging shop-windows flaunting bright gowns and rolls of cloth and ribbons and cottons and lace; and butchers and bakers and sweetmeat makers tempting the hungry; until they arrived at one of the finest restaurants in town.

Inside it was warm and crowded, the air redolent with the smell of rich cooking. Rippling waves of conversation spread across the room, rose and fell, dropped to a humming murmur only to be suddenly broken by a staccato shout of laughter from a celebratory party seated at a long table set against one wall. A flank of beef was turned upon a spit by two hollow-eyed boys while a perspiring cook basted the meat with fat from the drip pan beneath. Attentive waiters hurried through the kitchen doorway to return with plates and covered dishes and steaming tureens of soup.

A waiter took her cloak while Daniel went to speak to the proprietor, a completely bald giant who wore his beard in the French fashion and whose dress — were it not for what she took to be a chain of office hanging about his neck — made him almost indistinguishable from his guests. Daniel, she noticed, seemed to be engaged in a heated discussion with the bald man who, for his part, wagged his huge cannon-ball head from side to side and shrugged enormous shoulders in gallic apology.

Daniel returned looking downcast.

"I'm sorry, dear heart," he said, "we would have to wait an hour."

Her heart sank. Always of good appetite, she realised she was monstrously hungry and could not possibly wait an hour even to dine in such splendour.

"Unless . . ." Daniel was saying slowly.

"What?" she asked, hope rising.

"He says we could have a private room. Upstairs," he added looking embarrassed.

Elizabeth was delighted. Private supper rooms figured largely in the romantic "silver spoon" novels to which she was addicted — it had been her secret hope that Albert would have had the gumption to invite her to sup with him privately, but the fool had never even taken her to so much as a hot-pot supper. He really had been a great disappointment she thought, fretfully. But now she could dine alone with her betrothed, thereby being able to sip from the cup of wickedness without being called upon to settle the sinful reckoning.

She assented eagerly and the proprietor himself led them through a curtained alcove and up a flight of carpeted stairs to a long corridor above. There was a wine-coloured wallpaper and the gas jets burned low behind pink glass bowls. Paintings hung upon the walls and she paused to look more closely. Venus rose from the waves in one, and Psyche stepped from her bath in another, while a third portrayed the Judgement of Paris. Elizabeth blushed and hurried on.

The restaurateur unlocked the door, gave the key to Daniel, and bowed them inside.

She had never seen such a splendidly-appointed room; it quite took the breath away. The walls were draped in silk. Ornate gold mirrors reflected the light from a cheerful fire. Silverware was laid upon the table, and a magnificent sideboard held the most startling array of bottles and decanters she had ever seen.

Baldhead settled her into a brocaded chair at the table, gave each an enormous menu card and waited attentively for Daniel to order. She stared bewildered at the bill of fare and then looked helplessly to Daniel. To her unbounded admiration he dealt with the matter decisively.

"We'll take," he said, ignoring the jaw-breaking French, "a dozen oysters apiece. Oxtail soup. And roast sucking pig."

The proprietor scribbled industriously and bowed his gratitude.

"Wine, sir?" he suggested.

Daniel appeared to give the matter a great deal of thought, then looked across to her.

"What do you say to champagne?" he asked.

Champagne! She could hardly believe the evidence of her ears. Dear Daniel! And she had harboured such unworthy thoughts in the past; privately calling him oaf and boor and thinking him to be coarse and stupid, and yet here he was quite at his ease and ordering champagne as though it were the most natural thing in the world. Why, he was far more the gentleman than Albert Frazer could hope to be for all his fanciful education and breeding.

"Thank you, Daniel," she said, as

calmly as she could. "I think a little champagne would be splendid."

The man bowed and took himself off to execute their order, softly closing the door behind him.

"Oh, Daniel," she said softly, "I do love you."

The room she noticed was stuffily close and her feet hurt after all that walking.

"Do you think," she asked, "I could remove my footwear? My feet ache dreadfully."

"Of course you may, you goose," said Daniel. "You may do as you wish. The room is ours for as long as we care to use it."

She thankfully unlaced her boots while Daniel inspected the rows of bottles on the sideboard. She looked around for somewhere to hide her boots, positive that she would feel embarrassed should the waiter return and see them standing beside her chair. She settled on placing them behind a chaise-longue — the largest she had ever seen — standing by the heavily curtained window and covered in a mound of bright-coloured cushions. She plumped experimentally upon it and found it to be as soft and springy as any bed.

Daniel returned to the table carrying two glasses of sherry. She rejoined him and then her heart suddenly beat such a clamour of alarm that her breath caught in her throat and the blood drained from her face. She looked at Daniel, wide-eyed.

"Daniel," she said. "Oh, Daniel. Can you afford it? All this . . ." she waved a hand, "must cost a fortune!"

He smiled at her foolishness. "This and a great deal more," he said. "Once I am Master of the *Barracuda* I shall have not only a Captain's salary but I shall earn a five per cent cargo bonus, twenty-five per cent on cabin passengers and five per cent on steerage. And more beside. I reckon . . ." he calculated, lips pursed, "to be worth a thousand a year of any man's money."

A thousand pounds a year! The sum was beyond her comprehension. He grinned at her open-mouthed wonder.

"I told you it'd be worth the waiting for. Never settle for second best, I said. From now on we'll live in style. Mix in the best society."

It was incredible. Really incredible. And what an end to such an incredible day!

Surely there could be no more wonders after this?

But there were. There was the meal to be disposed of: oysters on the half shell washed down with champagne, rich tawny oxtail soup and the sweet and tender little suckling with fresh vegetables and baked potatoes, and all served by no less than two properly obsequious waiters—and then Daniel called for a second bottle of champagne for she found she had such an intolerable thirst—then the waiters cleared the table and tactfully withdrew leaving them at last alone.

She nibbled a ratafia biscuit and Daniel poured two glasses of sweet sticky liqueur. She sighed happily and expelled a breath.

"I'm so hot," she said. "And so full. If I eat another mouthful I shall burst."

Daniel lit a cigar, then loosened his tie.

"It is close," he agreed. "I wonder if the window will open?"

She followed him across and sprawled upon the chaise-longue while he parted the velvet curtains and struggled with the window fastenings.

"It's no use," he said. "I'm afraid we're battened in."

She leaned back against the soft cushions and stretched out her arms.

"Come here, Daniel." She took his head in her hands. "Daniel, my love. Oh, Daniel," she crooned. "Dear Daniel."

His hands fumbled at the multitude of buttons on her blouse. She moved his hand away, smiling into his eyes, and shakily began to unfasten them herself, her mind a tumult of incoherent thoughts, a ragbag jumble of fears and warnings and desire and yearning and, above all, an overwhelming sense of gratitude for such a wonderful, wonderful day.

"We are betrothed, Daniel," she heard herself whispering. "We should be married within the month."

He lifted her breast from her bodice and cupped it in his hand. Then lowering his head he kissed the small soft tender thing until she thought she would swoon with sheer pleasure. She felt strangely languorrous and, looking up, he read the acquiescence in her eyes. He left her side and crossed the room, turning down the gas jets to pale yellow orbs of light that hissed and popped softly within their tiny globular worlds of glass. He touched the fire with his foot and then sat on a chair to remove his boots while a shower of sparks ran up the chimney like a silent scream. She unhooked the waistband of her skirt and wriggled out of it thankful that she had, at the last moment, decided against wearing a crinoline. Really, female garments were too ridiculous for words. Then she lay full length on the chaise-longue and found herself gripped with a fit of shivering as though she had the ague. She closed her eyes and forced her mind to a numbing blankness. Having only the most nebulous notions of what was expected of her she determined at whatever cost to suppress all thought. She would not cry out nor give him the slightest cause for self-reproach. She heard him pad across the room and in a moment he was beside her.

Later they lay quietly side by side for a while, not daring to speak or move, and she felt a languid sleepy warmth stealing over her, and sighed in utter contentment, longing to sleep in his arms for ever.

"Dear Daniel," she murmured. "Dear, dear Daniel. Do you love me?" she asked. "Really and truly love me?" It seemed a ridiculous question to ask under the circumstances, but one to which she must have the answer.

"For ever, my sweet," he replied. "For ever."

12

ONCE the *Firefly* was clear of the Lizard she swept out into the Atlantic with the wind on her port quarter, made two long raking tacks, and caught the *Charlotte Rhodes* on the fourth day in longitude 9° 50 west, latitude 43° 18 north. Fifty-five miles north-west of Cape Finisterre, and 340 miles north of the Tagus.

James watched from the stern rail as the *Firefly*'s topmasts appeared over the horizon and she spread her wings and bore down upon them. He passed the telescope to Anne and she focused upon the red and gold Callon houseflag flaunting at the masthead.

"Which ship is she?" she asked.

"The *Firefly*," James replied. "One of Callon's crack western ocean packets with a bone between her teeth." He grinned. "Callon's dander must be up to detach such a ship from so profitable a service."

They watched the gap narrowing.

"What shall we do?" she asked.

"Have you finished sewing our house-flag?"

She nodded, surprised at his easy confidence.

"Fetch it," he commanded. "We'll show him our colours," and grinned again like a schoolboy.

Anne hurried below and scooped up the flag upon which she had worked so hard and lovingly. It was a blue burgee with a large white O surmounting a wavy white line and, she thought, the most beautiful banner in the world. She hurried back on to deck and watched James expertly roll the flag into a ball, bend it to the halyard and then run it aloft to the masthead where it broke to whip and snap defiantly in the wind.

But all the defiance in the world could not hold back the inevitable. At six bells in the afternoon watch the *Firefly* overtook them, its canvas piled high and towering above their heads.

James subjected its decks to a careful scrutiny.

"I thought so," he said with satisfaction. "Windy Davis is in command."

"Who?" she asked, laughing.

"Captain Davis," he told her, "has the reputation of being a man who likes plenty of searoom. The moment the sun touches the horizon he'll bring her round a point or two to starboard, mark my words."

"And what shall we do?"

"Take the inshore passage and cut a few corners," said James.

"Shall we beat him into port, then?" she asked.

James shook his head. "No. But we will be snapping at his heels, and that is all I require." He smiled at her. "I am not racing a ship, Anne, I am racing time."

She was puzzled.

"It is really quite simple," he explained. "I wrote to Senhor Braganza from Liverpool asking for the favour of a conversation and hinting that I had certain proposals to make which might be to our mutual benefit."

"You did not mention Mr. Callon?"

"No. Just enough to whet his appetite."

"But will it be enough?" Anne looked anxious.

"More than enough. If Callon had remained in Liverpool, then our conversation would be no more than a straightforward business discussion. But if Callon arrives first, eager to bargain, then Senhor Braganza's suspicions will be aroused. Believe me, Anne, that little Portuguee is nobody's fool."

The *Firefly* dropped anchor in Lisbon Roads at nine o'clock in the morning, thirty hours later.

A boatman answered the hail from the deck and rowed Callon ashore. He sat fuming his irritation in the sternsheets, turning his head once to look back at the sound of the *Firefly*'s crew raising hoarse voices in song as they breasted the capstan bars and dragged up the anchor from the mud of the Tagus:

"Awa-ay, Rio!
Fare-ye-well, ye Liverpool gals,
For we're bound for the Rio Grande."

By the time the wherry had bumped alongside the quay the *Firefly* had weighed anchor, crossed her yards and was reaching for the open sea again.

A cabriole drawn by a splay-footed bag of bones set Callon down at the Casa Braganza, Exporter de Vinhos, a building of deeply-recessed windows and painted an eye-aching white, overlooking the harbour in the Cidade Baixa district. Callon hauled upon the bell pull and a porter in olive green livery opened a sort of postern gate and bowed him into a cool courtyard fringed with palms and bowered with trellised vines. The porter transferred his responsibility to a clerk wearing a crumpled linen suit. He in his turn led Callon up a flight of stairs, through a wide ante-room to the private office of Senhor Braganza.

Firmino de Deus Braganza was a small dapper man of neat imperial beard and quick bird-like movement. He rose from his desk and greeted his visitor with outstretched hands and the gratification of a man welcoming home a favoured companion.

"Senhor Callon! This is indeed a pleasure!" His English was fluent and perfectly enunciated — almost too perfect were it not for a native tendency to overstress vowel sounds and slightly slur sibilants.

"Delighted to renew our acquaintance, Seenyoor," growled Callon, shaking hands and creaking his bulk into a basketwork chair brought forward by the clerk. Relieving Callon of his top hat, the underling bowed his way out through the wide double doors.

Braganza's white teeth seemed to flash across his face.

"You will take wine, of course, Senhor?" He glided across the room on soundless feet and poured thin cool pale-green wine into two tall slender glasses. "Vinho Verde. Your health, Senhor."

Callon drank thirstily while outside the sun boiled in an ultramarine sky and the cries of orange-sellers and fish peddlers and hawkers of laces and gums and spices were borne in through the wide casemented window.

Braganza raised his glass and stood looking out across the harbour. Callon wished irritably that the damned Portuguee would stop flitting about the room and sit down and come to business like a sensible fellow. He bottled his ire, screwed his features into an affable grin and fished a bundle of papers from his leather wallet.

"I called, Seenyoor," he began, "to discuss our new contract . . ."

Braganza raised his shoulders and spread his hands.

"Ah, business, business. Always business." He sighed. "You English are such demons of energy. If only my countrymen could be bitten by the same flea. Another glass of wine, Senhor?" He refilled their glasses while Callon took the opportunity to spread the new contracts upon the desk.

"I proposed," he said, "to reduce freight charges by two and one quarter per cent." He sat back with a self-satisfied air, waiting for Braganza to nibble the bait.

"I am overwhelmed at such generosity, Senhor," said Braganza. Callon nodded and sipped his wine, missing the irony in Braganza's voice.

The little man picked up the documents and carried them across to the window.

"You'll not find better terms elsewhere. I'll warrant it," said Callon, wishing again that the confounded man would sit at his desk like an Englishman instead of hovering around that damned window.

Braganza studied the papers with the time-consuming care of a man determined upon committing every word to memory. He paused from time to time to stare out of the window, apparently rapt in thought. Callon shifted restlessly in his chair.

"Satisfactory?" he asked, unable to contain his impatience the longer.

Braganza peered over the top of the contract. "More than satisfactory," he said mildly. "But might I be permitted the temerity to ask, why?"

"No more than you deserve," said Callon. "A practical expression of goodwill by way of return for a long and profitable association between our two houses."

Braganza smiled and looked out of the window again.

"And you were in such haste to bring me the good news that you came by packet ship? I am indeed honoured, Senhor."

This time the irony was unmistakable. Callon looked at him suspiciously. The man didn't miss much. He must have seen the *Firefly* dropping anchor—probably from this very window. In which case Braganza had probably seen him coming ashore. And that meant that he had been expected.

"It is one of my maxims that in matters

of business, principals should always deal with principals." Callon sat up in his chair, leaned forward and put the palms of his hands upon the table. It was a favourite posture when faced with opposition.

"An admirable sentiment," said Braganza.

"If you accept the terms," said Callon, getting down to business, "and you'll find none more favourable, perhaps you'll be kind enough to append your signature?"

Braganza shook his head. "Not yet, I think, Senhor Callon." Once again he turned to gaze out of the window. "I see that another British ship has just come to anchor." He took a brass-mounted telescope from its wall hanging, steadied against the window embrasure, and focused carefully.

"A topsail schooner," he pronounced. "Red canvas and flying a blue houseflag with the device of a white circle." Lowering the telescope he turned and smiled at Callon. "Do you know of such a company, Senhor?"

"It is new to me," replied Callon, ambiguously.

Braganza drifted back to the desk, sat in

his chair and pushed a box of cigars across.

"We will wait," he announced, smiling his thin, infuriating smile.

James had himself rowed ashore in the ship's gig by the Dandy and Scalplock. He left them at the quayside and, long acquaintanceship making him familiar with the port, set off on foot at brisk pace. The white stone houses rose in terraces from the shores of the Tagus. He walked through the narrow alleyways of the Alfama, passed the cathedral, and crossed the Rossio to enter the rectangular district of the Cidade Baixa.

The porter recognised him immediately and let him find his own way up the narrow stairway. He tossed his hat to Gussio, the clerk, and, pushing open the doors, entered Braganza's office.

Braganza beamed. "Ah, Captain Onedin. We have been expecting you. You are acquainted with Senhor Callon?"

The question was a politeness. James and Callon acknowledged each other's presence with formal nods and, on Callon's part, a wary look. James tossed his leather wallet on to the desk and, settling himself comfortably in a chair, accepted a glass of wine from Braganza. They smiled at each other like old friends.

Braganza settled himself behind his desk. His surface urbanity disappeared.

"Can we come to business, gentlemen?" he asked.

This was more to Callon's liking. He was nothing if not a fighter and the knowledge that he had the ships, the finance, the power and the influence, the product of a lifetime's scarred battles, gave him confidence.

"So it's the wine contract you're after, eh, Onedin?" He took another cigar, chewed and spat out the end. "This man," he said to Braganza, "has not an ounce of loyalty in him."

"Any man who demands loyalty from his fellows, Callon, must first earn it." James's eyes had a flat cold look.

"You took advantage of a position of trust."

"I took advantage of a business opportunity." James noticed that Callon's hand was shaking. The fool was working himself up into one of his famous tantrums.

Callon snarled: "No man of principle

would accept his employer's money and then betray his interests."

"There are two sides to that coin," said James.

Braganza intervened with amusement. "Gentlemen, if you please. The purpose of this discussion is to decide which of you will ship my produce. Your opinions are not at issue. My position, however, is abundantly clear. The contract will go to him who can offer the more favourable terms." He leaned back, spread his hands expressively and looked from one to the other; again he gave that idiosyncratic shrug of the shoulders. "It is a plain matter of business, gentlemen."

Callon thumped the desk. "I'll put an end to this lottery. A man with but one small ship to his name cannot compete with Callon and Company . . ."

"I'll soon have more," said James. He spoke quietly and seemed to be inspecting the toe of his boot as though bored with the entire proceedings.

"And where will you get 'em?" demanded Callon. "And the money to pay for 'em?"

"That," said James, "is my affair."

"He has neither money nor credit," snapped Callon.

Braganza regarded them reflectively. He picked up the contract between finger and thumb and then lowered it delicately to the desk again.

"And this is your offer, Senhor Callon?" he asked politely.

"I'll better it here and now. I'm prepared to offset any losses I might incur against my emigrant trade. You can have a five per cent reduction of present freight rates for the first six months, three and a half for the remaining six, and an option of renewal. You will also have six ships to call upon — and I'll guarantee to replace the schooners with brigs. There's capacity for ye." He sat back, snorting defiance.

"Rather too much capacity," murmured Braganza, gently. "I am sure my poor business could not keep six such magnificent ships fully engaged."

"I'll find work for 'em," growled Callon.

"Of course he will," said James. "They'll creep around the coast while your precious wine slops around in its casks losing body. And when he finds more profitable cargoes, you will whistle for his ships."

Callon hammered the desk again.

"There'll be no reneging on either side. It'll be there in black-and-white, all drawn up legal fashion. What do you have to offer?"

"My word," said James.

Callon puffed derision. But James caught the speculative look in Braganza's eye. James, as Callon's agent, had been dealing with Braganza for the past three years and was aware that the little Portuguee had a prickly sense of honour.

"Interesting," said Braganza. "And your offer, Captain Onedin?"

James knew the value of silence. He reached forward, helped himself to a cigar and lit it with care.

"I'll ship your wine free of freight," he said, and waited for their reaction.

For a moment Callon appeared not to believe the evidence of his senses, then he roared with laughter. "Damme," he said. "The chicken'll be a long time growing fat on that diet," and wiped his eyes.

Braganza smiled: "Indeed, I think you will find small profit there, Captain Onedin."

"Oh, I should find profit enough," said

James carelessly, "if I were to be your sole agent for the United Kingdom."

"Ah." Braganza closed his eyes.

Callon shook his head like a bull. "It can't be done," he claimed, decisively. "It's been tried, and failed. It is impossible to sail a ship on commission alone."

"I shall also require," said James, carefully, "an undertaking that my ships — and my ships alone — will have the concession of returning your empty wine casks."

Braganza's eyes opened. He nodded his head thoughtfully.

"It is possible."

"A wine cask," explained James, "makes a double journey — outward full, homeward empty. You pay freight each way. I am simply proposing to halve your freight charges."

Braganza considered. "And make it pay?"

"I will make it pay," said James, "because no one else," — he grinned at Callon — "because no one else will be allowed to carry a Braganza cask into, or out of, the country."

"It's too damn' clever by half," exploded

Callon. "If it's your empty barrels you're concerned about . . .?" He was appealing to Braganza. And at that moment James knew he'd won.

"It is rather more than just empty barrels. Which," he asked Braganza, "has the greater value? The cask? Or its contents?"

"The cask," said Braganza. "Every time." It was true. Casks were the bane of a wine merchant's life. Wine must be carried in matured wood, and that process could take three years. And there was a secondary problem; casks were continually going astray, or returned damaged — and then usually in small parcels of a dozen or so at a time.

Braganza looked the question at James: "You will undertake . . .?"

"To return your casks by the shipload. We will discuss the matter of their freight charges later." He looked pointedly at Callon.

Callon raised an empurpled visage and made one last attempt: "Seenyoor Braganza, I do beg of you most earnestly to reconsider. This man will bring you to ruin. He will surely betray your interests as he has mine. Think, before you decide, of the years of goodwill that have existed between our two houses; and I ask you to remember — without Callon and Company you would have no English trade at all."

He's gone too far, thought James, and watched Braganza.

"And when competition is no more, Senhor Callon," asked Braganza, "what then will happen to your freight charges? If I am to judge by past experience they will undoubtedly increase." He raised a hand as Callon was about to speak. "No, hear me out, Senhor." He left his desk and took up his habitual stance by the window, dreamily looking out at an indigo sea lapping white waves against the seawall's grey face. Then he turned to face them again. A mosquito whined into the room. James slapped at the back of his hand, leaving a smear of blood and crumpled wings. He flicked the body away and absently sucked at the bite on his wrist.

Braganza spoke carefully, dropping each word like a stone into a pool. The ripples reached out and touched each mind, bringing to Callon's a blaze of anger and to James the cool sweet scent of success.

"You have set me a problem, gentlemen. In whom am I to lodge my trust? With you, Senhor Callon — who spoke a few moments ago of the value of loyalty? Or to you, Captain Onedin, who claims to be a man of his word, a man of honour? You, Senhor Callon, come post haste with a contract in your pocket and the intent of persuading me sign before I can learn of Captain Onedin's counter-proposals. You will forgive me saying so, but to me that does not accord with your plea for loyalty. Or is loyalty for you a one-sided compact, Senhor? You have also spoken of the long and profitable association between our two houses, and yet — in all those years — your rates have always increased, never once reduced. Until now. Now, suddenly, you are prepared to serve me at any price. I must ask myself why. It is, I believe, the fear of competition and new ideas. The contract goes to Captain Onedin."

Callon stood up, picked up his leather wallet.

"You'll regret it," he said. "Believe me, you'll live to regret it." He walked to the door. "As for you, Onedin — you'll learn. You'll learn, by God." He pushed his way out through the double doors. They swung shut behind him and his footsteps clacked across the mosaic tiles of the ante-room like miniature thunderclaps. Braganza and James smiled at each other. Braganza turned an open palm toward James's wallet.

"Well, Captain Onedin? You have brought your contract with you?"

"No," lied James. He stood up. "I gave my word."

Braganza surveyed him thoughtfully.

"Reflect, my friend. A contract is no more than writing upon a piece of paper. It can be clearly understood. Its terms of reference are drafted by lawyers . . ."

"For lawyers," said James.

Braganza smiled. "But a man's word is his honour; and as such must not lightly be given, nor broken."

"When I draw up a contract," said James, "any man would be well-advised to read the fine print. But my word, I keep." He held out his hand. Braganza paused before taking it.

"For how many years?" he asked.

"Your wine will be carried free of freight aboard any ship flying the Onedin flag for as long as the Onedin flag flies."

Braganza shook his hand.

"Then it is settled," he said.

13

NIGHT following restless night Robert tossed and turned on a rack of despair. When sleep's harlot finger beckoned toward the terror-haunted realms of Nightmare he beseeched the mercy of God to bring oblivion. But the god of Avarice accorded his followers no absolution; instead Robert found himself plunged again and again into a purgatory where gold dissolved like water and forests of grasping hands reached out to pluck the flesh from his bones.

If the nights were an abomination, the days were little better. Four times daily the postman called, and every visit brought a fresh plague of bills, accounts to be settled, threats of dunning. The one hundred and fifty pounds seemed to have run through his fingers like sand. As fast as money came into the shop it was paid out again as a sop to the more importunate creditors; the shop itself was beginning to look as bare as Mother Hubbard's cupboard for he could no longer afford to replace the rapidly diminishing stocks; whichever way he turned he simply seemed to incur more and more debts. He cursed James, cursed him through all eternity, and read and re-read that damnable Deed of Partnership until the words lost all meaning and looked like nothing other than lines of little black ants winding their way across plains of white paper. It was a simple agreement on a share-and-share-alike basis; but implicit in the cursed legal jargon was the responsibility of each partner to shoulder the burdens of the other. What was worse, infinitely worse, was that James could not be called to account for losses sustained by the shop. The partnership referred to the profits of the voyage only. By seeking to protect himself Robert had simply fallen deeper into the mire. He was gripped with terror. Once a man tumbled into the abyss of penury there was no climbing out. It would mean a debtor's prison for himself and the poorhouse for Sarah. He had tried appealing to Cousin Wilberforce and Uncle Will Perkins, but to no avail; a man on the way to pauperdom has neither friends nor relations. Poverty was a malady to which there was no antidote.

The shop door bell tanged. Robert looked up and groaned in anguish as Mr. Simpson entered and planted himself before the counter as though set upon taking root.

"I'm sure you'll not mind my drawing your attention to this small matter," he said, with the air of a man come to demand satisfaction at any price. "An outstanding account, which I am sure has escaped your notice." Mr. Simpson flattened the bill upon the counter. "In respect of," he quoted, "five casks of freshly salted beef, delivered as per agreement, to the schooner *Charlotte Rhodes*, discount at ten per cent, and . . ." — he rubbed forefinger and thumb together — "our own little understanding."

Robert's heart sank even further. "Our own little understanding" was no more than a modest kickback. A sovereign for Robert's own pocket. A common enough practice, but one that Robert was more and more regretting. Mr. Simpson was by no means alone. Others had also shown their gratitude for the favour of his custom, and no doubt, like the wretched Mr. Simpson, would soon be beating on his shop door bawling for the return of their money and immediate payment for their confounded services.

"Discount," Mr. Simpson was saying, pointedly, "is for cash."

"Within the month is the usual practice," said Robert, determined to make a fight of it.

"Time's up," trumpeted Mr. Simpson.

"Fresh killed beef," said Robert.

"Ah," said Mr. Simpson, obscurely.

"Beef fresh killed it was not," said Robert, decisively.

"Delivered and accepted as ordered," countered Mr. Simpson.

"Offal," snapped Robert. "Not fit for carrion."

"Accepted after due examination." Mr. Simpson pushed the account forward.

"Subject to approval," said Robert, pushing it back.

"Approved as per personal inspection," snorted Mr. Simpson.

"But not by the ship's master," retorted Robert, triumphantly.

Mr. Simpson looked blank.

"Is is customary," continued Robert, seizing the advantage, "for the ship's master to defray all muniments for ship's stores. He — having satisfied himself as to character and quality — then reimburses the chandler — me — who, in his turn, disburses said payments to his customers — you. Custom and practice, Mr. Simpson. Custom and practice." He shook his head sadly. "If it were in my power to alter same, I would so do. Forthwith," he added, hoping this tarradiddle made sense.

Mr. Simpson's mind worked slowly.

"Custom *and* practice?" he asked, sagely.

"Common usage," threw in Robert for good measure. "All outstanding accounts settled promptly at termination of voyage."

"There are some mighty long voyages," said Mr. Simpson, suspiciously.

"Owners have quarterly accounts with bona fide chandlers," stated Robert. "I trust you are not challenging my bona fides, Mr. Simpson?"

"By no means, Mr. Onedin," protested Mr. Simpson hastily. "By no means."

Robert picked up the bill and jabbed it on the spike to join a dozen or so of its fellows. "Very well, Mr. Simpson," he said, smiling indulgently, "we shall say no more of it."

Mr. Simpson was not entirely convinced.

"I'll think on it, Mr. Onedin," he said. "I'll think on it." He walked to the door. "But I do not like bad debts. No, Mr. Onedin, I do not like bad debts."

The door clanged shut behind him and Robert, heaving a sigh of relief, mopped his face, and found that his hands were trembling. Many more Mr. Simpsons and he would be a nervous wreck. He thanked God that ships did not take on oats or hay; the foul-mouthed Mr. Jenkins would be more than he could bear.

"Who was that, dear?" asked Sarah, waddling into the shop from the living-room.

"Mr. Simpson demanding money," said Robert, holding his head in his hands. "Where will it all end?" he begged. "Where will it all end?"

"There, there," said Sarah consolingly, adding — for she was a woman with the misfortune of never being able to keep a still tongue in her head — "You should never have put your name to that document. I said so at the time."

"I only wish you had," snapped Robert, irritably. "But as usual, you left all the decisions to me."

"It is not a wife's place to contradict her husband," responded Sarah, virtuously. "And if you had spent more time concentrating upon the shop, and a little less in listening to James's get-rich-quick schemes, you would sleep the better o' nights and not snap your poor wife's head off every time I open my mouth." She held back a flood of tears long enough to implore him to show consideration, if not for herself, then at least for his unborn child; then, sobbing convulsively, she returned to the living-room.

That was another thing, thought Robert, bitterly, there seemed to be no peace from women these days. If it wasn't Sarah continually snipperty-snapping, it was Elizabeth waltzing around the house and singing at the top of her voice. Not that she was at home long enough for her presence to grate on his overwrought nerves. Life for her seemed to be one damned picnic after another. Daniel

Fogarty called each day and off she went without so much as a by-your-leave and leaving him, Robert, to manage the shop single-handed. And that brought another bone of contention for Sarah to gnaw over. "That girl doesn't know she is born. It is time she learned to stop treating our home as though it is a common lodging house and we her paid servants. I think you should speak to Daniel Fogarty; it is all very well for that young man — he has nothing to do all day but kick his heels until Mr. Callon's return — you must point out to him that Elizabeth has work to do. That girl seems to think that life is one long holiday. Really, Robert, you must exercise your authority; the responsibility for running this entire household is becoming too much for me."

But Robert considered he had problems enough without adding Daniel Fogarty's displeasure to his afflictions. For Daniel would soon be a man of considerable influence. As captain of the *Barracuda* it would be in his power to put many little commissions in the way of an honest chandler, particularly one linked by ties of marriage. Family was family and a contract for but one quarter of the *Barracuda*'s stores would settle all debts and put him on easy street for life.

So Robert held his tongue, tried to keep the peace, and wished — not for the first time — that he had taken a somewhat less contumelious woman to wife.

Far from being idle, Dear Daniel — like some good-natured Samuel shorn of his strength — had spent the past few days being paraded before a succession of uncles and aunts and cousins. But at last Elizabeth had relented and released him from the tedium of duty; and so today they found themselves sprawling on the grass at the top of Frodsham Hill, eating egg and cucumber sandwiches, and watching the tiny white ships skimming the surface of the river below like midges.

The hill was a massive buttress of sandstone rising sheer above the marshes at the narrow throat of the Mersey. Liverpool sprawled sixteen miles away in a straight line, and they took turns to squint through Daniel's pocket spy-glass at the ferries bustling across the river like little old ladies puffing and panting in a froth of crinolines.

Daniel seemed to instantly recognise every ship there ever was: emigrant ships bound for America and Canada; Yankee blood-boats; packet ships with soot-encrusted sails; French ships and German ships; outward-bounders and homeward-bounders all brimful of rich cargoes. The docks stretched as far as the eye could see, the bare ships' masts rising like thickets of reeds; and in the middle distance Frazer's yards where ships lay with ribs picked clean like the skeletons of mythical beasts.

They watched a newcomer rounding the Point, sails set and smoke billowing from its funnel, a rash of flags breaking out at its signal yards. Daniel focused carefully.

"A P & O boat," he translated. "Asking for a pilot and requesting pratique. Carrying mails from Gibraltar. She'd call at Lisbon . . ." They looked at each other and then scrambled to their feet.

"I wonder . . . ?" he mused.

She clapped her hands: "Mr. Callon! He *must* have taken passage. By tomorrow . . . " They stared into a wonderful future. "By tomorrow you will have your promotion!"

A wax-sealed envelope awaited Daniel Fogarty's return to his lodgings: "Mr. Callon presents his compliments and requires Mr. Fogarty to present himself at the offices of Callon & Company at nine o'clock tomorrow morning." It was signed by Agnew and kept Daniel awake until the sun, drowsing through the curtained windows, brought him the gift of a new day. He rose, washed from the pitcher of cool water, trimmed his beard and dressed with care. Then he quietly left the house and walked down to the docks.

The *Barracuda* lay at her berth, fenders out, white-painted sides stained with the scum of the dockside. To Fogarty's surprise she was already working cargo and — from the evidence of the hissing of a few unextinguished naphtha lamps — had been throughout the night. He made his way to the dock office where a sleepy-eyed clerk showed him the cargo manifests. She was bound for Melbourne and would carry a total declared value of £72,850 consisting of 6,253 pieces and packages of soft goods. 88 packages of fancy goods. 704 cases of glass including marble, china and earthenware. 1,300 casks of cement. 12 tons of sheet iron. 115 tons of galvanised iron. 164 kegs of nails. And 30 tons of iron rails.

He hung around the ship as long as he could, eyeing the rake of her masts, guessing at the number of berths and cabin accommodation. Then he made his way to a coffee house and drank four cups of coffee, his stomach churning with trepidation.

At two minutes to nine he presented himself at the outer office, relieved to find Agnew baring his teeth in an ingratiating smile of welcome and adding to his performance a repertoire of "Don't-forget-I-told-you-so" nods and winks. At least it seemed that Callon had not changed his mind, for Agnew was a man who took care to know on which side his bread was buttered.

He was ushered in to the presence promptly at nine.

Callon sat at his desk, picking his teeth and staring at a sheaf of papers as though his mind was weighted with other problems.

"Mr. Fogarty, sir," said Agnew, and slipped out through the door like an eel through a net.

Daniel stood waiting. His hands felt

clammy and his eyes suddenly seemed to be filled with sand.

Callon seemed to be in no hurry. He initialled a couple of documents then raised his bull head.

"Ah — Mr. Fogarty."

Daniel discovered that his tongue had inextricably become glued to the roof of his mouth.

"Good-morning, sir," he managed at last.

"You are not married, Mr. Fogarty?" Callon's thick beefy fingers drummed the desk top, his round eyes looked accusingly at Daniel.

"Not yet, sir. But the lady to whom I have been paying my addresses has done me the honour of accepting my avowals. We hope to be married within the very near future."

"Delighted to hear it," said Callon. He smiled sourly. "And you are not required to speak so formally. I prefer plain speaking, sir. Plain speaking. Perhaps I may one day have the pleasure of meeting the young lady?"

"We should be honoured, sir."

"Yes," said Callon. "Marriage, Mr.

Fogarty, is the mainstay of society. It brings stability. A man with a wife and family to support is a reliable man, sir. A reliable man. A married man, Mr. Fogarty, is a man who thinks before he acts. He is a man sensible of the responsibility he bears. And for those very reasons a man should not take upon himself the obligations of matrimony until he has made his way in the world. Do you not agree, Mr. Fogarty?"

"Indeed, yes, sir," replied Daniel, wholeheartedly.

"Indeed, yes, sir." Callon sniffed. "And to whom does an officer's first duty lie?"

"To his Owner, sir," responded Daniel without hesitation. This was one catechism he knew by heart.

"An officer's first duty is to the master, the master's to the Owner," corrected Callon. He smiled sourly. "I think you are perhaps a little over-eager for promotion, Mr. Fogarty?"

"No, sir. I consider that I owe my loyalty to the Company at all times."

Callon interlaced his fingers and was lost in thought for a moment. He sighed. "Loyalty," he mused. "Yes, Mr. Fogarty,

I do set great store by loyalty. And to whom," he asked, "does a wife owe her first duty?"

"To her husband, naturally." He almost tumbled into the trap. "And to her husband's interests," he added quickly.

"Which are identified with those of the Company. Exactly," said Callon. "And yet . . ." His fingers curled around the papers on his desk. He looked up quickly and the little round eyes bored into Daniel's. "And yet, I have been informed that the lady of your choice is none other than that Onedin moppet?"

There was a contempt in his tone that brought a surge of anger to Daniel's face.

"I am sorry, sir," he said stiffly, struggling to control his voice, "but I cannot remain in your presence if you insist upon traducing the good name of the lady I have had the honour of asking to be my wife." Why the devil, he thought bitterly, can't I learn to keep a guard on my tongue?

To his surprise Callon was grinning. "You stiff-necked rascal," he was saying. "Understand me, Mr. Fogarty, I care not a fig for your attachments, but I have no doubt that you have already heard something of the villainy of that perfidious rogue, James Onedin?" He spat out the words and crumpled the papers into a ball. "That man will be your brother-in-law."

"By the accident of marriage, not of choice," said Daniel.

"You fully understand the direction of my questions?"

"Of course, sir, and I appreciate your confidence. I would like to assure you that it is my most earnest ambition to remain in your service, sir, and to be worthy of your good opinion."

"H'm." Callon reflected for an eternity. "Very well, Mr. Fogarty," he said at long last. "I made one error of judgment." He smiled crookedly. "I hope I am not making another. It has always been my practice to promote from within the company whenever a suitable vacancy falls due. Such an opportunity is now open to you, young man. I speak of the command of the *Barracuda*. The berth is yours, Mr. Fogarty, if you have a mind for it."

"I am overwhelmed, sir," said Daniel.

"You will be overwhelmed with work," said Callon, drily. "She is due to sail in three days."

"Three days!" Elizabeth stared at him, white-faced.

"I'm sorry," said Daniel unhappily. "But there was nothing to do but accept with as good a grace as I could find."

"But surely — if you had explained? Told him you were to be married? Asked for leave?"

He shook his head. "I have had a month's leave. If James," he said savagely, "hadn't drawn Mr. Callon away on a wild goose chase we would have been wedded and bedded by now."

"James," grumbled Robert, "has much to answer for on his return. I intend to have a few sharp words with him myself."

They were seated in the living-room and, when Daniel hesitantly broke his news, had remained fixed in their positions like figures caught in a tableau: Robert reaching a spill from the fire; Sarah poised over her knitting needles; and Elizabeth, mouth open, leaning forward in her chair. Only Daniel seemed capable of movement, shuffling his feet restlessly and twisting the brim of his hat round and round and round in an agony of self-abnegation.

"There was nothing I could do," he

repeated. "It is a once-only opportunity." His eyes implored Elizabeth. "You must see that."

All Elizabeth could see was that her marriage prospects seemed further away than ever.

"How long?" she asked. "How long will you be away?"

"I'll make the fastest voyage on record, that I promise you," he swore.

"How long?" persisted Elizabeth, a cold fear clutching the pit of her stomach.

"The normal passage," replied Daniel carefully, "is around eighty or ninety days. But I'll clip a week off, believe me."

"Ninety days out, and ninety days back?" The future seemed to stretch into infinity.

"Add a month to six weeks, discharging and loading, eh, Daniel?" pronounced Robert, lighting his pipe before the spill charred his fingers to the bone.

"Soonest done, soonest mended," quoted Sarah, her knitting needles again clacking furiously. "You must learn to cultivate the virtue of patience, Elizabeth. Daniel will be back within a year; it is not an impossible time and does have the merit of giving you sufficient time to prepare your trousseau; one which will be worthy of the occasion."

"Everything will work out for the best," puffed Robert, placidly. "You mark my words."

It was so unfair. So totally, unreasonably and stupidly unfair. She plied Daniel with questions until that young man's head buzzed like a beehive and his eyes took on a harassed pleading look. But the one question she yearned to ask above all others could not be voiced in the presence of Robert and Sarah.

Eventually Daniel took his leave and she followed him to the shop door.

"Dearest," she whispered. "What if . . . ?"

He stared at her, his brown eyes frankly puzzled. She was uncertain, unsure how to proceed.

She tried again: "That night . . . ? Do you suppose . . . ? Oh, Daniel, you fool — what if I am with child?" Having blurted it out she felt ashamed of her ridiculous fears and wished she had not spoken, wished in the same breath that she knew more of the subject; she was sure that

that must be the way it happened, but the process defied all logic, although every nerve in her body screamed yes, yes, yes!

Daniel put his hands on her shoulders and tried to laugh her fears away.

"Silly goose," he said. "Lovable silly goose. Of course you won't have a child."

"Are you sure, quite sure?" she asked, trusting him.

"As sure as I am of your love," he told her. "Do you feel as though you are with child?"

"No — I don't know. How would I know?" she asked miserably.

"If you were, you'd know," said Daniel confidently. He hid his concern beneath a bantering voice. In truth he didn't know himself. It was certainly possible. But at this moment she needed all the comfort he could give her. Therefore, to spare her the added misery of doubt, he quelled his own uncertainties and hugged and kissed her fears away. "We'll be married," he promised, "the moment I return. You will wait?" he asked anxiously.

"Oh, God, Daniel . . . !" was all she could whimper.

"We'll be married by a convocation of bishops and before the eyes of the entire population. And, what's more, we'll have a houseful of children. You'll never stop having babies, I promise you," he laughed, as though promising her the gates of heaven. After all, he thought, it may never happen. He'd known people married for years before producing their first-born. No, he decided; it was very unlikely.

They met only twice more before the ship sailed, and then in the company of Robert and Sarah. There were no more picnics or visits to theatres and music halls. His days were spent in preparing the ship for its long voyage; hers in the shop, serving customers, scrubbing and polishing, and turning a faded dream over and over in her mind.

She watched the ship's departure from its berth, towed by a panting tug far out into the river, until the *Barracuda*'s sails ballooned and bellied in the wind like white explosions against the washed blue of the western sky.

Then the ship was no more and she turned and trudged home with the gait of a sleepwalker, slowly counting to ninety and back again, haunted by an unbearable sense of loss.

14

ANNE had finally accustomed herself to the fact that because a sailing ship heeled with the wind their small dining table would one day slope this way, the next day, that. But one thing to which she could not accustom herself was shipboard food. She spat out a mouthful, sniffed suspiciously at the glutinous mess of meat, and pushed away her plate.

"From whom did you purchase this pigswill, James?" she asked, wondering how a man otherwise so astute could so easily be gulled by swindling butchers.

"From brother Robert, of course," he replied, chewing stoically upon a lump of parboiled salt beef.

Anne wrinkled her nose and emptied her plate into the slop bucket.

"I know who had the better of that bargain."

James wolfed down the last mouthful with the appetite of a man utterly indifferent to the nature or quality of the fare set before him.

"A man must take his profit where best he can," he commented, placidly.

"Not at our expense," she snapped. "No housewife worth her salt would tolerate this offal for a moment."

He picked at a sliver of meat wedged obstinately between his teeth.

"A ship is not an hotel, Anne."

"Just as well," she responded tartly. "For it would have precious few customers."

James yawned, stretched his arms, and glanced at the chronometer screwed to the bulkhead. It showed ten minutes to twelve.

"Time to take the noonday sight," he said, and went to fetch his sextant.

She followed him to the tiny cubbyhole that served as chart-room.

"Will you teach me?" she asked.

"What?"

"The use of the sextant. It would pass the time; and I would like to have a grasp of at least the rudiments of navigation." She watched his face hopefully.

James raised an eyebrow. The woman's insatiable curiosity never ceased to delight and mystify him. From the moment they had set sail she had set herself the task of learning by rote not only the names of the sails, but the nature and purpose of each and every line, halyard and downhaul aboard ship, and by the time they had reached Lisbon she had taught herself to box the compass as well as any man among the crew. She had poked her long nose into every nook and cranny, from forepeak to lazareet; and the club-footed cook lived in mortal terror of her rasping voice, continual sniffing and tasting, and determination to have the galley as spotlessly clean as her own kitchen at home. And now she wanted to learn navigation? James wagged his head. She really was a most remarkable woman.

"Very well," was all he said. "If you have set your mind upon it, we'll see what we can do," and led the way on to deck.

The *Charlotte Rhodes* was deep-laden, her decks continually awash. According to Scalplock she had about as much freeboard as a frying pan and would ship water if sailing across a saucer.

At Lisbon James had discharged her shingle ballast and loaded 850 casks of Braganza'a wine: Madeira and Setubal chocked off in the bilges; above, on a floor of dunnage, he stacked red and white Daos, barrels of Lisbons and Colares; stowed against the after bulkhead were four tuns of the fashionable port wine. And that, James had considered, left space enough for an extra seventy or eighty tons of freight-paying cargo — if he could find it.

Braganza was a pillar of the local business community. A few introductions served their purpose: the *Charlotte Rhodes* topped off with 50 tons of olive oil and 35 tons of turpentine. That brought her down to her scuppers. But the empty deck space irritated James, so a couple more days tramping around and the free use of Braganza's name brought him a deck cargo of corkwood. The sheets of bark filled the waist of the ship and covered the hatches until the booms of the fore-and-aft sails had just sufficient clearance. It made life hazardous for the crew and gave the ship rather too much windage so that she tended to sail sideways like a crab.

It was horrible sailing weather. The sea was a confused cross-hatching of waves apparently engaged in private insurrection.

Pillars of spray rose and tore across the deck, stinging and blinding. The wind raced above the tumult, shouting and muttering, then dying to a whisper. The sky above was cold and blue. Far to the north and east a sulphurous bank of cloud spread across the horizon like a malignant tumour. The upper topsail was reefed and the flying jib taken in, but otherwise the ship bore all the sail she could carry. She lurched through the sea, wallowing and pitching and occasionally rolling with a slow pendulum swing that had the pots and pans clashing in the galley and the crew staggering like drunken men, cursing and reaching for handholds.

James braced himself against a stanchion, squinted through the eyepiece of the sextant, made a quick adjustment to the arm and then handed it to Anne. She had difficulty enough in finding the horizon, which seemed to lift and sink at a most alarming rate; the sun eluded her completely.

"Open the other eye," James advised, "and hold yourself steady." She followed his instructions, carefully moving the arm — or so she imagined — until suddenly, through the darkened glass, she caught a glimpse of the image of the sun reflected from the tiny mirror. It looked like a tiny yellow pill and leaped and danced like something insane.

"Hold it steady," said James. "Wait until the sun just touches the horizon, then tighten the clamp."

The sun's image whirled like a Dervish, zig-zagged rapidly from side to side and then disappeared from view. She readjusted the arm and the sun crept stealthily into the upper right-hand corner then, as though playing a secret but amusing game of its own, commenced to bounce between sea and horizon like a demented gutta-percha ball. She concentrated fiercely and, as it dipped once more to the line of the horizon, triumphantly screwed the clamp tight. Eyes watering from the effort of concentration, she passed the sextant to James. He read the altitude from the scale and grinned.

"I think you've got us making sternway."

She looked crestfallen.

"Come, now," he said, meaning it kindly. "You can't expect to be a Captain Cook at the first time of trying."

As he spoke his fingers were busy unscrewing the clamp and re-setting the arm to zero. He looked up, calculatingly, at the sun. Then he put the sextant to his eye and, balancing carefully, moved the arm with infinite pains along the scale, bringing the image down closer and closer to the horizon. She watched him, half-convinced that the very sun in the heavens was obedient to his will. He seemed to take an unconscionable time, but quite suddenly he screwed the clamp firmly, called: "Time!" and let the sextant hang loosely at the length of his arm.

She had watched the little ceremony daily without entirely comprehending; now she resolutely applied her mind to the business . . .

Mr. Baines, swaying easily on the tiny poop, held his huge silver turnip of a watch in a massive paw. At James's call of "Time!" he re-set the watch to noon, then — presumably to signify he had done so — struck eight bells upon the ship's bell. Thereupon the watch below tumbled out and the watch on deck went below. Obviously when James said it was noon, lo, it was noon. He really was a quite remarkable man, she thought, and followed him to their quarters and the tiny chart-room.

Anne waited for him to finish his calculations, knowing from past experience that he hated to be disturbed at these moments.

He worked methodically and with the trained habits of a life-time's practice. First he placed his sextant carefully upon the chart-room table, then he re-set the ship's chronometer from his own watch — which he, like Mr. Baines, had checked at noon. Then he noted the reading from the sextant scale. Next he opened the lid of a compartment at the end of the chart table. Here was kept a second chronometer swinging gently on balanced gimbals and ticking softly to itself in its dark and secret lair. It showed the time at Greenwich and never varied beyond one-tenth of a second a day. It was also, James had impressed upon her, the most expensive single item of equipment aboard the ship. He wound it carefully at noon each day; exactly the same number of turns of the key. He did so now, then checked the time against the ship's time before closing the lid of the compartment again.

He reached down much-thumbed

volumes of the Nautical Almanac, Traverse tables and Correction tables, and applied himself to industriously scribbling calculations in his work book. In a very few minutes he had finished. He took the chart from the chart table and quickly plotted the noon position. She peeped over his shoulder as he used a pair of dividers to measure the distance covered from noon to noon. She was unsure of the scale of the chart, but from the closeness of the positions the ship seemed to be moving at a snail's pace.

At length, satisfied with his work, James sat back in his chair, put his fingertips together and asked blandly:

"Well? What is it you want to know?"

"You have just measured the altitude of the sun. How," she asked, "do you translate that to the chart?"

He nodded approval. She had asked the right question.

"Principles first," he said. "Mathematics later." He paused long enough to marshal his thoughts and wipe the back of his hand across his forehead. He had developed a slight headache and his mouth felt as dry as a lime kiln. That beef was far too salty. He would speak to the cook. In future he must soak it overnight.

Anne noticed the gesture and thought for a moment that he was wiping salt spray from his face; then she noticed the tiny beads of perspiration. Strange, she thought it is really quite cool below.

"There are two requirements," began James, "for finding your position on any point of the earth's surface." He ticked them off on his long fingers. "Latitude. And longitude. For the one you require . . ." He picked up the sextant. "A plumb line. For the other . . ." He opened the lid of the chronometer compartment. "A time-piece. Noon aboard ship is determined by the moment at which the sun reaches its zenith. . . . Yes? What is it?" he snapped in answer to a polite tap at the door lintel.

Baines's bulk filled the entrance. He ducked his head and stepped into the chart-room.

"Beg pardon, sir, but one of the hands is took bad."

"Oh? What's the matter with him? Is he trying to come the old farmer?" A farmer was an idler.

"No, sir," said Baines. He looked worried. "I think it's ship fever."

The sick man lay in his bunk like a corpse in its coffin. The oil lamp, swinging from one of the low transverse beams, threw out a pale sickly light, making pearls of the beads of perspiration that clung to the man's face and matted his beard into a dank tangle of black hair.

The fo'c'sle seemed to sweat in sympathy with the victim, droplets of water dripping from the beams and carlins and running down the shipside in thin rivulets to join the inch-deep scum of seawater slopping about the deck. The air was foul and reeking with the stench of vomit. Six plank-sided bunks and a narrow deal table bolted to the deck took up all available space; it was as dark and cheerless as a dungeon.

James clamoured down the steep ladder and a suit of oilskins rustled and swayed across the room to embrace him in its clammy grasp. He pushed it aside and, unhooking the oil lamp, peered closely at the man's face.

His lips were dry and cracked, his eyes dull. He shivered continually. Spittle ran down the side of his mouth and his breathing was shallow. Looking more closely, James saw the tell-tale rose-red spots on chest and abdomen.

Cold air and a rush of spray hissed into the room as the fo'c'sle door was opened and closed; then Baines was standing at the foot of the ladder.

"Ship fever, sir?" he asked.

James nodded. "Looks like it, Mr. Baines. How long has this man been ill?"

"He heaved his heart up just after eight bells. The Dandy and Scalplock put him in his bunk. It is his watch below," Baines added, almost apologetically.

James reflected. A sick man aboard a merchant ship was always a problem. Sailing short-handed meant that no one could be spared to take care of him. There were two other men in his watch, of course, but now they would be called upon to do the work of three.

"Where are his mates?" he asked Baines.

"Sitting in the lee of the galley, having their munjee. They don't fancy the fo'c'sle."

James understood and could hardly blame them. Anyone forced to live in confined quarters tended to live in mortal terror of contagion; ship fever and gaol fever were common enough blights, and Death was not such a friend as to be welcomed with open arms.

"I'll see what I can do," he said, knowing there was no remedy other than the strength of the man's own constitution. The stuffy atmosphere was making his head ring and his eyes ache abominably. He led the way back on to deck.

The sails cracked and boomed in the wind, the bows lifted and dipped and seemed to shake angrily at the worrisome sea. Spray whipped across the deck to rattle like hail against the straining canvas. James staggered and Baines put out a supporting arm.

"Are you all right, sir?"

James shook him off. "Of course I'm all right," he snapped. The truth was he hated being touched and had a built-in resentment to being helped. He saw the Dandy and Scalplock peering around the lee side of the galley. He beckoned Scalplock.

"You. Come here."

"Watch below, sir," said Scalplock.

James eyed him frostily.

"Do you want to lose a day's pay?"

"No, sir."

"Then when I give a command, jump to it. You are not aboard a sloppy whaler now."

He scrambled over the stacks of cork-wood and made his way aft to his quarters. Scalplock, muttering, followed in James's wake.

Baines eyed the Dandy.

"You. Get forrard and keep an eye on your mate."

The Dandy protested: "He's sick."

"You'll be sicker," growled Baines. "Jump to it. Move!" he roared as the Dandy reluctantly made his way toward the fo'c'sle.

Baines looked around the horizon. To the nor' east the sulphurous clouds were banking high. He cocked his head and listened. A new sound at a different pitch to the familiar rush of water and shout of the wind. He heard it again: the long grumbling drum-roll of distant thunder. Pleased with his identification he headed aft to take up his station on the poop.

"Ship fever," pronounced James, entering their cabin. "No doubt about it."

Anne had come to her own conclusions but was sensible enough to hold her tongue in the presence of Scalplock, who had obediently followed James below and now stood ill at ease at the foot of the companionway. To a common fo'c'sle hand the master's quarters were a Holy of Holies where authority reigned supreme and there was no justice for the poor. So he stood with downcast eyes, shuffling his feet and dripping seawater on to the strip of carpet while James unlocked the medicine chest and rummaged among the pills and potions. He handed Scalplock half a dozen paper packets of Dover's Powder, a universal panacea in popular use since the seventeenth century.

"Mix one packet with water and give it him every two hours," he instructed. "And I want that fo'c'sle dry as a bone and clean as a whistle before the dog watch." It was unfair, he knew; a man's watch below was precious to him — the most hated cry aboard ship was that of "All Hands!" — wrenching men from the drug of sleep to stumble about the decks and clamber aloft like somnambulists. But it was the only way he could ensure that they paid attention to the sick man — left to their own devices the Dandy and Scalplock would certainly sneak off and bed down on a coil of rope beneath the fo'c'sle head. James did not believe in any form of bribery — it smacked of weakness — but he felt that under the circumstances a gesture was called for.

"And when you've finished," he added gruffly, "report aft for a tot of rum."

Scalplock knuckled his forehead and left to find the Dandy and break the bad news.

James removed his pea-jacket, tugged off his sea-boots and, feeling unutterably weary, his head ringing like a bell, stretched out on the lower bunk and tried to concentrate his mind on the problem that had bedevilled him for the past four days. Tomorrow noon they should bring up Fastnet at the southernmost tip of Ireland. The question concerned the ship's point of departure — the moment when he would have to decide whether to turn the ship to port, and out into the Atlantic in order to make the wearisome passage around the north of Ireland; or to starboard and try to beat up the St. George's Channel with the risk of being blown upon a lee shore. If only that devil's wind would shift! He would ask Baines's opinion. . . . Baines could smell a change in the wind. . . . The sick man would be buried at sea, of course. . . . Quarantine? Would the ship be quarantined . . . ? He tumbled into sleep like a man falling down a mineshaft.

Anne, dozing in a chair, awoke to a cataclysm of sound that wrenched her to her feet, her heart pounding madly. She blinked her eyes, trying to clear a confused memory that the room was afire. She must have overslept, she thought, for the cabin was as dark as night. And in that instant the room leaped into brilliant eye-aching light and a clap of thunder crashed overhead as though the heavens had split asunder.

She drew a woollen shawl about her shoulders and hastened on to deck.

It looked like the end of the world.

To the west the sky glowed crimson behind clouds the colour of beaten copper. To the north and east towering cumulus threw out tattered black banners and glowed and flickered with an eerie pulsing light. Lightning forked and flashed, searing across the sky with the sound of tearing canvas. Thunder rolled and crashed above their heads, numbing the senses with an ear-splitting tumult of sound. Around them the sea lay like wrinkled lead, slowly heaving as though pressed from below by some subterranean convulsion.

Anne looked around, lost in wonder, and saw that the crew had tumbled out on to deck and were gaping as though bereft of their senses. One swarthy man wearing gold earrings had fallen to his knees and was rapidly making the sign of the cross and babbling words she could not catch, but whose meaning was clear enough to offend her Protestant soul. She caught sight of Baines standing on the poop. His head was thrown back and he was looking with a sort of frozen horror at something immediately above his head.

She followed his gaze and became aware of the reason for the unusual darkness. An enormous black cloud hung above their heads, turning day into night. It hung so low it seemed that by raising an arm she could touch it. The edges had a fuzzy greyness that turned white in the lightning's glare. The centre was swollen like a great black bladder filled with water and ready to burst. The bulge seemed to dip and strain lower and lower. Then, not a hundred yards off the starboard bow, the sea began to boil. The waves slopped and chattered and reached up imploringly toward the massive bulge of the cloud. She watched, fascinated, not understanding, as the cloud seemed to draw itself together and then reached down a long dark arm to touch the water beneath. The waves hissed and spun and leaped high, twisting and turning to clutch at the black smoky column. Then with a roar the sea spouted upwards and sky and water met.

Baines came out of his trance.

"Waterspout!" he bellowed. "Wear ship. All hands wear ship. Wear ship for your lives!"

The crew hurled themselves at the sheets and braces, the terrified helmsman spun the wheel, and the ship began to turn sluggishly.

All the water in the world seemed to fall upon them. It poured down in a solid sheet, a roaring cataract that had men stumbling blindly, drowning on their feet.

Anne breathed in and inhaled water; gasping she opened her mouth and swallowed water; the pressure of water flattened the lids against her eyes. She could taste salt water. Breathing was an impossibility and the sheer weight of water seemed to be beating her to her knees. She bowed her head and, cupping her hands over her face, made a pocket of air. It was impossible to move; she had lost all sense of direction; so she remained, crouched over the sanctuary of her fingers, until the waterspout, drawing up more and more of the sea into its central maw, began to rotate faster and faster until, driven by its self-generating impetus, it gradually spun away toward the north and east.

The torrent eased at last and became no more than a drum-beating downpour. Rods of rain, like brilliant fiery streamers in the flash and the flare of the lightning, hammered the flooded decks into a multiplicity of miniature fountains.

Anne felt bile in her throat. She stared around her, stunned and dazed. The ship seemed to be waterlogged. Even through the driving rain she could see that the decks were completely awash and level with the sea itself. One of the jibs had carried away and the remnants hung like a useless sodden rag. Some of the crew lay like logs, others crouched whimpering in corners. The wheel spun uselessly and the booms of the fore-and-aft sails lurched and banged from side to side. She saw Baines haul himself to his feet, spew out a mouthful of water, retch violently before looking around and assessing the situation. He seized the wheel and steadied the *Charlotte Rhodes* on course; then he raised his voice to a hoarse croak and to Anne's surprise the apparent corpses straggled to a semblance of life. The ship, too, which she was certain must founder, seemed determined to survive. She rolled sluggishly, the bows lifted, the accumulation of water spilled from her scuppers and cascaded along the deck to sweep Anne from her feet and bring her up with a bone-jarring crash against the lee rail. She clambered to her feet as the wind suddenly gathered force and howled across the sea. Baines was already putting the *Charlotte Rhodes* under storm canvas but the hands hauling themselves aloft were too late to save the topsail which blew out with a noise like a pistol shot.

Anne felt exhausted and her soaking garments weighed heavily on her.

She returned to the cabin and stood in an ever-growing pool of water looking down at the sleeping James. She started to laugh. He, the master of the ship, had slept through it all like a child. Then she noticed that he was bathed in perspiration and that his breathing was shallow and uneven, rasping and gurgling in his throat.

15

THE Western Ocean is a lonely place. A desolation of storm-torn seas and fierce biting winds; the most turbulent stretch of water on the surface of the globe; 3,000 miles wide and two miles deep; a savage battleground strewn with the bones of ships and men; when the Atlantic rose in fury there were few survivors.

Driven by the relentless westerlies, the waves marched in ranks to hurl themselves against the rock-bound bastion of Ireland, the most westerly outpost in the unending war between land and sea. The sea had raged, sapped and mined, hacked its way into the ramparts and tumbled the outworks into bights and estuaries and rock-strewn inlets that turned Ireland's western shores into one of the most dangerous stretches of coastline in the world.

Anne had made James as comfortable as she could by dressing him in his nightshirt and covering him with a mound of warm dry blankets. Then she sent for Mr. Baines.

"It's ship fever, right enough," pronounced Baines.

Anne disagreed.

"Nonsense," she said briskly. "It is the result of eating tainted meat and drinking foul water."

"If that be the case," said Baines, "there'd never be a seaman standing on his feet. All shipboard meat is of poor quality, ma'am, and drinking water soon loses its freshness after a day or two at sea."

Anne strove to keep an edge of irritability from her voice. "Any housewife knows the difference between meat of poor quality and meat which is infected."

"It is well known, ma'am, that ship fever is a contagion of the air and is best cured by the purifying action of clean ocean winds." Baines's features had set in stubborn lines. Anne decided to pursue the matter no further — there was little point in antagonising the man. If her conviction was correct and James and the seaman were stricken with food poisoning she would need Baines as an ally, not an enemy.

"Very well, Mr. Baines," she said.

"Call it what you will. In the meantime, as you will take command of the ship until my husband recovers, please feel free to use the chart-room as you wish. You will find the sextant in its box and the chart shows our last noon position . . ." She broke off to find him staring at her in consternation.

"Me, ma'am ?"

"Why ever not ? You are the ship's Mate. Next in order of command."

"Oh, I can handle the ship well enough. No fear on that score. It's the manner of calculating position that'd have me baffled." He looked uncomfortably embarrassed. She stared at him in perplexity.

"I don't understand. Just what is the difficulty, Mr. Baines ?"

He looked more embarrassed than ever.

"I don't have the lettering, ma'am. I never had no schooling, you see ?"

She stared aghast at the implication.

"Is there no one aboard ship who could . . . ?" She realised it was a forlorn hope; it was doubtful if any member of the crew could so much as scrawl his name, much less struggle with the problems of navigation.

"No one but yourself, ma'am," said Baines.

Her heart seemed to stop.

"But I know nothing of navigation."

The giant looked at her as though she were being wilfully obtuse.

"Cap'n Onedin showed you the manner of using the sextant. It's just a matter of plotting the altitude on the chart."

She sighed. "I am afraid there is rather more to it than that, Mr. Baines."

"I see no difficulty," he said, perversely. "There are books enough in the chart-room. I've seen Cap'n Onedin making use of them many's the time."

Anne understood. To the illiterate books were the source of all knowledge. The key to a magic door which, once opened, would resolve all problems.

"I'll do my best," she said.

She must have sounded doubtful, for resentment showed on every line of his features.

"If I had the lettering I shouldn't trouble you. But I haven't, so the matter rests in your hands. There's nothing else for it."

She realised there was another reason for his discontent. He was now officially in command of the ship; it must therefore gall him to be forced to apply to a petticoated female in order to, literally, find his bearings.

"I shall give you all the help I can, Mr. Baines," she said, tactfully.

"Thank you, ma'am." If anything he was more rigid than ever. "What course shall I set?"

She hadn't the remotest idea.

"I think we should keep to the same course for the time being," she answered with as much confidence as she could muster.

"Nor' by west a half west, steady as she goes," he said, then paused long enough to look down at the unconscious James. "Ship fever," he stated unequivocally, and tramped resentfully up the companionway to the deck above.

James stirred restlessly. Saliva ran from one corner of his mouth. She bathed his face and tried to guess at his temperature. His forehead burned to her touch and he ground his teeth and tossed and turned vainly trying to throw off the swaddling blankets.

She opened the medicine chest and read

the List of Contents pasted on the lid. It bore the heading: "Scale of Medicines and Medical Stores suitable to Accidents and Diseases arising on Sea Voyages. Issued by the Board of Trade in pursuance of the Merchant Shipping Act, 1854." It consisted of fifty-two items inclusive of scissors, splints, needles and thread, syringes, lancets (2), pestle and mortar and one piece of tape. She ran her eye down the list of medicaments and found little of use beyond 2ozs Laudanum, 6ozs Simple Ointment, 1 dozen Opium Pills and 4ozs Paregoric. There were also such eccentricities as an ounce of Powdered Ginger, a yard of Adhesive Plaister (in tin case) and four ounces of Tincture of Rhubarb.

She shook her head and, closing the lid, wondered what ills of the flesh seamen were heir to that would account for such capricious remedies. Then she made her way to the chart-room.

She sat at the desk and gave herself a few moments to compose her mind. Above all, she told herself, she must think clearly and not panic. Fortunately she had an accurate memory and, if anything, an over-active brain; which was why, bored with shipboard life, she had set herself the task of memorising the vocabulary of the sea, and patiently observed James busy at his chartwork.

There were, she knew, two methods of calculating position when out of sight of land. By dead reckoning — simple but unreliable, according to James — and chiefly used when cloud cover made observations impossible. The other was by observation of sun and stars and called for accuracy and at least a working knowledge of mathematics.

Very well, dead reckoning it would be. "A lazy man's navigation," James had once told her, adding with that sour smile, "And sometimes a dead man's."

She fished out the chart and spread it on the chart table. The principle was simplicity itself: all it required was knowledge of the ship's course and the number of hours from the last observation. She looked at the chronometer. It showed five minutes to six o'clock. Nightfall was closing in. She lit the oil lamps, then applied herself to the problem of plotting the ship's course and position.

Her confidence grew as she worked.

Tongue protruding from the corner of her mouth, she used the parallel rulers to step off the course from the noon position: north by west a half west, Baines had said. She drew a continuous straight line to the uppermost edge of the chart. The ship had progressed for six hours at an average speed of . . . ? She bit her lip and then realised there was a ready-made solution to hand. Please with her perspicacity, she picked up the dividers and measured the distance traversed between noon and noon of the previous day. The scale at the edge of the chart gave the distance as 123 miles — say 5 miles an hour — 5 knots for six hours would put the *Charlotte Rhodes* 30 miles ahead of its noon position. It was really childishly simple, she thought, and would serve the purpose for twenty-four hours, by which time, with God's blessing, James should have passed the crisis and be sufficiently alert to show her the mathematics of the business. Yes, she decided, between them they would manage.

She looked at the chart again and made a neat X at the six o'clock position and then encircled it with an O. The position was quite close to the top of the chart, she noticed. Tomorrow a continuation chart would be required, but she would deal with that problem when it arose. James would advise her. She looked at the ship's snail-track staggering from top to bottom of the chart in a series of zig-zags, each representing a correction of course. It was a pity, she thought, that the chart was simply a grid-iron of lines of latitude and longitude and showed no vestige of land. Her imagination played tricks with her. The *Charlotte Rhodes* was nothing but a tiny X in an immensity of ocean. But there was safety in distance. Searoom, James and Mr. Baines called it. She became a little more self-critical and admitted that she had probably made minor errors of calculation. She had not allowed for leeway — the sideways movement of the ship through the water; and of course to escape the waterspout the ship had turned and run to the west. For how long? Half an hour perhaps? She shrugged off a feeling of unease. Over so short a distance any error in her reckoning would amount to no more than a couple of miles. And what was a couple of miles in the vastness of the ocean wastes?"

She came out of her reverie as the ship heeled and she heard the sound of bare feet slapping on the deck above, hoarse shouts, the rattle of yards and the bull-whip crack of slatting sails.

Putting her cape about her shoulders she hurried on to deck again.

The sun had set, leaving a pale orange afterlight across the western sky. Veils of rain trailed across the sea like lost wraiths. Toward the east a night of crystal stars climbed into the heavens.

She noticed that the motion of the ship had changed from its usual unsteady flat-footed wallowing to a more spirited advance, lifting and plunging its head, throwing twin fountains of water over the bows.

Baines greeted her without animosity.

"Wind's veering to the south'ard and freshening, ma'am. I've brought her round a point," he added. "Might as well get the best out of her. Wind and sea behind suits her a treat."

Her mind busy with fresh calculations, she asked: "What speed will we make, Mr. Baines?"

"Now we've got rid of that damn' nor'

easter we'll reel off the knots," said Baines. "Mind you, we're low in the water so she'll tend to drag her skirts a bit, begging your pardon, ma'am. I reckon we'll make maybe seven knots."

Seven knots? That meant by midnight they would have covered another 42 miles. She peered into the compass binnacle and read off the new course from the swaying card: north a half west. Almost due north. And if the wind was veering it could shift right around. It really was becoming most complicated.

"Please let me know of any further alterations of course, Mr. Baines," she requested, and then was suddenly conscience-stricken. "How is the sick man?" she asked.

"Died half an hour ago," said Baines, matter-of-fact. "I knew it was ship fever. Said so all along."

"Died?" Something seemed to be wedged in her throat. She couldn't breathe.

"Best enter it in the log, ma'am."

"Yes," she said dully. Oh, God, James!

"And perhaps you'll read a word or two over him. It's the practice, ma'am," he added.

"Now?" she asked stupidly. She couldn't believe that death could strike so swiftly. Ill of eating bad meat had been her conviction. But if she was wrong and Baines right? Baines was experienced in these matters. Ship fever? Ship fever, gaol fever, Irish fever. Unhappy soubriquets that covered a multitude of ills. Cholera. Typhoid. Typhus. Each synonymous with overcrowding and bad hygiene; and each bringing death in its train.

Oh, God, James! Bewildered and terrified she stared at Baines.

"Now?" she repeated. "Now?"

"Not until daylight, ma'am. It wouldn't be Christian," he said. "Not at night."

"Very good, Mr. Baines," she said, and hurried below again.

James's skin was ice cold. He lay shivering, teeth chattering, eyes wide open and unseeing.

Anne piled on more blankets and his eyes rolled wildly in his head. He tried to speak, but only succeeded in producing an incoherent jumble of nonsense. She found the brandy bottle and forced a little down his throat until he choked and spluttered.

Water, she thought. He must have water to drink.

She scurried away to the galley and found a kettle steaming and hissing contentedly to itself. The club-footed cook glowered balefully as she drew off a panful of boiling water.

"In future," she snapped at him, "all drinking water is to be boiled first. Is that clear?"

His toothless mouth opened in a gape of dull-witted incomprehension. She had no time to argue with the blockhead.

"Every drop of water. See to it."

His rheumy eyes watched her skirts disappear through the doorway then he curled up again on his straw palliasse. Tears of laughter ran down his cheeks: "Biled water," he spluttered. "By the Holy! Biled water!"

Most of the blankets had tumbled to the floor and James was threshing about wildly when she returned. She put down the pan of hot water and replaced the blankets. She found that she required all her strength to restrain him. His cheeks were sunken and his skin had the look and touch of dried parchment.

While waiting for the water to become more temperate, she rummaged through the medicine chest and found the 2oz bottle of laudanum. She poured hot water into a cup, added a few drops of the laudanum, then, propping James's head up, coaxed him to drink. He gulped and slopped the liquid at first then swallowed greedily. She waited. He mumbled a little and then in a few minutes relaxed and fell into a sound sleep.

She determined to sit with him through the night, but first she must again apply herself to laying off the new course on the chart. She walked wearily through to the chart-room and tiredly ruled off the new course. The additional 42 miles brought the midnight position within an inch of the top of the chart. She must find the continuation chart. Midnight would be time enough, she thought drowsily.

Returning to their cabin, she drew her chair close beside the bunk, fixed her gaze firmly upon James, and promptly fell asleep.

And while she slept the erratic wind veered even further to the south and west, gathering strength and carrying before it a fine obliterating rain that covered the ship like a shroud.

And every hour the *Charlotte Rhodes* ploughed steadily toward Fastnet and the barren surf-bound rocks lying beween Mizen Head and Cape Clear.

16

THE sun had risen and painted the sea an ochrous yellow. The Atlantic rollers were wide and unbroken, rising and falling, gently pushing the ship forward. The wind was contrary, at one moment gusting from the south and west, the next shifting to the south-east. Every change of direction brought the crew tumbling out, half asleep, cursing and swearing, to haul on sheets and braces as the *Charlotte Rhodes* staggered from one tack to the other.

The rain was as fitful as the wind. Long grey curtains that swept across the sea to envelop the ship in an icy downpour, drenching them to their skins until their teeth chattered in their heads. Then the early morning sun would break through again to draw curling fingers of steam from the evaporating moisture on the decks.

Baines was bone-weary, irritable, and more worried than he cared to show.

It was that damned witch-woman. This morning she had been up betimes harassing the cook. She had condemned the harness cask of meat and, shrilling like a fishwife, insisted upon its contents being dumped into the sea. Then she had had the head knocked off the remaining cask and picked over the meat as though she were shopping in a market. Half of that had also been condemned. God alone knew what she imagined they would live off if the wind backed to the north. They would be blown out into the Atlantic and probably starve to death, he thought, morosely. Then the damned virago had given the cook elaborate instructions — she seemed to have a mania for boiling everything — insisting that good salt beef was to be thoroughly boiled for at least an hour. And all drinking water also! She was mad, quite mad. The crew, faced with a breakfast of hot water and meat as tough as rubber, were sullen and angry, and who could blame them? Baines was resentful of her damned interference with matters that did not concern her. Her function was to nurse her husband and to extract their position from those navigation books. God, if only he had learned to read! He'd have been master years ago. He'd have had command of a packet ship by now as like as not, and be living off the fat of the land!

The ship's position worried him. Every instinct crawled with apprehension. A lifetime's experience had bred an almost clairvoyant sense of danger. He assumed that they were approaching the St. George's Channel — the stretch of water between the mainland and Ireland — and had therefore obediently kept the ship on its heading. He would feel safer once they sighted land; he could sail the ship from point to point with ease. And land could not be far away. When the — so-called — bad meat had been disposed of, the seabirds had come from nowhere to gorge themselves to repletion. Even now, standing listening to the confounded woman droning on with the burial service, he could see the birds resting sleepily on the water, digesting this unexpected benison. They bobbed on the surface, lifting and falling with the long slow swell, like so many white plumes dropped from the sky.

The motion of the sea itself bothered

him. The rollers raked unbroken from horizon to horizon and the troughs were wide. They were sailing over deep water, he was sure. At the entrance to the Channel the sea bed shelved rapidly and the colour of the sea invariably changed to a noticeably lighter hue.

A long green slime glided past the ship. Seaweed. Land *must* be near to hand. He looked up toward the man he had posted at the masthead. The wretch stood at the cross-trees, shelving and beating his arms.

Baines returned his attention to the service, which seemed to be taking an interminable time. "Just say a few words," he had told her, and meant just that; but, contrary as ever, the confounded woman was preaching as though she was in a pulpit.

The body, sewn into its canvas shroud, lay on a plank. The Dandy and Scalplock had one end resting on their shoulders and waited only for the Mate's order before heaving their one-time shipmate over the side. Scalplock appreciated a funeral at sea. It showed respect and gave a never-ending topic of interest for the remainder of the voyage. His stomach rumbled rebelliously and he determined to tackle the Mate immediately afterward. Boiled meat was unhealthy, every seaman knew that. All the good was taken from it. And the flavour. Scalplock liked his meat gamey and perhaps with a pickle or two. They had discussed the matter at length at breakfast and he had been elected spokesman. Salt beef they had signed for, and salt beef they would have. In the meantime, he listened to the service. The woman, for all her faults, read it very nicely. She put it very well, he thought.

"Man that is born of a woman hath but a short time to live, and is full of misery. He cometh up and is cut down like a flower," recited Anne; thinking, Oh, God, James, James, James!

She had wakened from her vigil feeling stiff and wretched. One of the oil lamps was smoking, filling the cabin with acrid fumes. The thin grey light of a false dawn filtered through the skylights. James lay so still and quiet that for one heart-stopping moment she thought he had died in the night; then she noticed that he was breathing shallowly. His hand lay outside the blanket. It was warm to the touch and the pulsebeat slow and steady. She made him as comfortable as possible, added a silent promise that she would return as soon as circumstances permitted, and then steeled herself to face the duties of the day.

"Forasmuch as it hath pleased Almighty God of his great mercy to take unto himself the soul of our dear brother here departed," she intoned . . .

"Land-ho! Land-ho!" bawled the masthead lookout.

Their heads craned to follow the direction of his pointing hand.

"Where away?" shouted Baines, already swinging himself into the mizzen shrouds.

"Dead ahead," the lookout called back.

Baines, scrambling aloft, paused once to look down upon their upturned faces.

"Dump him," he ordered brusquely, and ran hand over hand to the cross-trees.

Anne opened her mouth to protest against the sacrilege, but the end of the plank was promptly raised and the body slid into the sea, while the seabirds rose in a cloud to skim the surface and cry dismay.

Baines, perched forty feet above the deck, squinted his eyes and peered ahead. Then he called down to Scalplock to fetch the telescope. Shading his eyes, he could just make out the dark shadow of land above a thin white pencil line at the edge of the horizon. Breakers, for certain sure. He looked away to starboard. For a few moments the spread of the fore-topsail hid his view. Then, as the ship rolled and pitched, he caught a glimpse of a tall slender shape with a froth of white surf about its base. Christ! he swore, and slid down to deck. Grabbing the telescope, he ran forward and raced up the foremast lee rigging to perch himself astride the topsail yard. He focused the telescope and the foreshortened distance sent fear coursing through his veins like rivers of ice. It was worse, much worse than he thought. Over to port he could see a long finger of land poking out into the sea, almost invisible beneath the smoking spray thrown up by the Atlantic rollers. To starboard, the tall column of a lighthouse on its perch of rock.

"Wear ship! Wear ship!" he screamed

hoarsely. "Bring her round! Bring her round!"

The sheer urgency of his voice galvanised the crew into action. They raced for sheets and braces as Baines almost hurled himself to the deck below. Every man aboard knew the danger without being told; a wind on the quarter and land right ahead could only mean one thing — they were in imminent danger of being blown on a lee shore.

The spanker sheets were hauled in and fore and mainsails braced to shiver.

"Ready about!" roared Baines, and the helmsman put up the helm. The jib sheets were rapidly overhauled and the weather forebraces eased until the *Charlotte Rhodes* turned her head and began to run before the wind. Then the spanker was braced full, the booms swung across and the ship heeled upon the opposite tack.

Baines mopped his face, and Anne noticed that the crew, instead of following their usual practice of leaving the watch on deck to coil the ropes neatly upon the belaying pins, remained at their stations waiting tensely for the next order.

The manoeuvre had given them a

breathing space and was carrying the ship across the wide bay, but toward the outthrust headland of Mizen Head. They had gained time but lost sea room.

Anne looked over her shoulder and was astonished to find the coastline so near. She could see and hear the roar of the breakers. The enormous cliffs seemed to have leaped toward them.

Baines licked his lips and judged the distance between the ship and the tip of the headland. He must now bring the ship around until it lay close-hauled and sailing almost into the teeth of the wind. It was a decision which required nicety of judgment and a disciplined crew. If the *Charlotte Rhodes* was caught aback there would be no second chance; she would simply make sternway and be pounded to pieces on the rocks. If he made the decision too soon she would be embayed with the same result — it would simply take a little longer. Too late and she would never clear the headland.

"Luff her!" he bawled.

The jibs rattled down. The spanker held the wind and swung the stern around. The hands standing by the fore and main sails tailed on to the sheets and hauled the booms across. The sails shivered and flapped as the ship's head swung into the wind. The helmsman put the helm down and concentrated his gaze upon the set of the sails. Sweat poured down his face. The hands standing by the jib halyards waited, straining their ears for the expected command. The pounding of the surf seemed to be the only sound they could hear, would ever hear.

"Jibs!" shouted Baines, and the jibs soared up the stays to boom and balloon in the wind.

"Haul in your sheets!" screamed Baines. "Haul in your jib sheets!"

He could have saved his breath. The crew slaved until their lungs were bursting and hands bleeding. Slowly the jibs tautened, shook once or twice, then steadied, cracking in the wind.

The *Charlotte Rhodes*' head came round and she clawed her way to the south and the open sea.

Baines expelled a breath of relief.

"Steady as she goes," he told the helmsman and then called to Scalplock.

"Mr. Duncan."

Scalplock looked up in surprise. Only Mates and petty officers were addressed as Mister.

"Muster the hands for a tot," said Baines. "And as of now you are second in command. You'll stand watch and watch with me."

"Aye, aye, Cap'n," grinned Scalplock. "Mate's pay?" he asked, cunningly.

"Mate's pay," agreed Baines. He leaned over the poop deck rail and scowled down at Anne. "As for you, Missus, your place is with your husband. Get below and stay below. I've had my fill of book-learning."

Anne was about to answer, but his angry face and a few sniggers from the crew warned her that she had better hold her tongue. Dejected and dismayed, she returned to their quarters.

To her surprise Baines followed her below.

"The keys to the rum locker, if you please." He held out his hand with the attitude of a man who would brook no argument.

"For the crew," he added shortly. "They've earned it."

Anne led the way through to the chart-room. Still in the grip of rage he barely glanced at James. She gestured wearily to the keys hanging from a nail.

"Fastnet," he said. "Fastnet and the Mizen! And you had us heading straight between. Almost had us beached. You put us at grave risk, ma'am. Every man Jack."

"I'm sorry," she said, tiredly. "I didn't know."

"Didn't know?" He shook his head at the enormity of her ignorance. "What's the sense to book-learning if you didn't know? It was your business to know, ma'am."

"I'm sorry," she said again.

"Sorry?" he raged. "Of what use is sorry? Sorry don't mend dead men's bones. Sorry don't excuse good salt beef to waste over the side. The crew on hot water and short commons! There'll be no more boilings of meat and water aboard this ship, by God!"

He unlocked the cupboard door beneath the chart table and fished out the small keg of rum.

"Ship fever is a contagion of the air,"

he pronounced. "It does not spring from chandler's meat!"

"No doubt we shall know the truth shortly," she said.

Baines stared at her.

"If your surmise is correct I doubt any of us will survive. Unless we put into port."

He frowned, trying to work it out.

"Can't hardly do that. Nearest safe port'd be Bantry."

He scratched his head. "The Irish are a wild lot and their whole country's rife with fever, it's well known. In any case, we'd be quarantined no matter where."

"A ship is only quarantined for fever, Mr. Baines. Not because of contaminated food."

"Ship fever . . ." he began again.

She held up a hand.

"Think about it, Mr. Baines. Think carefully."

He shouldered the keg.

"I have yet to enter the man's death in the official log. When I have done so I will read it to you. Then you, as the officer of the deck, will be required to sign."

"You know I can't. If I'd had the

schooling I'd have been master of my own ship by now. Those with book-learning have all the advantages." The sullenness had returned to his face.

"I could teach you to write your name," she said.

He stared at her as though she had announced the performance of a miracle.

"My own name? Seized, wrapped and parcelled?" His free hand described a series of loops in the air.

She laughed. "And with a round turn and two half hitches for good measure."

He put down the keg.

"By the Holy," he said. "By the Holy I believe you means it." Suspicion clouded his face. "Why should you want to do that?"

"I'll strike a bargain with you. Until my husband recovers you sail the ship; I navigate."

He shook his head. "We've given that a fair trial already. Near enough brought salt water shrouds to us all."

Anne looked at him levelly. "And in return I will teach you to read and write."

It took him a moment to digest the information.

"My characters?" he asked

She nodded.

"And figuring?" he asked quickly, as though sensing a trap.

"And figuring," she agreed solemnly.

He considered carefully.

"Once I know the lie of the land I can find my bearings."

"Exactly," she said. "Within sight of land the employment of the ship will be entirely in your hands."

He brooded. "The thing is, ma'am, we're close-hauled and heading south. Looking for sea room, you understand?"

Anne followed his reasoning. Their present course would take them far south into the Atlantic until it was safe to turn the ship and try again. The problem would simply repeat itself: it was impossible to lay off an accurate course without first knowing the position of the ship. But there was a solution to at least half the problem scratching at the back of her mind.

"I am sure I could find our longitude," she said. "Quite easily."

Baines rubbed his chin, unsure, and looked at the woman's long face bobbing in eagerness at the end of its thin neck. If this odd creature could teach him the mysteries of book-reading he'd have little to lose and much to gain. He had already made up his mind to take the only course open to him. To head south until his instinct told him it was safe and then run across the wind, edging eastward toward the Channel and Land's End. He had all the deep water man's fear of being within close reach of the land pursued by a wind that shifted halfway around the compass every hour. Given the choice, he would have preferred to heave-to in the open sea and simply wait until Cap'n Onedin recovered. But since the blasted woman had pitched virtually all their food over the side he had little option but to run for home and sail by guess and by God.

He nodded: "We'll try it once more, ma'am," and hoisted the keg to his shoulder again.

"I'll have no drunkenness aboard ship, Mr. Baines," she warned, sharply.

He grinned at her: "I know ships and the seas and the winds that blow. I can handle men drunk or sober, but — begging your pardon, ma'am — contumacious, parsimonious females I will never understand." He tapped the keg. "Take a little wine for thy stomach's sake. Scripture, ma'am."

She bared her teeth in a grin of acknowledgment.

"I have every confidence in your exercise of authority. Mr. Baines. Which brings me to my second point. I shall be in charge of the commissariat."

"Commis . . . ?" He paused, bulking in the doorway.

"The cook is to carry out my instructions at all times. I shall expect your full support."

He was exasperated. Of all the disputations . . .! Then he shrugged resignedly. There was simply no arguing with the woman.

"Very well, ma'am," he agreed. "You tend to the boiling of the meat and I'll see to it that they swallow every morsel."

"Thank you, Mr. Baines," she said, and returned to her work at the chart table.

Anne waited until Baines had left and then tried to compose her thoughts into some sort of order. A fugitive memory twisted and turned through the corridors of her mind. A bright clear day — the sun sparkling on the waters — four days homeward bound from Lisbon — far out in the Atlantic — they had finished breakfast and were strolling on deck. "I wonder," she had mused, "what they are doing at home at this time?" James had smiled, glanced at his watch and said, "Probably just getting out of bed and rubbing the sleep from their eyes."

She clung to the thought: breakfast time aboard ship was waking time ashore. Therefore there was a time difference. Of course! That is why the clock was altered daily. But the clock kept ship time and not shore time. She ran her fingers through her hair. It was really very complicated.

On deck the quartermaster struck two bells. Automatically her eyes went to the clock. Nine o'clock already. . . . She frowned in perplexity, then recollected James calling, "Time!" and Mr. Baines resetting his watch and striking eight bells. Suddenly she understood. Longitude was no more than the difference between ship and shore time. That was why the accuracy of the GMT chronometer was of such importance! All that was required was to transpose hours and minutes of time into degrees and minutes of longitude.

The method eluded her for the space of twenty minutes. Then she sat back, satisfied with her calculations. It really was so childishly simple, she thought. The earth rotated once every twenty-four hours. 360 degrees divided by 24 gave a result of 15. Therefore 15 degrees of longitude equalled one hour of time.

She spent a self-congratulatory forty minutes checking and re-checking her theory and now only longed for noon to come so she could put it to the final test. There remained the problem of finding their latitude, of course, but after her success with longitude she anticipated little difficulty in that direction. No doubt Mr. Baines was right; the answers would be found in the navigation books.

She was brought from her reverie by a groan from the cabin.

Hurrying through, she found James retching and vomiting over the side of the bunk.

She put the pail before him and held

his head. He finished and lay back gasping as she wiped his face. His eyes opened. He focused with difficulty, then gripped her arm. His jaw opened and closed in an effort to speak coherently.

"Sail plain, Plain Jane," he said with the greatest urgency. His fingers held her forearm like pincers. "Plain Jane," he repeated. "Sail plain, Plain Jane, Plain Jane," and his voice died away to a mutter until he once more lay still and quiet.

She tucked his arm back beneath the blanket. "Is that what he thinks of me?" she thought bitterly. "Plain Jane?"

The cook saw her approaching in a flurry of rustling skirts. He began to clatter his pots and pans in a frenzy of impotent anger. Anne lifted lids, peered, tasted and sniffed. She paused at a huge cauldron, fished out an unappetising lump of bone and gristle, wrinkled her nose in a snort of distaste and then popped the meat back into the pot.

"It is to be fast-boiled, you understand?" she snapped at the scabrous-looking wretch. "And I shall require a nourishing broth from the liquid. Add lentils, peas, barley and . . . what else do you have?"

He wiped his streaming nose.

"Nuffin'," he said.

"Can you make dumplings?" she asked.

"No," he shouted triumphantly. "Can't make dumplin's. Don't know how."

"What sort of cook are you?" she demanded.

"A bilin' water cook," he crowed, flapping his hands. "A bilin' water cook."

"Fetch me the ingredients," she commanded. "Suet . . ."

"Don't have no suet," he screeched.

"A lump of fat and flour. I'll show you how," she said.

"Show me nothin'. Nothin' at all. My galley," he yelled. Capering with rage, he picked up a skillet and brandished it above his head. "Gerrout, gerrout, gerrout, bilin' water bitch. Gerrout o' me galley!"

She backed away from the madman, out on to deck, followed by his shrieks and squawks.

Baines loomed beside her, plucked the skillet from the enraged cook's hand and shook the old bag of bones until he rattled.

"You want to go over the side, Johnny

Oilcake?" he rumbled. "Feed the fishes, you bone-bag? You do as the lady says. And I want to hear 'please' and 'thank-you-ma'am'. D'ye hear me, piss-bag? Begging your pardon, ma'am." He released the quivering wretch, who immediately rolled his eyes and pleaded, "I want me tot." He licked his lips. "It in't fair. Not right by Articles. All hands to muster for a tot. It's me entitlement." He cringed as Baines raised a hand the size of a ham.

"I'll give you entitlement," he growled. "When the lady gives a lawful command, you jump to it, or I'll 'entitle' you to a deep Atlantic bath. Move, you Johnny-jump-ashore! Move!"

Tears started from the red-rimmed eyes, then he knuckled his forehead and scuttled back into the galley. Baines turned good-humouredly to Anne.

"I promised my support, ma'am, and my support you shall have."

His breath, she thought, was strong enough to scorch bark from a tree; but she had seen enough of seaboard life to know that discipline was not maintained with kind words and soft phrases.

"He is of a somewhat cantankerous nature," she smiled.

"Any more trouble, you let me know. I'll take the tar out of him," said Baines. "You hear?" he roared. "You hear, old Reach-me-down? What set him off this time?" he asked Anne.

"He said he didn't know how to make dumplings. I offered to show him . . ."

Baines thrust his head into the galley.

"Dumplings," he bellowed. "Dumplings for all hands, you old bag o' wind. Eight bells sharp, or I'll know the reason why." He turned back to Anne. "He knows," he said. "He's been making dumplings these past ten years. He's the worst cook I ever did ship with, but he knows how to make dumplings."

"Then why did he fly into such a paddy?" she asked.

"All cooks is mad," said Baines. "They got to be, otherwise they'd never venture to ship as cooks. Stands to sense."

"Perhaps," she ventured, "he feels resentment because he has not had his share of the rum issue?" The rest of the crew certainly had, she noticed. They were lolling around in relaxed groups, drinking deeply from tin cups as though the fiery liquid was mother's milk. Even the helmsman had his share and balanced himself easily at the wheel, pausing occasionally to take a satisfying draught from his tin mug. God knows what James would say if he knew, she thought. But the ship, no longer close-hauled, was scudding away to the south and west and no one, least of all Mr. Baines, seemed to have a care in the world.

"He can't hold his liquor," Baines was saying. "He's a poor enough hand with the vittles sober; drunk he couldn't boil water without burning it." He tapped his forehead. "He's a softy, y'see, ma'am. Shipped aboard a slaver in his younger days. It is said that the sights he saw turned his brain, but in my opinion, ma'am, he's always been a softy."

"It is the judgment of God," she said pitilessly. " 'Fools because of their transgression and because of their iniquities are afflicted.' Scripture, Mr. Baines." She nodded politely and, leaving him to stare after her, made her way aft to the cabin.

James seemed to have passed the crisis. His pulse beat strongly and he lay in a deep calm sleep, breathing easily and heavily. Anne dropped to her knees, clasped her hands and offered thanks to God for his goodness and mercy; then she made her way to the chart-room, and opened the chart drawer to look for the continuation sheet. Her heart galloped into her throat and she cursed herself for a stupid, arrogant, mindless fool. She spread the chart on the table top and there, before her, lay a detailed projection of the Irish and Welsh coastlines at either side of the St. George's Channel.

She could have wept with anger and frustration. She had naught to blame but her own perverse nature! If only she had had the wit to open the confounded drawer earlier they would never have stood in to danger. Through her own pride and stupidity she had brought them to the brink of disaster. The fault was hers, and hers alone. If she had had the gumption to look out this new chart last night she would clearly have seen the southern tip of Ireland looming ahead of them. What the devil do you imagine charts are for? she asked herself savagely. Overcome with self-recrimination she sat for long minutes in a state of stupor. Then she roused herself and examined the chart with growing interest. As long as it was here she must make full use of the information it contained. For an hour she busied herself with ruler and dividers; then she called for Mr. Baines.

He arrived in great good humour and wreathed in a cloud of rum.

She showed him the chart and waited for the outburst, fully expecting him to rant and rage at her for a dimwitted ninny. But he merely puzzled over the outlines for a full minute and then announced: "I seen this somewhere's before."

Relieved beyond measure, she pointed out the main features: "This represents the south-eastern coast of Ireland and over here, the Pembrokeshire coast of South Wales."

He grunted, searching his memory, and then stabbed a forefinger down. "That'll be Tuskar . . . and over here . . . Strumble Head. The Smalls is to the south'ard. Am I right?"

She nodded.

"If you can indicate our position, ma'am, I can take me bearings. You've done well, ma'am. Very well indeed. By God, we'll make a navigator of you yet." He beamed at her with pride as though she had drawn the chart herself.

She tapped the desk below the chart. "Our position is somewhere down here," she said, and watched his face closely.

"Ah," he said, puzzled.

"However, if we could steer north by east, making due allowance for leeway, I think we should bring up the Welsh coast in the hours of daylight, Mr. Baines."

He spanned his enormous fingers across the chart.

"Don't look far," he said.

"About one hundred and eighty miles," she told him, and waited hopefully. This time she wanted the decision to be his.

He calculated slowly. "That'll be around midday tomorrow, I reckon?" He grinned at her, delighted. "Leave everything to me, Missus. From now on everyting'll be plain sailing."

Plain sailing? She looked at him, gaping like a fool.

"Plain sailing, did you say, Mr. Baines? Plain sailing?" *Sail plain, Plain Jane,* James had said. *Sail plain.*

"Rule o' thumb," said Baines. "Point to point. Landmark to landmark. Leave it to me, Missus. In two days' sail we'll be home and dry. God send us fair winds," he added piously.

He tramped out, ducking his head in the doorway, and she could hear him above deck roaring orders.

The ship pitched and yawed, bucked into the sea; the booms and yards creaked and she could hear the hiss of rope running through greased blocks; then the crew's voice raised in a chant as they sweated on downhauls and sheets:

> "We're gettin' paid off in Liverpool
> To blow our money free,
> To sup and booze and chase the
> whores,
> And forget the bloody sea . . ."

"Anne . . . ?"

At the sound of his voice she almost jumped out of her skin. Coming to her feet she half ran, half stumbled through to the cabin.

James was struggling to sit up in his bunk, part-raised on one elbow, his head wagging weakly from side to side. He had difficulty in focusing his eyes.

She ran to him, weeping. "Oh, James! James, James . . ."

He blinked at her in alarm, listened to the stamp of feet above.

"What is it?" he demanded. "What's the matter?" and tried to swing his legs over the side.

"Nothing," she cried, half-weeping, half-laughing. "Nothing is the matter. Everything is just fine. Just fine."

James stared at her in amazement. Did the creature always give way to tears when she was in good humour? His stomach hurt and his head rang and he felt as weak as a kitten. He had a confused memory of lying down and. . . . My God, he thought in panic. We're heading for Fastnet! He heaved himself upright and his head swam.

"Where are we?" he asked.

"You are not to worry," she said, pushing him back. "Everything is in hand. We are heading towards the Welsh coast. There is plenty of time, James. Mr. Baines calculates that we should not sight land until about noon tomorrow."

"Baines!" said James. "The man can't count beyond ten. Who is navigating?"

She smiled a secret smile. "Mr. Baines and I have learned to trust each other's judgment."

"I'd rather trust Providence," he snapped. "Fetch me my trousers."

She shook her head firmly. "No, James. You have been ill. Seriously ill. Your strength will return slowly. First you must eat. Remain where you are — do you understand me?" She spoke in a no-nonsense voice, as though addressing a recalcitrant child. He sank back, finding that he lacked the strength to argue the point.

"I shall fetch some broth from the galley," she told him, and only then realised that she herself had had nothing to eat for twenty-four hours. "We shall dine together," she added, and her skirts whisked from view as she hurried on to deck.

James sighed and relaxed. She really was a most remarkable woman, he thought. Remarkable.

The *Charlotte Rhodes* berthed in Liverpool fifty-two hours later. James shook hands with the pilot and then made his way ashore.

Robert was waiting to greet him, hopping from one foot to another, his jowls quivering with anxiety. He seized James by the hand and pumped it heartily.

"Thank God you are back, James," he greeted. "How much profit have we made?"

17

IT wasn't fair, Elizabeth thought, miserably. It simply was not fair.

From the moment Daniel's ship had disappeared from view she had been relegated to her position of household drudge. Her situation seemed to be, if anything, harsher than it had ever been. Long before sunrise Robert's hammering upon the bedroom door would drag her from the warm clutch of sleep. Numb with cold, she would button herself into her clothes, fingers fumbling, and yawning as though her jaws would break. Then she would drag herself downstairs to light the fires and prepare the breakfasts while Robert, looking more and more haggard each passing day, would mope and fidget around the shop, hoping to catch a few early-morning customers.

To add to her woes Sarah had lately taken to having breakfast in bed, and become so finicky about her food; the bread was to be thinly sliced and just smeared with butter; the eggs lightly boiled and with a touch of fresh mustard — of all things! — at the side of her plate; the tea must be freshly brewed in a china pot, and one morning it must be strong enough to melt a spoon, the next so weak it could barely climb out of the spout. And she had a catalogue of complaints that seemed to lengthen with the day, until Elizabeth came to dread the moment the creak of the stairs would herald Sarah's appearance. She would stand swaying in the doorway, holding her monstrous belly and clucking peevishly while she waited for Elizabeth to plump the cushions before piloting her across to the sofa, where she would spend the remainder of the day munching broken biscuits, drinking quarts of barley water and catechising Elizabeth on her household duties: had she aired the sheets? shaken the mattress? opened the window? swept the carpet? emptied the chamber pot? cleaned out the grate? It was bad enough, in all conscience, when they were in the same room together; but no matter in which part of the house Elizabeth found herself — upstairs in the bedroom searching for a non-existent pot of salve, or down in the cellar struggling with a scuttleful of coal — the hateful, demanding voice would resound through the house, screeching unintelligible commands; and if Elizabeth, instead of replying at once, muttered beneath her breath, the voice would rise to a wail when both Elizabeth and Robert would rush in, convinced that the labour pains had started.

These were the moments that struck terror to Elizabeth's heart. She had tried to question Sarah, but it was so extraordinarily difficult to frame an enquiry of so delicate a nature without exposing oneself to dangerous suspicions. In fact Sarah welcomed any opportunity to discuss her condition at interminable length, and dwelt upon her sufferings with an obsessive detail that froze the marrow in Elizabeth's bones but only served the purpose of leaving her more bemused than ever. "How? When did you first know you were with child?" she had once asked. "That," Sarah had replied disapprovingly, "is not the sort of question to which you should require an answer until you are married, Elizabeth."

Whenever she had a free moment, Elizabeth would retire to her bedroom to pick over the gleanings from her latest crop of information: babies took a long time in the making—a nine-month seemed to be the most commonly held opinion. And yet, if this were so? She rapidly counted on her fingers back to the day Sarah had made her first momentous announcement and Robert had opened a couple of bottles of wine and their father had sat in the corner grinning like a stone ape and congratulating Robert as though he were the finest fellow alive. That, she calculated, had been exactly seven months ago. She remembered the day distinctly because it was the day that Mr. Jenkins's old horse, Greybeard, had fallen down dead in the street, breaking the shafts of the cart, and Mr. Simpson had offered ten shillings on the spot, and he and Mr. Jenkins had almost come to blows as a result. Seven months? That meant two months must have elapsed before Sarah was sure. And it was now almost two months since she and Daniel. . . . No. It couldn't be! She tried to reason it out: people married and had babies. The

Reverend Mr. Samuels, who was not only an ordained minister of the gospel but, as a family man, had practical experience of these things, regularly proclaimed that babies came from God. When Robert had told him that Sarah was expecting, Mr. Samuels had smiled and announced that God had blessed their union. That must be the answer. You prayed for a baby. That would certainly account for Mrs. Samuels being blessed with ten children, and that termagant Sarah having to wait four years for her first. Yes, she decided, prayer must be the answer; and it therefore followed if you prayed for the gift of a baby, equally you could pray not to have one. So Elizabeth prayed every night and promised, as an act of penitence, to be obedient to Sarah's every whim until she was delivered of child, and to take on the extra burden of the household duties without a word of complaint.

And then, two days before James's return, trudging up the narrow stairs with Sarah's breakfast tray, a sudden howl from the bedroom raised the hair upon her scalp, and Robert had come pounding up the stairs, shoving her to one side and spilling boiling hot tea down her dress, and plunged into their bedroom, only to reappear in a moment white with fear and bawling at the top of his lungs for her to run and tell the midwife that Sarah had started.

Elizabeth had run all the way with Sarah's yells and screams ringing in her ears. She hauled at the bell pull and hammered at the door until a first floor window opened and Mrs. McCready's round red moon-face peered down and demanded to know who was a-pounding at a poor body's door in the middle of the night. "It's seven in the morning," screeched Elizabeth, "and you are to come at once. Mrs. Onedin's in labour." "Away and hold her hand, hinny," said the moon-face. "I'll be along presently. It will be five shillings and my breakfast," she shouted after the departing Elizabeth.

Elizabeth returned to find Robert at the top of the stairs, wringing his hands in anguish and grinding his teeth at every squeal from the bedroom.

"The midwife?" he hissed. "Where is she?"

"On her way," said Elizabeth and turned to make her escape. Robert seized her by the arm and half-dragged her toward the bedroom.

"Take care of her, Elizabeth," he pleaded. "Take care of her. I'll hurry Mrs. McCready along. And the shop. Must 'tend to the shop." Terrified out of his wits, he scuttled away downstairs leaving her alone with the near-demented Sarah.

Sarah's howls had subsided to sobs and moans. She lay on her back in the enormous half-tester bed and seemed to be boiling with perspiration. The great mound of her stomach was covered with an even greater mound of bedclothes and every so often Sarah would thrash her legs, roll her eyes until the whites showed and whimper like an animal.

Elizabeth was paralysed with fear. If the baby was born now she would be held responsible for its survival and she had not the remotest idea of what to do, nor even how it would be born. She found that her knees were beginning to shake; then bile flooded into her throat and she turned and retched into the basin.

"The midwife," wailed Sarah. "Fetch the midwife. The doctor," she suddenly shrieked. "Send for the doctor!" Then, to Elizabeth's horror, the contractions began, and Sarah rolled and threshed and kicked around the bed, roaring and weeping and yowling and calling upon God at the top of her lungs until Elizabeth put her hands over her ears and, running to the window, leaned out and screamed for somebody to send for Mrs. McCready. Then she turned back into the room and all she could think to do was to try to straighten the bedding as fast as Sarah kicked it off.

Gradually Sarah's nerve-wracking repertoire of screeches and screams subsided and she lay gasping and chattering, a bedraggled pasty-faced creature plucking at the sheets with taloned fingers and rolling imploring eyes round and round the room as though seeking an escape from her tormented body.

There was a tramp of hurried feet upon the stairs and the sound of Robert's urgent voice, then the door opened and Mrs. McCready bustled in, red moon-face dispensing "good-mornings" and "ho-

ho, what-have-we-heres?" like some pantomime Dame come to amuse the children. But once divested of cloak and bonnet she showed that she knew what she was about. Elizabeth was packed off to fetch and carry. First a tin bath; then kettles of hot water and pans of cold; and when Elizabeth had panted up the stairs with yet another pan of water: "And a wee pot of tea, hinny, wi' a cup for yesel', you look as though you need it, child." Mrs. McCready's buttonhole eyes had looked into Elizabeth's with an unfathomable wisdom: "There's naught for you to fear — I promise you'll not feel a pang," and she rocked her mountain of flesh in a wheezing eruption of laughter. But the shrewd eyes held their gaze: "No doubt but ye'll be having one yesel' one fine day, eh?" Then she turned her attention to Sarah, prodding and probing and talking fifty to the dozen: "Ye'll have a fine big healthy bairn, and it's going to be borned whether ye like it or no, so ye'd best make up ye mind to it. If it's any consolation to ye, it'll soon be over, and I've not lost more than five this year. I always tell my ladies to fix their minds upon one simple fact: Ye can walk doon the street of any town ye choose in the whole wide world and never the once will ye clap eyes on a body that wasn'a borned at some time nor anither."

Elizabeth did not wait to discover whether the thought brought comfort to Sarah or not, but hurried away to the kitchen to brew a fresh pot of tea and worry herself sick over Mrs. McCready's searching gaze. Waiting for the kettle to boil, she suddenly realised that here at last was someone who would know. The midwife could, as it were, give a professional opinion. She would say that she was inquiring on behalf of a friend, that should satisfy Mrs. McCready's curiosity. Mrs. McCready had said that she required breakfast as part payment, so she would ask her then. It was, she encouraged herself, no more than obtaining confirmation of her own reasoning. There was only one tiny niggling doubt that wriggled and turned at the back of her mind: the novels she read portrayed fallen women who had babies; it seemed hardly likely that they could have prayed for the blessing of children. On the other hand, she could now readily understand why some of them went demented.

She was pouring water from the kettle into the pot when Sarah suddenly entered into a fresh bout of agonising yells and howls that brought Robert trembling from the shop to stand at the foot of the stairs, mouth open and perspiration trickling down his face. Then he stumbled into the living-room and poured himself a massive tot of medicinal whiskey with hands that shook as though he had the ague.

Elizabeth left the teapot to stand on the hob and joined her brother at the table. She laced and interlaced her fingers, bit the ends of her thumbs, and finally put her hands over her ears and screwed her eyes tightly shut; but still the terrible clamour rang through the house. Then, quite suddenly, it ceased. She and Robert looked at each other. Strangely, the silence seemed even more unbearable. Robert's lips moved in prayer: "Oh, God, oh, God, oh, God. Oh, please, God. Oh, please, God. Oh please," he chattered senselessly. She, too, was praying silently. "Not me, please. Not me. Ever."

Then a new cry broke the silence. A thin

wail like the mewing of a cat. It rose and fell, rose and fell, gained in strength, then fell away to silence again.

Elizabeth stared at Robert as though she had never seen him before.

"My God, Robert," she said. "You are a father!" and they both began to laugh hysterically. Robert picked her up, swung her off her feet, hugging and kissing her in an ecstasy of relief.

"By God," he swore. "I'd not go through that again for a thousand pounds!"

He poured more whiskey and they toasted the child and Sarah and Robert and herself, and one to absent friends, meaning Daniel, and she felt quite dizzy as the scorching liquid went down her throat like a stream of molten lava.

Robert, in his excitement, even offered her a cigar, and Elizabeth, half drunk, accepted it and coughed and choked and spluttered and howled with laughter until Mrs. McCready called from the stairwell above, "Mr. Onedin. You may come up now."

They pulled themselves together and she followed Robert upstairs.

Sarah had a mannikin look about her

as though a stranger had taken possession of her body and washed away the pain. She lay almost buried beneath the bed linen with a tiny swaddled whimpering bundle tucked in one arm. Mrs. McCready stood by with a proprietorial air, the great moon-face redder than ever, beaming and bobbing with approval. She had evidently been busy, for the counterpane was spread neatly, the bolster and pillows plumped, Sarah's hair had been brushed and the perspiration wiped from her face. There was, however, a faint sickly smell in the room which Elizabeth could not account for until she caught a glimpse of bloodied towels and the carmined water in the tin bath pushed beneath the bed. It might have been the whiskey, but she suddenly found that the room had disappeared into a whirling darkness and that she was unaccountably seated on a chair with her head between her knees and heard Mrs. McCready's voice coming from a great distance: "There, there, my hinny, it's nothing mair than a fit o' the vapours." Then she coughed and spluttered as a burned feather was held beneath her nose and Mrs. McCready hauled her to her feet and guided her downstairs, leaving Robert to gloat over son and wife.

Elizabeth sat shakily at the table while the midwife went in search of the teapot and cups and saucers.

Returning, she sniffed Elizabeth's breath then poured two cups of hot strong tea, topping up her own with a generous helping from Robert's medicinal whiskey.

Elizabeth obediently gulped down the sweet liquid while Mrs. McCready eyed her thoughtfully.

"Ye're in trouble, aren't ye, lass?" she said eventually.

Elizabeth burst into a flood of tears and poured out the whole sorry tale.

"Aye," said Mrs. McCready, stirring her medicinal tea. "Ye're twa months gone, so ye'd best fetch the feller that pupped ye and drag him to the altar afore he can deny his responsibility. Men are demons for denying responsibilities."

"I c-can't," sobbed Elizabeth. "He's sus-sailed for Australia."

"Australia, is it?" sighed the midwife. "That Australia must be a boon and blessing to seafarers. They is scallawags all."

"Not Daniel. He — he will return."

"Too late for your little keepsake to be born in wedlock," said Mrs. McCready coarsely. "Australia is more than just a spit and a cough away." She helped herself to a little more medicinal whiskey.

Elizabeth wailed: "What shall I do? What shall I do?"

"What's done canna be undone," pronounced Mrs. McCready. "Ye canna hope to hide it, so ye must bear it. Is there anyone you can confide in?"

"No!" cried Elizabeth, thinking of Robert and Cousin Wilberforce and Uncle Will Perkins. "I'd die of shame!"

The round moon-face looked at her sympathetically. "I doubt it," she said drily. "Ye've been popped and pupped, my lovey. Take my advice and speak to your brother the moment he comes downstairs."

Elizabeth shook her head. "I couldn't. I couldn't."

"Ye'll no find a more opportune moment. You catch him now, my dear, the whiles pride has him by the forelock. He'll be in as forgiving a nature as you are ever likely to find him; all fathers — even the worst rapscallions that haunt the face of the earth

—are in high fettle on the day of their first-born. Strike while the iron's hot, my girl, you'll never have another opportunity the like. Leave it too late," she warned, "and you'll be more likely to find ye'sel' pitched into the street."

Elizabeth's brain no longer seemed to function. "Pitched into the street"? Like that unfortunate creature in *Mrs. Miller's Sin*. Why must it happen to her? Why couldn't she die of consumption instead, like the governess in *The Ordeal of Harriet Thorndyke*? It was unfair. So dreadfully unfair. Why should she be punished for . . .?

They heard Robert's feet clattering down the stairs. Mrs. McCready hurriedly poured two stiff cups of medicinal alcohol and, as an afterthought, one for Robert.

"Swallow it down, lovey," she hissed, and Elizabeth, stomach churning, obediently gulped a mouthful.

Robert appeared in the doorway, wreathed in smiles and rubbing his hands together in a fervour of self-congratulation.

"It's a boy. A fine boy, every inch an Onedin. He's taking his first meal at this very minute. By God," he crowed, skipping into the room, "but he's a greedy little monster. He's like a little fat pup." He took the cup of whiskey from Mrs. McCready and raised it high. "To the first of the Onedins. The first but not the last. Not by a long chalk, hey?" and roared with laughter at his own joke.

They raised their cups and Elizabeth managed to summon a weak smile.

"Been celebrating, have we?" asked Robert, cheerfully emptying the remainder of the bottle into their cups. "And good cause, by God. No matter, there's plenty more where that came from. Close the shop, Elizabeth. Close the shop. I declare today to be a public holiday. A holiday from the public, hey, hey?" And in high good humour he unlocked the cupboard and fished out another medicinal bottle while Elizabeth stumbled through to the shop like a sleepwalker.

When she returned Robert was standing, unopened bottle in his hand, mouth agape, disbelief written on every line of his face. Mrs. McCready put an arm about Elizabeth's shoulders.

"The poor sweet child," she said. "She's been took advantage of."

Robert was galvanised to life.

"You — slut!" he roared.

Mrs. McCready put a warning finger to her lips and raised her eyes to the bedroom above.

"Fortunately the gentleman has promised to honour his obligations. There, there, my child," she murmured, but loud enough to catch Robert's ears. "It will be the dearest loveliest babba in the whole wide world. A dear little girl, if the signs are right."

"There'll be no bastards born in this house," snarled Robert. "You can pack your traps, Miss, and take yourself off to your paramour."

"Come, come, Mr. Onedin, this will never do. It will not do, you know. The child is in need of love and affection . . ."

"Good God, woman," howled Robert. "Hasn't she had enough of love and affection yet?"

"Someone to care for her," continued the implacable Mrs. McCready, "until the gentleman returns. To claim his own," she added dramatically.

"Gentleman!" snorted Robert. "Which fine gentleman, you jade?"

"D-D-Daniel," sniffed Elizabeth.

"D-D-Daniel, indeed! I'll D-D-Daniel him!" growled Robert. But some of the venom had gone from his voice to be replaced by a face-saving bluster. He lowered himself into a chair and uncorked the bottle. If the man was Daniel Fogarty — and he had no reason to doubt it — he was faced with a poser. The master of the *Barracuda* was not some jumped-up reefer to be sent packing about his business. On the contrary young Fogarty would be a force to be reckoned with. Mr. Callon seemed to have a high opinion of his qualities and Mr. Callon, in Robert's often expressed opinion, was a man of sound judgment. If this little matter could be kept quiet — perhaps she could have the child discreetly somewhere? Sarah's folks were country born and no doubt would be glad of a few extra shillings a week. The child itself would be no problem; it could be farmed out and none the wiser. Yes, indeed, an obligated Captain Fogarty with strings to pull on the behalf of his benefactor would make a very useful brother-in-law.

"Are you quite sure that the man is set upon marrying you?" he demanded.

"Of course," said Elizabeth. How could anyone possibly think otherwise? Dear, dear Daniel. If only he were here!"

"Do you have it in writing?"

"No," she said. "Why should I? We saw each other every day."

"That much," he grunted sourly, "is only too obvious. Very well, Elizabeth. Although I cannot for one moment condone your infamous conduct, your unseemly and dissolute behaviour, your shameless and degrading loss of virtue, your unpardonable deceit of this household, I am prepared to help share the burden of the cross you bear." He raised a hand. "No, do not thank me yet. First hear me out. You will not move from this house unescorted, or without my express permission. Is that clear? Nor must one word of this shameful disclosure go beyond these four walls." He smiled ingratiatingly at Mrs. McCready, jangled some coins in his pocket and poured her a liberal cupful of whiskey. "I am sure Mrs. McCready fully comprehends the need for discretion?"

"You can rely on me, sir." The moon-face nodded solemnly. "My lips is sealed, sir. My lips is sealed." To prove it she opened her mouth long enough to empty the contents of the cup down her throat. "Discretion is the keystone of my persession. You can rely upon McCready, sir. Silence is McCready's stock-in-trade. Allow me the privilege of wishing yourself, your good lady, and your bonny wee son, all the health, wealth, and happiness this world can offer, and a place reserved for you and yours in the next." She dabbed her eyes with a piece of torn linen and remembered to hold out her empty cup. "You are a Christian gentleman with a Christian heart."

"Thank you," said Robert, pouring again. He looked sternly at Elizabeth. "Go to your room, Miss," he ordered. "And pray to the Almighty for the forgiveness I cannot find in my heart to extend."

Elizabeth rose from the table and blindly left the room with the memory of Sarah's screams and agonised threshings accompanying her like a vision of hell. "Not me," she pleaded silently. "Not me. Oh, please, not me."

Robert leaned forward as the door closed behind her.

"Now then, Mrs. McCready," he began,

lowering his voice to a conspiratorial whisper. "I should appreciate the benefit of your professional advice."

Elizabeth lay on her bed staring at the ceiling, watching her life slowly crumble into dust.

It wasn't fair, she thought miserably. It simply was not fair.

18

ELIZABETH looked up from serving a customer as the shop door bell tanged and a glowering Robert stumped in followed by James. James's cheeks, she noticed, seemed sunken and his complexion pale beneath the tanned skin and his eyes had a slightly feverish look; but he was evidently in full command of his faculties and quite unaffected by Robert's tantrums; if anything he seemed mildly amused.

" 'Morning, Elizabeth," he called, cheerfully enough. Then paused, noticing for the first time the dark circles beneath red-rimmed eyes, the pallor of her countenance and a certain dejection of spirits quite alien to her usual temperament.

"What ails Elizabeth?" he asked Robert, following him through to the living-room.

Elizabeth pricked up her ears but could only hear a muttered answer from Robert, then James's voice saying, "She's sickening for something. I've never known the child look so pasty-faced." Then another mutter, mutter, mutter from Robert.

She finished serving the customer and tip-toed to the curtained entrance and listened, trembling with anxiety, to the fragments of conversation.

Robert said, "In need of fresh air — moping and pining for that rascal Fogarty — mumble, mumble, mumble — send her to the country — stay with Sarah's kin — best place — hard work — fresh air — plain food — mumble, mumble, mumble."

And James's voice: "Your concern does you credit. But I'd not send a dog to stay with Sarah's folks . . ."

Robert: "Mumble, mumble, mumble."

James: "Well, have it your way. If you think it best. Now let us take a look at the latest addition to the Onedins."

Robert: "Growl, growl, growl."

James: "Business can wait a few minutes. Don't look so downcast, man. We're almost out of the wood."

Then the chairs scraped back and she heard the tramp of feet heading upstairs to the best bedroom.

She crept back to the counter and busied herself polishing the brass weights while she thought over the implications of her eavesdropping. Evidently James had, as yet, no inkling of her fall from grace. It was equally evident that Robert had determined upon packing her off to wait out her time with Sarah's parents and have her baby in picturesque rustic squalor.

Elizabeth had only visited the clod-hoppers once, and once had been enough. The Stirlings inhabited a tumbledown cottage with a dirt floor, leaking roof and a total absence of glass in the windows. There was no garden and they thought themselves lucky to be allowed to keep a pig. Sarah invariably referred to her father as a farmer, with the implication that he was a gentleman of some substance. The picture she painted bore little resemblance to reality. The Stirlings were, in fact, farm labourers. It is true that old Stirling did once rent a smallholding, but a series of bad harvests and an outbreak of cattle disease broke him completely and he had been driven to hiring out the labour of himself and his family to the tenant farmer. His wages were eight shillings a week supplemented by six shillings for his eldest son, half a crown each for wife and daughter-in-law in harvest time, and twopence for the youngest who acted as a bird-scarer. They dined off skimmed-milk cheese and coarse bread for lunch, and made a late supper of potatoes and cabbage. They were, not surprisingly, brutish in soul and manners. The prospect of remaining more than a few minutes in their company drove Elizabeth frantic with fear. She could not endure such a life. She would die first. Yes, she would die. Her imagination spun a fantasy: she lay on a bier, covered in a white shroud, surrounded by flowers, still and silent in the peace that passeth all understanding, while the sorrowing family filed past, begging forgiveness. Then Daniel would appear like an avenging angel and, flinging his arms wide, would call down the wrath of heaven upon their heads. It was a very satisfying scene, the only difficulty being that she would not be alive to witness it. Perhaps she was not really dead, but had taken a phial of something which counterfeited death? Yes, that would be far the more satisfactory. That way she could have her cake and eat it. She would rise as though from the dead, strike Robert and Sarah with accusing eyes, and Sarah would collapse with a brain-storm and Robert would be stricken with paralysis . . .

Another customer arrived at that moment wanting a penn'orth of candles, a ha'porth of tapers, an ounce of hard cheese and to gossip about the advent of the new baby.

"Mother and child doing as well as might be expected, Mrs. Furlong," Elizabeth told her, listening to the footsteps moving about the bedroom above.

"As well as might be expected?" queried Mrs. Furlong, nodding a knowing head. "A difficult delivery?" she pursued hopefully.

"No trouble in the least," said Elizabeth, hacking at the cheese and wishing the garrulous crone would take herself off.

"A gentleman baby, or a lady baby?" asked the garrulous crone.

Elizabeth dropped the cheese on to the scale pan. "A boy. Seven pounds twelve ounces," she said flatly. "Will that be all, Mrs. Furlong?"

Mrs. Furlong eyed the balance suspiciously. "That cheese is underweight," she announced.

Elizabeth added a piece of rind and wrapped the cheese quickly in a piece of tissue paper.

"Tuppence three farthings, if you please."

"Book it, dearie," said Mrs. Furlong. "I'll settle as usual at the end of the week. Seven pounds twelve ounces? A fine plump little man, I expect? He'll need feeding at that weight. Aye, he'll require a deal o' milk. But good milk makes for good bones, I've always said." She would, no doubt, have said a deal more if Elizabeth had not interrupted rudely, "I am sorry, Mrs. Furlong, but I am afraid I have no time to stand here gossiping."

"Gossiping, is it?" Mrs. Furlong's wattles turned a rich purple. "A body asks a polite inquiry from the kindness of her heart and is accused of gossiping by an uppity Miss too idle to wipe her own nose. You can tell Mrs. Onedin when she recovers that she has had the last of my custom. No, don't bother," she trumpeted imperiously. "I shall tell her myself!" and, sweeping her purchases into her shopping bag, Mrs. Furlong slammed from the shop.

Elizabeth heard movement from the

room above, the bedroom door squeaking open and James's voice calling: "Take good care of yourself, Sarah. He's a bonny child. A chip off the old block." Then the door closed and by the time the brothers had made their way downstairs again and entered the living-room Elizabeth was at her listening post.

There was the clink of glasses and "Your very good health" from James, and grunt, grunt from Robert, after which they settled down to an incomprehensible but angry debate about full and empty wine casks and invoices in, and invoices out, and bills of lading, and bills of this and bills of that; and Robert banging his fist upon the table and roaring that he would not have it, damn it, he would not have it! And James's stiff-necked tones telling Robert that he was a dunder-headed, addlepated fool who thought he could make a fortune simply by scratching his name upon a sheet of paper. Then Robert in a fury of anger calling James swindler and cheat and liar; and James answering levelly: "If you do not care for the partnership, tear up the agreement."

Robert yelling: "What of my debts?

Queer Street. Ye'll have us all in Queer Street!"

James sounding bored: "You rid yourself of one encumbrance only to saddle yourself with another. Very well, put an end to the partnership and I will undertake to settle all outstanding accounts."

Robert: "Grunt?"

James: "Grunt, grunt."

Robert: "Two hundred and forty-eight pounds from Frazer's alone. Where will you find the money?"

James: "My affair. Mumble, mumble."

Robert: "Mumble, mumble, mumble."

James: "You have my hand on it."

Robert: "Grunt, grunt. Don't ever try to make my fortune again, James. I can't afford it."

At that point the shop door bell clanged and she jumped away guiltily from the doorway to see Mr. Simpson marching purposefully into the shop waving a copy of his overdue account in one hand.

"I wish," he announced with the air of a man resolved to die before he would give an inch, "to speak to Captain Onedin. Tell him it is a matter of some consequence, if you please." He straddled his legs, clasped his hands behind his back and stood as sturdy and immovable as an oak.

"Certainly, Mr. Simpson," said Elizabeth, glad of the opportunity to intrude upon the discussion before the wind of their discourse shifted and blew her way.

She poked her head through the curtains. Robert was standing by the fire, the partnership papers held out toward the flames. James was lolling easily in a chair and puffing contentedly at one of his favourite long thin black cigars. Robert waved the papers. "Not only outstanding accounts, James. I have had to dip into my pocket. This venture of yours has already taken every penny I possess. I have been dunned . . .!"

James waved a careless hand: "Let me have a rendering and you shall be paid in full."

"When?" demanded Robert.

James sighed. "Within the next few days. Certainly before I sail again. Now, for heaven's sake, man, burn those damned papers before they burn you."

"Here's an end to partnerships," said Robert, thrusting the papers into the fire.

James, Elizabeth noticed, seemed to relax and a thin smile touched his lips as the papers curled then burst into flame.

She coughed. "There is a Mr. Simpson asking to see you, James. Says it's a matter of some consequence."

James turned his head.

"Ah, the butcher," he smiled. "Come, Robert, we must not neglect Mr. Simpson. His account shall be settled first."

"He's your affair now," said Robert. "Not mine." He gestured to the heap of paper ash in the fire. "Partnership's at an end."

James rose lazily from the chair, cigar clamped between his teeth. He tweaked Elizabeth's cheek.

"You look peaked, Elizabeth. What you require is a long sea voyage. That would soon bring the roses back to her cheeks, eh, Robert?" Grinning, he followed her through to the shop, affecting not to notice the crimson blush that seemed to flow from the tips of her toes to the crown of her head.

"Ah, Mr. Simpson," said James cordially. "I have been looking forward to our meeting. Kind of you to save me the trouble of calling upon you."

"No trouble," said Mr. Simpson, presenting his bill. "Just settle that account and there will be no trouble whatsoever."

"Ah," said James, picking up the bill. "Due of R. Simpson, Butcher and Purveyor of Poultry and Game. Of 17, Cotton Hey. 5 casks of freshly salted beef at 30 shillings per cask. Casks returnable as per invoice. Total, Seven pounds and ten shillings. H'm. That seems quite in order, Mr. Simpson." James took out his purse and counted out seven sovereigns and four half crowns. "If you will oblige me by receipting the bill, Mr. Simpson?"

Mr. Simpson fished a stub of pencil from his pocket, licked the end, and leaned forward to endorse his signature.

"I shall require it as evidence," said James in the same pleasant even tone.

Mr. Simpson looked up blankly, pencil poised in mid-air.

"Evidence? Evidence of what?"

"I was taken seriously ill and one of my crew died through eating your 'freshly salted beef'. Should there be an inquiry, naturally I shall be expected to furnish evidence as to the source of supply. Sign here, if you please, Mr. Simpson."

Mr. Simpson stepped away from the bill as though discovering it to be coated with venom.

"There was nothing wrong with the meat when it left my premises," he protested, but clearly shaken at the suggestion of interfering officialdom.

"That," said James calmly, "is a matter of opinion. My own opinion, for what it is worth, is that contaminated offal can in no way be described as 'fresh salted beef'."

"It was sold fair and square to Mr. Onedin, Chandler," said Mr. Simpson, licking his lips.

"Who bought on your recommendation."

"You'll never prove it."

"My ship was given a clean bill of health," said James remorselessly. "Which is more than can be said for the offal you supplied."

"Slander," piped Mr. Simpson.

James wagged his head sadly. "Bad for business, Mr. Simpson. Bad for business."

"I'll not bandy words with you," snorted Mr. Simpson, grabbing the bill and stuffing it back into his pocket.

James shovelled his money back into his

purse. "I'll not hold it against you. This time," said James.

The butcher blinked at him.

"I must store my ship for another voyage." James smiled his thin smile. "Better the devil you know, is an old adage, but a true one, I think."

Mr. Simpson hesitated and was lost. The meat had been of poor quality, even by the standards of chandler's meat. He knew it. Robert knew it. And, he suspected, this devil Onedin also knew it. But he also knew that he dare not pursue the matter further. Once word got around that a man had died of eating of Simpson the butcher, he was finished. On the other hand, as a regular supplier of ship's stores — even through a middleman such as Robert — he would be assured of future profits.

"I apologise for the error, Captain Onedin," he said with true shopkeeper's civility. "And I would more than appreciate the favour of your custom in the future."

"Then we shall say no more about it," said James cheerfully. "But remember, Mr. Simpson — quality meat in future. Quality meat."

"The very best, sir. You have my word

on it," said Mr. Simpson, edging from the shop. "You'll have no further cause for complaint, I assure you."

"We'll give it a trial, Mr. Simpson," James called after him. "We'll give it a trial. Well," he said to Robert as the shop door closed behind the departing butcher, "that's one account settled." He rubbed his hands together. "Now for Frazer's."

"You'll find old man Frazer a tougher nut to crack than a poor shopkeeper," said Robert.

"We shall see," said James. "We shall see."

Frazer's yards lay between Queen's Basin and Coburg Dock and squatted at the side of the Mersey like a strange shanty town set beside a forest of stricken timber. Massive stone slipways reached up from the black water toward the launching cradles and building ways. Half-completed ships' hulls reared high above James's head as he picked his way across the yard; passed the saw-mill where sawyers ripped forests of trees into mountains of planks, passed the kilns and drying rooms, the chain shops, the boiler houses that supplied steam to the clattering machinery, the ropewalk with its spinning frame and men and women walking endless miles, backwards and forwards, twisting the cordage into running rigging and great cable-laid hawsers, and chanting mournfully as they plodded along:

> "It's a dreary day for a pittance o' pay.
> Twist and turn,
> And turn-about . . ."

He ducked beneath scaffolding and huge timber shores where carpenters hammered and sawed, re-planking the hull of a bluff-bowed coastal trader damaged in collision; walked past a site office where a harassed yard foreman bawled orders to a group of grinning draymen off-loading bales of fresh-picked oakum, leaving their great shire horses to jingle their harness and push their noses deeper into canvas feed-bags.

He came to the outbuildings where a three-storey structure of sandstone was flanked by the long, low profiles of the sheet-metal and plating shops. A brass plate beside a solid oak doorway indicated that the centre building was, indeed, the offices of "John Frazer & Son. Ship Builders & Repairers".

The door was closed — presumably to keep out the din of the nearby sheet-metal workers. James twisted the massive brass knob, pushed the door open and entered a foyer of tiled walls and mosaic floor. A flight of marble stairs flanked by a wrought-iron balustrade curled away to his right. To his left was a small cubbyhole. As he paused to take his bearings a gnome with a tortoise head and wearing porter's olive green livery emerged.

"Yes, sir?" asked the gnome.

"No, sir," said James curtly and headed for the stairway.

The gnome scuttled across the floor.

"Beg pardon, sir," it begged. "But which office was you wanting?"

"Mr. Frazer," said James, halfway up the stairs.

"Name, please, sir?" yelped the gnome.

"Onedin. Cap'n Onedin," James called back, and the walls rang and echoed "Onedin . . . Onedin . . . Onedin."

The tortoise mouth opened and shut. "I'll announce you, Cap'n," it said huskily, and as James ran up the next flight of stairs the porter hurried to his lair to blow urgently into the mouthpiece of a voice-pipe.

James strode along a wide corridor. A hum of voices rose from closed doors at either side. The corridor ended in a T junction. James hesitated a second and then turned left, reasoning that John Frazer's private office would be sited to overlook the shipyard.

A door opened quickly and a tall fox-faced man with a neatly-trimmed beard barred James's path. Fox-face bared his teeth in the practised smile of the professional charmer.

"Captain Onedin? I am afraid Mr. Frazer is engaged. If you could state your business . . .?" The voice had the same mechanical quality as the smile; empty and indifferent.

"Who are you?" demanded James, rudely.

"I am Mr. Frazer's confidential clerk. If you . . .?"

James interrupted: "I am not in the habit of dealing with under-strappers," and had the satisfaction of seeing a flare of anger behind the calculating eyes.

The smooth voice found a brittle edge. "I have told you, Captain. Mr. Frazer is engaged."

"Then disengage him," said James brusquely. He took out his pocket watch and snapped open the face. "Tell Mr. Frazer I give him five minutes precisely. Otherwise I take my business elsewhere."

Fox-face hesitated.

"Very well," snapped James. "If you won't tell him, I shall." He took a half pace forward.

The smile seemed to be nailed to the fox-face by two dimples.

"One moment, if you please, Captain Onedin. I will see what I can do."

James watched the man walk to a heavy teak door, straighten his narrow shoulders, tap politely and then enter the room.

Listening carefully James thought he could distinguish three voices: the modulated accents of the ninny fluting above deeper rumbles. There was a pause, then a short burst of laughter. Within half a minute the door opened again and the clerk returned. He looked down his nose at James.

"Wait here, if you please," he said,

curtly. "Mr. Frazer can give you a few minutes at the conclusion of his present engagement." He turned and pushed open the door of his own office. James followed him in, shoving the door against plaintive protestations of hurt dignity.

"I have no intention of kicking my heels in the corridor," he growled, and plumped himself into a chair. It was perfectly obvious that there must be an ante-room to the great man's office; he could not imagine Sam Cunard, for example, hanging around a draughty corridor at the behest of some long-nosed quill-pusher.

The quill-pusher sat behind a small desk and made a pretence of being immersed in work while keeping eyes and ears alert for a whisper from his master in the room behind his back.

The small office was quite comfortably furnished, with panelled walls, a coal fire whispering in the grate, a velvet upholstered sofa and a pair of comfortable armchairs at either side of a marble-topped table upon which was spread a fan of daily newspapers.

James picked up a copy of the *Liverpool Herald and Shipping Gazette* and, burying his head in its pages, listened intently to the mutter of voices from the next room. He had the selective ear of the sailor, and in a minute he thought he had identified one of the pair. A short gusting laugh that could only come from Callon confirmed his suspicion. James cursed himself — he could not have chosen a worse time. Frazer and Callon were business acquaintances of long standing, and bosom friends into the bargain; their confounded families seemed to live in one another's pockets. James decided that he would leave the moment his five minute ultimatum was up. He fished out his watch and looked at the time. Two minutes to go. The clerk caught the gesture and his own eyes floated to the clock ticking monotonously above the mantelpiece. Then there was movement in the other room; the corridor door opened and Frazer's voice bidding Callon "good-bye". "Take care, now, George." And Callon's guffaw followed by "You watch yourself, John, or you'll be skinned like a cat." More loud laughter, then Callon's heavy boots ringing down the corridor.

The intervening door opened and old man Frazer himself looked into the room.

John Frazer was known to be a hard man and his appearance did nothing to belie his reputation. He looked as though he had been rough-hewn from oak and then weathered by the winds of time. His hair was iron grey and he shaved clean with the exception of long mutton-chop side whiskers. His eyes looked like two cold flints and his voice had a gritty quality that emerged as though forced by the power of will through a mouth like a steel trap.

"Cap'n Onedin?" he grated. "Come in, if you please."

He ushered James into his private office politely enough, pausing only to rasp at his clerk: "I am not to be disturbed again. I trust I make myself clear, Benson?"

The room was large and richly furnished. Behind a monster desk of polished rosewood a wide bay of mullioned windows overlooked the shipyards. A bank of voice pipes with ivory mouthpieces hung down from one wall. The carpet was of fine India work and the walls wainscotted, curtained and hung with pictures in ornate gilt frames. In pride of place, above the green-fringed plush pelmet, hung a painting of the "Death of Nelson", on either side of which stood alabaster busts of the late Admiral. In the stead of the usual bronze figurines and Parian marble statuettes there was a collection of toy brass cannons, a three-pounder cannon ball of pitted surface, a model of the *Victory* and a splinter of wood in a small velvet-lined glass case.

On the desk were rolls of draughtsman's Lines Plans showing profile, half-breadth and body plans. An ornate silver inkstand had been pushed to one side and in the centre of the desk stood a scale model of a three-masted full-rigged ship.

Frazer closed the green-baize door and walked to the desk.

"What's your opinion, Cap'n?" he asked, indicating the ship model.

James was impressed. He examined it with an experienced and loving eye.

"Superb," he said. "By God, but there's power there."

Frazer squeezed his bulk into a chair as massive as himself.

"I'm building a pair for Callon's Australian wool trade. Aye, she's power enough, Mr. Onedin. 18,000 square yards of canvas to drive her. She'll be a composite: teak planking on iron frames and built to carry two and a half thousand tons. £25,000 apiece, Mr. Onedin. Can you match that?"

Frazer, James noticed, seemed to be quietly enjoying himself. "Mister" Onedin instead of "Captain" and he'd been kept standing like a schoolboy. Evidently Frazer, damn his eyes, was indulging in a little bear-baiting. So his friend Callon must have been shoving his oar in.

James hooked a bentwood chair toward him, sat down and fished out one of his cigars.

"I hope to do better than that," he said.

"But not yet awhile, eh?" asked Frazer. "And I am not aware," he rasped, "that I gave you permission to fill the room with your foul cigar smoke."

"I am not aware that I asked for it," said James. He stood up. "I have heard a great deal about you, Frazer. Apparently I was misinformed. You are a fool. Good day to you, sir." He took a step toward the door.

"Sit down, young man," said Frazer.

James turned slowly and deliberately locked his gaze with the older man's.

"Sit down, sit down," repeated Frazer irritably. "And don't try to stare me down. I can play that game all day."

James returned to his chair feeling that thus far the game was even.

Frazer leaned back. "I have also heard a great deal about you, Onedin . . ." he began.

"From Callon, no doubt?" suggested James. "Understand me, Mr. Frazer. I did not go into the shipping business in order to win friends."

Frazer shook with laughter. "Poor George. You certainly tweaked his nose until the tears ran. But never forget, Mr. Onedin, that George Callon is not a notably forgiving man."

"And I am not a notably penitent one," responded James.

Frazer grinned like a gargoyle. "You are a man of pepper, Onedin. I like pepper in a man. Now then, in what manner can I oblige you?"

"First," said James, "if you and I are going to do business together, we'd best start by clearing the decks." He took Frazer's accounts from his pocket and tossed them on the desk. Frazer picked them up, glanced quickly at the figures, then turned an angry face upon James.

"Am I to understand," he demanded, "that you have the impertinence to waste my time with your damned pettifogging accounts? I employ clerks to deal with trivia." He reached for the summoning bell on his desk.

"I pay clerks," said James evenly. "I deal with principals."

"Then pay the damned bill and have done with it," snarled Frazer.

"I can't," said James calmly. "That is why I am here to ask for an extension of credit."

"I was wrong," said Frazer. "It is salt you have, young man, not pepper."

"It is no great hardship for a man of your standing to wait a month or so for a matter of two hundred and forty-eight pounds, eight shillings. If you choose to press me I have no doubt that I can raise the money within a day or two . . ."

Frazer smiled grimly. "You might find that a trifle more difficult than you imagine. I reminded you a few minutes ago that George Callon was not a man to be lightly crossed. He cuts quite a figure in the world of commerce — you might find credit hard to come by, Mr. Onedin."

James shrugged. "If Callon is asinine enough to bray his troubles from the house-tops, then more fool he. I care not a fig for Mr. Callon's opinion on any matter on this earth. I am concerned with the future, Mr. Frazer, not the present, and assuredly not the past."

"Your own future, I take it?"

"Why not? A man without a future is a dead man."

Frazer drummed his fingers upon the desk, then looked across at James. "Give me one good reason why I should oblige you, and you shall have your extension."

"I can give a dozen."

"One will suffice."

"Callon is mortal."

"We are all mortal, Mr. Onedin."

"But I have a longer lease of life."

"You regard yourself as an investment for the future?"

"I know of no other kind."

Frazer considered for the space of an eternity.

"I think, perhaps, I should hear a little

of this future you plan for yourself, Mr. Onedin."

James allowed himself to relax a little, paused long enough to marshal his thoughts and then spoke quickly and fluently.

"You are aware of the reason for the difference between Mr. Callon and myself," he began.

"I know his side of the story," said Frazer drily.

"My side is of no importance," said James. "What is important is that I now have the pick of the Portuguee wine trade in my pocket. I can furnish proofs," he added. "Written proofs. My patron is a Senhor Braganza — a gentleman who also cuts quite a figure in the world of commerce."

Frazer grinned crookedly.

"Callon had six ships employed in that trade," continued James. "In a twelvemonth I intend to employ a dozen. Within two years the Portuguese and Spanish coasts will be mine."

"I can see, Mr. Onedin, that when you and ambition walk hand in hand it behoves the rest of the world to give way. However, I don't quite see myself cast in the role of spectator, young man, so perhaps you will oblige me by explaining just what part I play in your scheme of things?"

"Ships," said James briefly. "We're in the same line of business. You build 'em, I sail 'em."

"Not on credit," grunted Frazer.

"I shall charter at first," said James. "Then buy. Then build."

The older man looked into the young man's eyes, saw the light of fanaticism, looked further and saw the past; his own past raising a spectral head to stare him in the face. He sighed; it seemed such a long time ago.

"I also started my business from scratch, Mr. Onedin." He put the accounts into a desk drawer. "You have four months. You'll pay off every penny within that time, or I join forces with Callon and break you."

James stood up.

"You tell your friend Callon," he said, "to keep his ships out of my waters."

19

AFTER leaving the yards James walked past the graving docks, crossed the footbridge between Queen's and Wapping Docks and stepped out upon the dock road.

A boiling tide of hay carts, brewers' drays, horse buses, cabs and pedestrians surged, broke and reformed about a flock of terrified sheep on their way to the cattle ferry. A hansom, light, fast and elegant, mounted one wheel upon the pavement. The hub, grazing James's elbow, left a smear of axle grease upon his suit. He cursed the driver fluently and a lady's maid, loaded with shopping parcels, blushed and hurried on with downcast head.

The hansom stopped a few yards further along and Albert leaned out. "Ahoy, Onedin!"

He hopped down from the cab, paid off the driver and loped toward James.

"I knew I recognised the walk," he said

cheerfully. "Head up, elbows out, shovin' the commonalty off the pavement; that, I said to myself, can be no one but Onedin."

James rubbed at the grease stain on his coat.

" 'Morning, Frazer," he said grumpily. "I thought you in a hurry to be off somewhere?"

"The horse had more spirit than myself. I was on my way to visit my father, but I can assure you, your company gives me more pleasure than the prospect of his. Would you care to take a little refreshment? There is an excellent little spirit-room just around the corner. You could have your coat sponged at the same time." He took James's arm. "This way, old man."

"The French Dolphin" belied Albert's off-hand description and was, in fact, a pleasant tavern whose bow windows bulged into the street with an air of conviviality.

They made their way to the snug where the landlord's daughter, a buxom creature with a hare lip and a laugh like a fractured gas pipe, greeted Albert like a long-lost friend and served them with cups of brandy punch.

"Well?" said Albert raising his cup.

"Well?" said James raising his.

They sipped their drinks reflectively and stretched their legs before the fire.

"Miss Elizabeth keeping well, I trust?" asked Albert, stifling an over-elaborate yawn.

"Pining for her far-away lover," answered James, cruelly.

Albert looked despondent.

" 'Obstacles'," pursued James, mockingly, " 'are there to be overcome.' It is a poor horseman who falls at the first fence." James yawned. Making idle conversation tended to bore him and he had no other thought in his mind beyond a mild interest in taking the young fop down a peg or two.

"Pining, you say?" Albert looked unhappy. "She really is smitten with that chap Fogarty?"

"Well," said James casually. "He is going up in the world, and Elizabeth always did have a taste for the creature comforts. I am afraid you muffed your chance, Frazer."

Albert sighed.

"Bear up, man," said James callously. "There are plenty more fish in the pond."

"Not for me," said Albert. "I love her."

"Good God!" James stared at the love-sick dolt. "There's no accounting for taste."

Albert drained his punch and gloomily prodded at the fire with the sole of his boot.

"Be sensible," James urged. "Even if it were possible your family would never permit it."

"Damn my family," snapped Albert irascibly.

"The damning would be somewhat one-sided," said James drily. "But if you have set your mind upon it you are not likely to find a better opportunity than now."

"Oh?"

"Good grief, man, where are your wits? Here is a young girl, moping and pining about the house, her intended sailing for the far ends of the earth, and all you can do is sit around wringing your hands."

"I don't believe she cares for me," said Albert.

"Pah! A young girl's fancies chop and change with the seasons. It is enough that you care." James began to wonder how on earth he had allowed himself to become involved with Albert's petty problems of the heart.

"Do you think she could be persuaded?" asked Albert, hopefully.

James shrugged, tired of the game. "I have no idea. In any event I think you are unlikely to have the opportunity — certainly in the immediate future. Elizabeth has been a little off-colour lately and Robert has recommended that she spends a little time in the country with Sarah's folks."

"Really?" Albert brightened considerably. "My sister Harriet has a place in the country. A villa with an acre or two of rough shooting, ornamental garden; that sort of thing. One or two hacks in the stables if she cares for riding; and Harriet is quite famous for her parties."

James was learning to interpret Albert's habit of understatement; the villa with an acre or two was no doubt a mansion the size of Buckingham Palace surrounded by parklands the size of a county.

"You can but ask," he said.

"Would you?" asked Albert.

"What?"

Albert shuffled his feet.

"Do your own damn courting," snapped James, then relented. "Very well. I'll mention it. You write a note of invitation.

From there on I wash my hands of the entire affair."

"This," said Albert, "calls for a drink."

Elizabeth was overwhelmed with the news that she was to be invited to a country house party. The invitation could not possibly have arrived at a better time. She was sick to death of Robert's accusatory gloom; anything, even the prospect of staying with the sluttish Stirlings, would be more tolerable than the constant complaints and reproaches to which she was subjected; but this most glorious and unexpected of invitations, dropped so casually by James, raised her spirits to miraculous heights. Albert, she decided, was the kindest hearted man alive; and she had treated him so cruelly.

She packed and repacked and haunted the postman until the formal note of invitation arrived in a thick lemon-coloured envelope containing an embossed card which read:

Mr. and Mrs. Fowler Dickson
Request the Pleasure of the Company
of
MISS ELIZABETH ONEDIN

at Their Country Residence
ARKWOOD MANOR HOUSE
on Saturday, October 12th

RSVP

On the back was written: "As Mr. Albert Frazer will also be among our guests may I recommend that he be permitted to act as your escort?

Most sincerely
Harriet Fowler Dickson"

"I am going away," she told Robert. "To stay with friends."

Robert didn't care. He was tired of looking upon her sickly face and reproachful eyes, and he had the problem of Sarah's Churching to contend with. There seemed no end to expense these days; and James was not the slightest help; he was walking around cock-a-hoop, chivvying Mr. Simpson and ordering stores as though money grew on trees. But at least the man had had the grace to start repaying some of the money owed. Robert, in fact, was too busy, too distraught and too tired to even inquire as to where Elizabeth was going, much less question her as to the identity of her new-found friends. Not that it would have made the slightest difference, for Sarah soon enlightened him.

Sarah had made her first appearance downstairs three days after the birth of little Samuel — they had decided, after long discussions and reference to the family bible, to name the child after Robert's father and it was to be christened Samuel Robert by the Reverend Mr. Samuels on October 26th. Sarah mooned about the house like a pale wraith, crooning over the child and weighing it almost every hour on the shop scales.

Robert had not, as yet, mentioned Elizabeth's misfortune to Sarah; he had decided to wait until she was strong enough to bear the blow with equanimity; there would be time enough when Elizabeth's situation became self-evident and by then — he secretly hoped — Sarah might well have made the discovery for herself. Women seemed to have an unerring instinct for these things.

Sarah, therefore, joined Elizabeth in crowing over the invitation card and the household was once more in an uproar of stitching and sewing and washing and ironing and trying-ons and trying-offs, and such a turmoil of ribbons and bows and ruches and flounces that Robert was at length driven to taking his meals in the shop and sending out for a bottle or two to take the taste of Elizabeth's cooking away. God help the man who married her, he thought. He would need the stomach of an ostrich and the digestion of a goat.

On Saturday morning Albert arrived in the family brougham handling the reins himself; and Elizabeth screamed that she was not ready and that her hair was a sight, and Robert poured Albert a drink and eyed him sympathetically. Then Elizabeth came mincing grandly into the room looking as though she had stepped straight out of a bandbox, and they bundled her hat boxes and baggage and parcels into the carriage, and Albert flourished the whip and the smart matched pair of greys broke into a canter and rounded the corner followed by a horde of cartwheeling urchins.

Robert mopped his brow.

"Peace at last," he said.

While James tramped the town chasing up cargo for the *Charlotte Rhodes*, Anne sat at the parlour table almost buried under a mound of correspondence. She copied the names and addresses of the wine merchants from a list supplied by Braganza and wrote to each explaining that Mr. James Onedin had the honour to inform them that he was now the sole and accredited agent for F. de D. Braganza of Lisbon and all future shipments would be executed by Mr. James Onedin to the complete satisfaction of customers. Mr. James Onedin further begged and requested that all empty casks, kegs, barrels and tuns, the property of Senhor F. de D. Braganza, be returned to the premises of Mr. James Onedin at the above address. Carriage refunded on receipt of invoice.

"Where do we find the money?" she had asked James.

"Braganza pays," he had told her. "I simply invoice his account."

Fortunately their finances were improving. With James's commission and the freight on the cargo of olive oil and corkwood they would be able to keep their heads above water for the present.

Her father was something of a trial. He and James did not hit it off from the start.

James had an ingrained dislike of excess and the old man regarded his son-in-law with the utter loathing of the failure for the successful. "Not a penny piece to his name," he would grumble. "Robbed me of me ship and daughter, and struts around as though he has the keys to the Treasury in his pocket. He'll sink without trace one of these days, mark my words; and take us with him."

Anne wondered how on earth she had put up with her father all these years. "James has kept to his bargain," she would tell him tartly. "You have a new suit, food in your stomach, and a shilling for your pocket."

"Charity money and charity food. That son-in-law of mine begrudges every mouthful. One tap upon the table and he's sniffing the air like a bloodhound. He's a vinegar face," the old man would roar. "Naught but a sour-visaged vinegar face." And Anne would sigh and slip him an extra shilling from her housekeeping. "It's hard when you've known better days," he would say. "Very hard," and take himself off to sit in the tap-room grumbling to his cronies.

James returned at lunch time as hungry as a hunter and as pleased as a dog with two tails.

"I've found a cargo of coal at a freight of eight shillings a ton," he told Anne, shovelling mutton pie into his mouth. "The ship is stored and ready to sail. I shall clear for Lisbon the moment she is laden."

"What of Senhor Braganza's casks?" she asked. "Surely they should be arriving shortly?"

He gulped down a mouthful of pie.

"If you will attend to the invoicing I shall arrange with Robert for storage. With luck there should be a shipload awaiting my return."

Anne looked disappointed.

"Can't I sail with you again?"

He eyed her in surprise, washed down the last of the pie with a mouthful of tea, secretly pleased with her request. She really was a quite remarkable woman, he thought. Quite remarkable.

"I imagined that you would have had your fill of voyaging?"

"You promised to teach me navigation," she reminded him. "And, for my part, I gave Mr. Baines my word that I would teach him the three 'R's."

"Very well." James grinned. "The schoolship *Charlotte Rhodes* sails with the morning tide."

Webster, seated at the head of the table, had been listening beetle-browed and clouding with resentment.

"And what is to become of me?" he rumbled. "I suppose I must accustom myself to being left alone to fend for myself?"

"Nonsense, Father," replied Anne sharply. "You know perfectly well that Mrs. Grossmith looks in every day; she has agreed to cook your meals, wash your linen and clean house as she did before."

"For a price," added James.

The old man snorted. "So I'm to live off kettle broth and that drab's left-overs again, am I?"

James yawned. "I don't doubt but you've eaten worse in your time."

"I have," growled Webster. "But that don't mean I have acquired a taste for it."

James spent the afternoon supervising the loading of the *Charlotte Rhodes* and then called upon Robert.

"No," said Robert firmly after listening to James's request. "I will not be responsible for casks, empty or full. You tend to your business, I tend to mine."

"Naturally you would be recompensed for your trouble and storage space paid for at fair rates."

"I seem to have heard this song before," said Robert, sourly. "You seem to forget, James — our partnership is at an end."

"You will not be required to dip your hand into your pocket for so much as a farthing. You simply store the casks and collect the invoices, for which service you will be paid. What could be simpler?"

"There's a catch," said Robert. "There always is."

"You will act as my accredited agent, and I will give you a note of authorisation to that effect."

"And that, no doubt, is the catch."

"Dammit, man," shouted James. "All I am asking is the use of your cellar for a week or two, I am not proposing to turn you out of house and home. Do you want the business or don't you?"

"Storage space?" asked Robert suspiciously. "Nothing else?"

"Good God, Robert, what else can you do with an empty cask?"

"How much are you expecting to pay? In advance, mind."

"Two shillings a week."

"Three."

"Half a crown. I could hire Mr. Jenkins's stable for less."

"Half a crown," agreed Robert. "But I warn you, James, if there is any trickery I shall pitch your casks into the river."

James counted out thirty shillings. "Three months in advance."

Robert pocketed the money. "It will go toward little Samuel's first Christmas present."

James yawned. "I'll take my leave now," he said. "Give my regards to Elizabeth when she returns. If she returns," he added with a grin.

Robert stared. "What do you mean by *if* she returns?"

"I was having a chat with young Frazer," said James casually. "I never saw a man so love-sick and moon-eyed, and I hope I never live to hear such drivel spoken again. If Elizabeth has a grain of common sense she will reel him in while he's swimming around with his mouth open."

Robert was gaping at him.

"But she can't," he protested. "She can't. She's . . ." He bit his lip. ". . . promised."

"Fogarty has a fancy for her, that's true; but he's not here, and Albert is. Elizabeth could marry into wealth and power. I don't believe she will think twice."

"She'd better," said Robert grimly, and told James the story.

"Why the devil," snarled James, "didn't you stop her from going, you dolt!"

"How the devil could I possibly know that you and young Frazer had been busily scheming behind our backs?" demanded Robert.

The brothers glared at each other.

"My God," said James. "If she fathers another man's child on to him!"

"She can't . . .!" Robert stared aghast. "She wouldn't . . .? No. Marriage is out of the question. The Frazers would never agree." He wiped his brow.

"I doubt," said James, "their opinion will be canvassed. I believe Albert has it in mind to persuade her to elope."

"He told you that?"

James nodded. "I am afraid that I put the idea into his head."

"We must put a stop to it, James. At once!"

"How?" asked James. His brain had recovered from the initial shock and was working quickly. An elopement. A premature birth. It could succeed. "How?" he asked again. "I shall be sailing first thing in the morning. Do you fancy riding over to this damned manor house and announcing our sister's shame to the world at large?"

Robert licked his lips. It would take more courage than he had.

"We could write," he suggested lamely.

"Pah!" said James. The notion was not worth discussion. "No, Robert. We keep our mouths shut and leave well alone. You tell no one. No one, you understand? Not even Sarah." Especially Sarah, he thought.

"But . . ." protested Robert weakly. "But when the child is born . . .? I mean — dammit, James, Albert can count."

"No one will know beyond Elizabeth and the two of us. He may suspect, but I doubt that he will voice his suspicions in public. It is a family secret, Robert, and we close the door on it here and now."

20

ELIZABETH had a splendid weekend.

"Dear Heart," she wrote to Daniel. "I am spending a few days with friends in the country. I think of you always and keep your likeness by my bedside and each night cover it with kisses (and send more and more and more to you now. Oh, that you were here, dear Daniel, Daniel dearest!)." She paused and chewed her pen. "Dearest Heart I have the most momentous news! ! ! ! !" She stopped again and, staring down at the expensive pale blue paper and purple ink wondered how to continue; then took the plunge. "I am with child! ! ! Yes, it is true! ! ! I am to have Our own dear little one. Dear, dear Daniel, you do not know how happy it makes me!" That she thought, was an untruth, but God would surely forgive a little lie. "Our child, dear Heart," she continued. "Ours! Yours and mine! Oh, how I long for your homecoming and to cover your dear face with kisses. Hurry, hurry back to me, my own sweetest dearest Man. We shall be so happy together, dear Heart, so very very happy and I promise I will always be a good kind and obedient wife to you. (Obedient to your Every Wish! ! !) Oh, my sweet, my beloved, I do love you so much my heart breaks at the thought. I will write to you each and every day and think of you every minute of every hour.

Your Own, Very Own! loving and longing,
Elizabeth"

She read it through quickly, splashed a few tears on to the paper, added a PS. "The tear stains are for you.", sealed the envelope and addressed it to: Captain D. Fogarty, Sailing Ship, Barracuda, c/o Callon & Company, Goree Piazzas, Liverpool.

She placed the envelope on her bedside table and leaning back against the soft downy pillows luxuriated in the enormous four-poster bed.

It had been such a wonderful, wonderful weekend, and — what is more — she had been invited to extend her stay for a few more days after the other guests had left! She wished she could remain in this splendid house with these splendid people and never, never return.

She remembered her first feelings of awe when the carriage passed through a pair of enormous ornamental gates and the horses stepped so proudly along a winding drive that twisted and turned through a fairyland park, and then stopped, steaming and champing at their bits, beneath a pillared portico; and a groom appeared from nowhere to hold the horses' heads and a coachman helped her down and unloaded her baggage and liveried servants bowed and scraped and ushered them inside the most magnificent house she had ever seen. And Albert, dear Albert, had taken her arm and held her hand because she was trembling, and greeted the servants by name and joked with Thornton, the butler and Mrs. Keene, the housekeeper — although at first, she recollected with a blush of shame, she had mistaken these aloof personages for their hosts, and just, barely just, stopped herself in time from dropping a curtsey. Then, before she could gather her wits, they had been ushered into a drawing-room full of people laughing and talking, and Albert introduced her to an absolute sea of faces and she had lowered her eyes and blushed prettily and bobbed and curtsied until her knees ached. It took her a long time to identify the guests, and some she never remembered until their departure; but she was able to single out Albert's sister Harriet and Mr. Fowler Dickson and Albert's cousin Hector and Hector's wife Mirabelle who was French and had a cast in one eye.

Harriet had been kindness itself, welcoming her warmly and kissing her cheek and telling her that Albert should consider himself a very fortunate young man to find such a charming companion. And Mr. Fowler Dickson, who must have been fifty if he was a day and had a booming voice and a booming laugh, took her two hands in his and boomed, "That young rapscallion doesn't deserve you, m'dear. Eh, Harriet, what, what, what?" and tugged at a bell pull and she found herself passed over to Mrs. Keene who inquired if she would care to take a bath before dinner? A bath! She had never known such luxury except once at Uncle Will Perkins'.

The bathroom had quite taken her breath away. Uncle Will Perkins would surely have had an apoplectic fit at the sight of such a pagan temple. The floor was of pink and black marble and the walls of white stucco with nymphs and little fat cupids in relief, while a palladian portico held, in place of a garden vista, a mirror that ran almost from floor to ceiling. The bath itself was encased in elaborately carved wood panelling, and a coal fire ensured that the bather would not catch a chill.

She had floated blissfully in the warm scented water until a discreet tap at the door announced the arrival of Julia who, Elizabeth understood, was to be her own personal lady's maid for the duration of her stay. Julia dried her off with a great soft woolly towel and then shepherded her to the bedroom.

And that was yet another wonder. Panelled and carpeted with a four-poster bed hung with silk curtains at the head to keep the sleeper's face free from draughts, and a dressing table with pots and powders and creams and lotions and silver-backed hair-brushes, and a marble-topped wash stand with two sunken basins and a copper ewer of water, and a massive wardrobe at least eight feet tall with a long plate glass mirror affixed to the door. And there, laid out on the bed, beside her under garments, was a magnificent dinner gown in frothing pink with a card attached from dear Albert hoping she would not be put out by accepting this small measure of his esteem and trusted that she would do him the honour of wearing it at dinner? Put out! She could have shrieked with delight.

She had sat at the dressing table while Julia combed and brushed her hair and gossiped away about the guests and who was who and what was what. She gathered that the tall young man with the stammer was the Honourable somebody-or-other and had lately returned from a year's wanderings in the valley of the Nile, and a fat man with a patch over one eye was a retired Admiral, no less, and the angular lady with the racking cough and heavy eyebrows was, in fact, a real genuine Ladyship and the short fat dumpling with a wart on its chin was the Ladyship's daughter. She had also learned, to her astonishment, that Harriet, who could not possibly be more than twenty-seven, had had no less than seven children. "She was married at seventeen, y'see, M'm," Julia had told her, mouth full of hairpins. "Her first was born short, if you follow, M'm?"

"Short?" Elizabeth had asked, imagining that poor Harriet had been delivered of a dwarf.

"Short of uns time, M'm. Mm, hold still if you please, M'm. Us reckons the Squire'd had a taste o' the comfits afore a-buying of the box, if you follow me, M'm. Mm?"

Elizabeth did and stored away the information.

"They're very clannish, the quality," Julia had added, speaking to Elizabeth as a confidante rather than a mistress. Lady's maids, it occurred to Elizabeth later, were no doubt adept at summing up the status of their charges. "Pleasant enough, and they can be generous to a fault, as long as you know your place. But a whisper of scandal and it's 'hang one, hang all', if you follow, M'm? And now, if you please, M'm, we'll try the dress, but half-petticoats only, M'm."

The gown fitted beautifully and the reason for half-petticoats became embarrassingly obvious; the neckline was cut so dangerously low that Elizabeth had been convinced that if she expelled a breath the upper part of her body would have tumbled out. But Julia had soothed her fears and told her that it was the height of society fashion and that all the other ladies would be exposing their — well — monuments, and giggled: "You has the carriage for it, M'm — some of 'em walk as though they was made of sticks instead of bones — and you have as pretty a pair as I ever did see. The gentlemen's eyes'll pop out of their heads, if you follow, M'm?"

Elizabeth, staring at her image in the mirror, had followed only too well. But, as Julia said, she had the grace and the carriage to carry it off.

Albert had escorted her in to dinner. The gown of bunched tarlatan covering the whalebone frame of the almost circular crinoline swaying from her hips made a faint susurration of sound as Albert conducted her to her place at the long table. This was the first time she had ever worn a full crinoline, her own being a half-crinoline of cane which always created problems of movement and seating; but the whalebone was pliable enough for her to push the hoops forward beneath the table while Albert, waiting politely behind, eased the chair beneath her.

She had found herself at the lower end of the table seated between Albert and the retired Admiral who, throughout the meal, huffed and hawed and sent his single eye roving around the assembled decolletages like the searching beam of a lighthouse warning voyagers of dangers ahead. Mr. Fowler Dickson sat as of right at the head of the table with Harriet to his right and the Ladyship to his left. Then there was Albert's cousin Hector with his French wife, and the young man from the Nile valley, and the plump young ladyship with the wart sitting next to a square-shouldered young man with an eye-glass and military bearing. The remaining faces were blurs; voices a pattering murmur that purred and plashed just beyond the range of hearing; but the men were so handsome in full evening dress and the ladies like so many parakeets in bright plumage, and many with far greater displays of balcony than herself, she had been glad to notice; and there were liveried footmen and a seemingly endless train of the most exotic dishes and wines and sauces which really left very little time for conversation. . . .

Oh, it had been so wonderful! And the day following, being the Sabbath, they had driven to the village church in a convoy of carriages and she had sat in the Fowler Dicksons' private pew while the household servants and the tenants and the villagers disposed themselves in the body of the church and listened with proper humility to the parson extolling the generosity of the squire and preaching the virtues of thrift.

In the afternoon she and Albert had taken an after-lunch stroll through the grounds and Albert told her that Harriet was the eldest of his three sisters, one of whom, Charity, was married to a cotton broker and lived in Manchester, and the other, Prudence, had married into banking and lived in London. Mr. Fowler Dickson, it seemed, owned two thousand acres of farm land and a coal mine and the hope of a seat in Parliament in the Tory interest.

Later, as the afternoon grew chill and a miasma of autumnal mist rolled across the grounds to clothe the bare trees in a pearl-grey light, they had turned and wandered back toward the house. Then, at the conservatory, Albert had pushed open the door and ushered her inside and there, in the strange green gloom had taken her in his arms and kissed her, and she hadn't felt in the least guilty because she was so happy, and Albert was really one of the kindest of men, and she had been less than grateful for that disastrous evening at the opera, and when all was said and done there was no real harm in a stolen kiss or two. Naturally dear Daniel must never know, but Albert, in his way, really was quite a charmer.

In the evening she had been invited to play the piano-forte and Albert had accompanied her, singing: "Drink to me only with thine eyes" and "Where e'er You Walk" in a quite pleasing tenor, and the Ladyship's daughter had given a rendering of "I Dreamt I Dwelt in Marble Halls" in a simply dreadful off-key voice and blushingly received a sympathetic round of applause. Then she and Albert had played a rollicking duet and afterwards sang "When Other Lips" and "The Last Rose of Summer" together. . . .

It had, all in all, been a really splendid evening; and to crown it all Harriet had whispered, as they were making their "good-nights" and "farewells", that she and Mr. Fowler Dickson would esteem it an honour if Elizabeth would consent to be their guest for a day or two longer. How could she possibly say "no" to such a delicious request?

She fell asleep finally, dreaming of marble halls and regiments of liveried servants and a strange-looking Daniel Fogarty with the features of Albert Frazer.

She awoke to the sound of the curtains being withdrawn and Julia bringing her a cup of hot chocolate and the latest gossip: after the ladies had retired last night the retired Admiral had drunk so much that he had fallen out of his chair and was presently confined to his bed with his head in a bandage and swearing like a Dutchman; and Albert and his cousin Hector had almost come to blows at one point in the evening; and early this morning cousin Hector had ridden off in a huff with his Frenchified wife who was as mean as ditchwater and had the temper of a harpy; oh, and young Mr. Frazer would be staying on for a few days longer, "and we can all guess why, M'm, if you follow me?"

Elizabeth blushed and dressed and went down to breakfast and then she and Albert went for a ride on a pair of the most docile horses you could imagine; and they rode for miles and miles across Mr. Fowler Dickson's estates which seemed to extend across half the county; and they had lunch at an inn with a thatched roof and a signboard bearing a wheatsheaf and a sickle, and where Albert quite took her breath away with a wholly unexpected proposal of marriage.

She turned crimson and lowered her eyes.

"I c-can't," she said. "It isn't possible."

"Fogarty?" breathed Albert, two red spots burning high on his cheek bones.

She nodded dumbly and started to weep. It was so unfair, she would be wife to a common sea captain and never, never be invited to such a wonderful house ever again.

"Can't you forget him?" asked Albert.

Oh, if only she could! She shook her head and Albert leaned forward and wiped the tears from her face.

"It wouldn't be possible, Albert dear," she said, searching for an excuse. "Your p-parents would never c-condone it."

"Do you like me?"

She nodded: "Of course, Albert. Of course I do."

"Do you love me?"

She didn't know. Perhaps she did. It was all so very confusing. Albert was so kind and considerate. She stole a look at him. He was sitting with such an expression of mingled misery and anxiety on his face that she didn't know whether to laugh or cry all over again. She wanted to be honest, but equally she didn't want to hurt him. "I don't know, Albert," she said. "I think I do, but I don't know."

"Would you marry me if it were possible?" he persisted.

She fell into the trap without thinking.

"Of course I would, dear Albert. But we know it is impossible." That had been the answer Eliza had given the Honourable Gregory Maltravers in *The Trial of Lady M*.

"We could elope," said Albert. He dropped to one knee and took her hands in his. "Please, Elizabeth. Say you will."

She gaped at him: "Elope. . . . !"

"Why not?" he asked. "My parents can hardly object to our marriage once it has taken place."

"But Albert. Dearest," she said. "Your parents would never forgive you. Or me," she added. It was impossible, of course. Unthinkable. She carried Daniel's child. She could not. Would not. Dare not. But . . . ? Julia had said that Harriet's first-born had been born prematurely. And the quality closed ranks when threatened with scandal. No. She must not. And then she thought of the misery that lay ahead. Robert and his everlasting moaning and groaning — and the moment that virago Sarah discovered her condition life would simply become unbearable. And she was to be packed off to have her baby in that hovel of the Stirlings. It would die, she was sure, die of some foul disease. That and that alone would be justification enough. She could make the sacrifice for the sake of her child, just like Polly Perkins in *A Child of Chance*.

"D-do you really mean it, Albert? Really and truly mean it? Would you risk all for me?"

"Say you love me," he demanded.

She clutched his hands to her.

"Oh, yes, yes, yes, Albert. I do, I do, I do."

"That is all I required to hear," said Albert. "We shall take the overnight train for Glasgow and be married at Gretna Green tomorrow morning."

"But . . . ?" It was impossible. Utterly and ridiculously impossible. "I can't," she protested. "Not now. Not at this very moment."

"Why not?" asked Albert.

"Well — I have nothing to wear." Reason seemed to elude her.

Albert dipped his hand into his waistcoat pocket, took her hand and slipped a diamond ring over her finger.

"This is your passport." He smiled. "It will, no doubt, be the shortest engagement on record."

She stared at the ring.

"Oh, Albert," was all she could think to say.

Albert had thought of everything. They changed trains once and then had a first class compartment to themselves until the train gulped to a stop at a wayside station an hour before dawn and a mangled voice announced that they had arrived at Greetna Grin.

They left the train, travel-stained and weary, and Albert hired a cab which took them about two hundred yards to a small hotel called "The Runaway".

Albert signed the register with a flourish and a smirking porter guided them to their room.

It was a small room dominated by a double bed with brass rails and printed instructions on the back of the door describing the route to the famous blacksmith's shop. The rest of the furnishings were mean and of poor quality. There was a cracked basin and a pitcher of stale-looking water on a rickety wash stand, an oaken wardrobe and a chest of drawers.

Elizabeth looked about with alarm.

Albert smiled reassuringly. "Any port in a storm," he told her. "The moment we are married we shall stay overnight in the finest hotel in Carlisle and spend our honeymoon — where? Where would you like to go? London?"

"Anywhere," she said miserably. "Anywhere but . . ." She stared around the shabby room. "Anywhere but here."

"You are fatigued after the journey," said Albert. "I shall take a stroll while you — um — tidy yourself." He kissed her tenderly. "I shall be back within the hour, my love."

The door creaked and closed behind him. Elizabeth sat on the bed feeling utterly wretched; the excitement that had sustained her throughout the journey was now replaced by an abysmal depression. Tired and dejected she lay down and fell asleep.

She awoke startled to the sound of a key turning in the lock. The door groaned open and Albert entered. He looked pale and tight-lipped with anger. She sat up and stared at him in alarm, her first panic-thought that his parents had somehow followed them.

Albert sat beside her, put his arm about her shoulders.

"I am sorry, my love," he said. "I'm a fool. A damned, inconsiderate, stupid fool. I should have made inquiries. I should have known!" He beat his fist on his knee. "I should have known!"

"Known what?" A tumult of fears churned through her stomach.

"They have passed a law," said Albert. "They have passed one of their damnable interfering barbaric laws. The confounded blacksmith cannot marry us unless we can prove a three weeks' residential qualification."

She looked at him in dismay.

"But . . . ?"

"Can you ever forgive me?" he asked miserably.

"Three weeks . . . !" She was rapidly counting. In three more weeks she would be. . . . Oh, dear God, was there no escape? "We shall never be married," she wailed. "Oh, Albert. Dear, darling Albert!" Suddenly marriage to Albert became the most important thing in her life. "What shall we do," she wept. "What shall we do?"

"I shall do the honourable thing, naturally," said Albert. "I shall return you to the bosom of your family and accept full responsibility."

She took his hand.

"No, Albert. We shall share the responsibility." She took a deep breath. "If we must wait three weeks — so be it — we shall wait three weeks. Together."

Albert raised his eyes and read the assent in the deep blue of her gaze and the crimsoning blush that suffused her features.

"Who is to know, Albert?" she asked softly. "Who is to know?"

21

"WILLIAM," said Anne for the twentieth time.

The chalk squeaked laboriously across the slate. "Wilyum," wrote Baines. "Willeeyum," he pronounced hopefully.

Anne tried again. "Double-yoo-I-double ell-I-A-M, says William, Will-i-am," she enunciated carefully.

"Will-I-am," repeated Baines and wrote: "Wilyam".

"I am Will," said Anne.

"I am Will," said Baines dutifully, and wrote: "I am wil".

"Two ells, Mr. Baines, if you please."

"I am will," wrote Baines.

"Will I am," said Anne quickly. "Will I am. Will I am."

Baines scrawled industriously.

"Hrrmph," said James coming down the companionway. "Mr. Baines, your watch on deck, I think."

"Aye, aye, sir," said Baines thankfully.

"Will I am. Am I William? Will I am." He put down his slate and headed for the deck.

"Is he mad?" asked James.

"I am afraid," smiled Anne, "that Mr. Baines's scholastic achievements are doomed to encompass a rather narrow field. But he progresses. He progresses."

"Does he, indeed? Well, now it is your turn, Madam." He seated himself in a chair and put the tips of his fingers together in the attitude of a schoolmaster. "Explain to me, if you please, one method of finding latitude by observation of a celestial body?"

"Oh, dear," said Anne. She put the end of her thumb in her mouth. "Ah, yes. By observation of the pole star which is fixed above the pole and from which all lines of latitude are measured?"

"Too easy," said James. "We'll try an observation of the sun."

"Oh, dear," said Anne again.

"Latitude by sun meridian altitude," prompted James.

"Sun meridian altitude," groaned Anne.

"Here are some figures," said James cheerfully. "Observed meridian altitude, zenith distance and declination. Apply that data and the answer will give you our present position. I shall be on deck if required." He grinned at her and made his way out again.

She worked for an hour at the problem until her head was spinning; then, clutching the results in her hand, she made her way on to deck to discover that the ship was coming to anchor in Lisbon roads.

"James! You monster!" she said.

James grinned his lopsided grin. "We might have been playing blind man's buff in thick fog." He glanced at the results of her calculations. "And you would have had us dropping anchor in one of Senhor Braganza's vineyards. You subtracted instead of added the sun's total correction."

"Oh, dear," said Anne. "I shall never learn."

"Don't lose heart," said James. "Take a leaf from Mr. Baines's book."

Baines stood beside the helmsman, his lips moving as though in prayer.

"I am Will," he muttered. "Will I am."

Senhor Braganza's clerk Gussio met them at the quayside to present the Patrao's compliments and beg that he be permitted to conduct Capitao and Senhora Onedin to the Quinta Brancosvinhedo when Senhor Braganza would personally express his deep regrets for being unable to welcome their arrival himself.

Leaving Baines to handle the discharging of the cargo of coal, James and Anne followed Gussio aboard a tiny steam ferry which puffed and snorted its way across the Tagus, unceremoniously elbowing barges and big-sailed fishing boats from its path and hooting derisively at the shaken fists and spluttering oaths of infuriated fishermen.

An open carriage awaited on the south bank and they set off on the Lisbon road toward Setubal while the hills and churches of Lisbon grew smaller and smaller across the water behind them. The narrow road, a dusty ribbon stitched with black hedgerows, climbed steadily. Then, topping the ridge Anne noticed the air becoming redolent with the soft sweet scents of cedar and gum. The road descended, and they passed a quinta, a large white farmhouse with green painted shutters, and lowing oxen trampling the mud of the farmyard. Anne pointed to a tall building alongside the quinta with arched supports beneath.

"It is the *lagar*, Senĥora," Gussio told her. "Where at the time of the *vindima* the uvas . . ." He flapped his hands, " . . . the grapes are walked, you unnershtand? Below are the bodegas for the barrels."

"And now perhaps you understand why oaken casks are life-blood to Senhor Braganza," James said to Anne.

They passed through a dusty village full of donkeys and children and, as the road wound down the hillside, saw terrace after terrace after terrace cut into the slope of the hill; and peasants with wickerwork baskets strapped to their backs winding their way between the terraces, prodding at the soil and distributing handfuls of straw and compost over the vine roots.

The carriage turned off the road and bumped its way along a rutted track until they arrived at another quinta, larger and better cared for than the other. It was a long low cool building with a terraced patio and an arbour which led to a small grotto and water-garden. Around it were clustered the outbuildings where the wine was made.

The Overseer doffed his straw hat and bowed deeply then spoke quickly to Gussio in hissing Portuguese.

"This fellow," said Gussio grandly, with the city man's contempt for the country dweller, "will guide you to the Patrao."

They followed the Overseer who seemed to think it incumbent upon him to walk backwards most of the way, continually removing his hat, and showing blackened teeth in smiles of encouragement.

Senhor Braganza was walking despondently between the brown terraces, pausing every so often to stoop, pick up a handful of soil, let it dribble through his fingers before tossing it away.

But he greeted them warmly enough, taking Anne's two hands in his and then kissing her cheek with continental enthusiasm. "Senhora Onedin. This is indeed a pleasure. Had I but known that I was to have the honour of your company, dear lady, I would have arranged that my wife and son be on hand to entertain you."

"Please, Senhor Braganza, I do assure you that I would be most put out if I thought for one moment that my visit would inconvenience you in any way."

Anne would never accustom herself to these confounded Portuguese politenesses.

Braganza shrugged his shoulders and spread his hands. "My wife will be desolated." He turned and spoke to the Overseer in a torrent of spluttering sibilants. The Overseer bobbed his head and ran back to the quinta as fast as his bowed legs would carry him.

"Welcome to the Quinta Brancos. You must be fatigued after your journey; I have therefore arranged for a little refreshment. If you will permit, Senhora, I have a matter of grave business to discuss with your husband."

James put an arm about Anne's shoulders "My wife, Senhor, knows more about my business than I do myself."

"Ah, that my wife would take such interest," sighed Braganza. "You English have all the advantages."

"What is the trouble, my friend?" asked James.

For answer Braganza poked at the soil at the roots of the withered vine plants. He pulled one of them free of the soil, shook it and pointed to the dry and deformed root system.

James was no green-fingered gardener, but even he could tell the difference between diseased and healthy stock.

"The Ravager," said Braganza, simply. "The Destroyer."

James blinked.

"The what?"

"It is a beetle. Nothing but a tiny beetle. But last season, Senhor, that tiny creature destroyed the entire property of my unhappy neighbour. This year, Senhor Capitao, it is my turn, I am sorry, my friend, but I am ruined."

"Is there no remedy?" asked Anne.

"Only one. These cultivated vines must be grafted on to new wild stock."

"Where lies the problem?" James looked puzzled. "Surely wild vines are not so scarce?"

"The problem, Senhor," replied Braganza, "is that the only wild vine known to be unaffected by the Ravager is to be found in North America. And I must have them without delay."

"Then your problem is resolved," said James, calculating freight rates. "My ship is at your disposal. How many will you require?"

"One hundred and fifty thousand," said Braganza.

James brightened. That had the smell of steady work and guaranteed profits.

"It would require three — possibly four — crossings for a ship of the *Charlotte Rhodes*' capacity."

Braganza shook his head.

"It must be one voyage only, Senhor. I require those vines in time for the spring planting. In three months, my friend, or I am finished."

James saw the prospects of quick profits rapidly diminishing. But the solution was obvious.

"You must charter a ship of sufficient capacity."

"I have searched the entire coast. But this is not Liverpool or London. The only vessels available are bound for the Mediterranean — Africa — India — Brazil. Anywhere it seems but North America."

"Surely, Senhor," said Anne. "One shipload of thirty thousand would be better than none?"

"Senhora Onedin," said Braganza, gravely, "we will return to the quinta and take refreshment, and I shall tell you a little about the production of wine."

The November skies were dull and a cool wind was blowing, so they sat indoors and dined off delicious shrimps and the inevitable *bacalhau* — a dish of salted cod, tender lobster, and tiny clams cooked with sliced pork — washed down with a bottle of pale dry Bucelas, while Braganza talked on until night crept toward the house and soft-footed servants moved about quietly, lighting the oil lamps and piling more sweet-smelling logs upon the fire.

James had been brooding, only half-listening to his host. He leaned forward suddenly.

"There may be a solution," he said. "You, Senhor, know all there is to know about the production of wine, but ships, my friend, are my business."

"I shall be in your debt forever," said Braganza.

James scratched his nose. "Now for once you are talking like a sensible man," and grinned hugely.

"And your plan?" requested Braganza.

"Let me sleep on it," said James. "Tomorrow we shall all return to Lisbon," and would say not another word. In fact he had an uneasy suspicion that perhaps it was the wine talking. His idea was simple enough. Perhaps too simple, he thought.

"There she is," said James and pointed to a graceful white barque lying at her moorings in mid-stream. "Flying a Portuguee ensign, so she probably has a Portuguee owner."

"What of it?" asked Braganza, puzzled.

"Light ship. Moored — not anchored. And neither loading nor discharging cargo."

"She is not for charter, if that is what you have in mind. I told you, James, I had inquiries made of every ship on the coast; and the *Pampero* was one of them." He sounded disappointed. Chartering was out of the question.

"The *Pampero*? Pampas storm?" James reflected for a moment. "I'll wager she was once a down-easter. Yankee-built from Yankee timber, for a pound." He seemed pleased with his deductions. Braganza was mystified.

"What of it?" he asked. "Is it important to know where the ship was built?"

"I have been told," said James, "that there are men who, from the taste alone, can name the vineyard that produced the grape that made the wine."

Braganza smiled. "Each man to his trade."

"That ship was built for speed. She was designed to make the passage from New York to 'Frisco in a hundred days."

"So?"

"So the Americans built a railway line across the isthmus of Panama and the days of the down-easters were over. Most were scrapped but a few were sold — but buyers for that class of ship are few and far between. Thirty and more sails to handle. Two acres of canvas. Narrow in the beam and sharp in the bows. They were built to carry people rather than cargo. No use for the China tea trade because a ship built of soft wood is a wet ship. But she'd suit our purpose. Buy her, my friend. Buy her."

"Buy her? How?" Braganza spread his hands. "Even if the owner would sell . . ."

"He will," said James. "Anyone will sell anything if the price is right. She is probably worth around seven and half thousand pounds. If her owners are not keen on selling you may be forced up to ten thousand. But she'd be worth every penny."

"You move rather too fast, my friend," said Braganza. "In the first place I am no ship trader . . ."

"But I am," said James. "I'll not stand by and see you ruined." He smiled crookedly. "I need your trade."

"Ten thousand pounds!"

"Weigh the cost against your vineyards."

Braganza shrugged. "I suppose I can but try."

"No," said James firmly. "Not you. Me. When I want to buy a vineyard, I'll come to you."

"You will sail her yourself?" asked Braganza anxiously.

"You give me a half share in her, and I will undertake to sail her out at a profit and return within fifty days with your vines."

"One moment, my friend. Suddenly I find I am not only to buy a ship I do not want, but I am also to give half to you. I think you drive too hard a bargain, James."

"You'll travel a long road before you find a better. Give me a five-year option to buy out your share. In the meantime we share half the profits of each and every voyage as equal partners. I'll make a start by loading her with salt and corkwood, and topping her off with a few casks of your wine, if you've a mind for it. Come," he urged, "how can you possibly lose? Five years' profits, then half your purchase price refunded; and your vines shipped free of charge — for no man can make a profit out of himself."

Braganza smiled. "Not all men perhaps," he said drily.

"Are we agreed?" asked James.

"It is known, I think, as robbing Peter to pay Paul. And I suspect that I am Peter." He paused. "Who will pay for refitting and repairs? Peter, or Paul?"

"You will incur no expense on that score," said James. "I will keep her in a seaworthy condition. After all, it is to my benefit. I intend to own her."

"First," said Braganza, "let us discover if her owners are prepared to sell."

Senhor Porfiro Diaz smiled apologetically and regretted that he could be of so little assistance. "I am, alas, but the agent," he told Braganza. The good ship *Pampero* was in fact owned by the ship's master, Capitao Tomas.

"Would he be prepared to consider an offer?" James asked through Braganza.

The pair chattered away in voluble Portuguese.

"He says," translated Braganza, "that Captain Tomas is a difficult man to deal with. Apparently he lives aboard with his wife and family. It is my impression that Senhor Diaz would welcome a change of ownership."

"Good," said James. "We'll take him with us. He can introduce us to the difficult Captain Tomas and add his powers of persuasion to ours. Although I think we will find that money talks loudest. Ask him why the *Pampero* is not loading cargo, and why he refused your offer of charter."

Diaz again smiled apologetically and shrugged his shoulders.

"He simply says that the Captain is 'difficult'," said Braganza.

They hired a boat and rowed out to the *Pampero*. The ship's sides towered above them and her companion ladder had been hoisted clear of the water. A ship high in the water and with her gangway hoisted inboard was as safe and impregnable as a fortress with its drawbridge up.

They circled the vessel while James and Diaz bawled their lungs out. The ship remained as quiet and still as a tomb.

"No one at home," said James. "Very odd. You say he has wife and family aboard?"

"Perhaps they are ashore? Shopping perhaps?" suggested Braganza.

James pointed to the companion ladder. "In that case, how do they propose to get back aboard?" He picked up an oar and hammered at the ship's side as they rounded the quarter.

"Ahoy!" he shouted. "*Pampero*, ahoy!"

He cocked his head, listening, and thought he heard a faint answering cry.

"I'm going aboard," he announced.

"How?" asked Braganza.

"Up her mooring lines." James removed his jacket and boots. "If I slip, you can pick me up. But warn our friends here

. . ." he indicated the two oarsmen ". . . to take care with that boathook."

They rowed to the mooring buoy at the stern and James reached up and grasped the heavy hawser. It was difficult to find a handhold around the eight-inch rope and the first few fathoms were covered in slime and weed. The hawser dipped and swayed and by the time he had clambered as far as the stern rail James felt that his arms were being slowly pulled from their sockets. He reached out and, taking a grip of the lower taffrail, swung himself aboard.

The *Pampero* had a high poop deck beneath which would be the accommodation for officers, first class passengers and the master's quarters. Entrance was by way of two heavy teak doors, one on the starboard side, the other to port. At sea the weather door would be kept closed and access would be by the lee side door.

James tried both and found them firmly locked. He hammered his fist against the solid timber and might as well have hammered against a rock; the teak would be two inches thick and designed to stand up to the heaviest sea. Finding that he was having no effect other than bruising his hands, James started to walk forrard toward the waist of the ship. Then he thought he heard the faint cry — or was it cries ? — again. He trotted up the ladder to the poop deck and put his ear to a ventilator. There were muffled sounds of sorts, unidentifiable because of the distortion of sound made by the bell mouth of the ventilator cowling. He put his mouth to the ventilator opening and called: "Ahoy! *Pampero*, ahoy! Ahoy!" His voice returned like some disembodied spirit doomed forever to repeat the pronouncements of the living. "Oy-oy-oy," sang the ventilator and the others accompanied their fellow in lower key: "ahoy-oy-oy-oy-oy" they piped until the cadence died away to be replaced by the familiar slap of water and the protesting creak of the rigging.

It was odd, thought James, very odd, as he clattered down the ladder to the main deck. No ship was ever left deserted; there was always a shipkeeper. He stared around. The hatch coverings were trim and firmly battened down, the decks clear, running gear neatly belayed to fife rails. A shimmer above the black spout of the galley funnel caught his eye. He pushed open the heavy door. The fire beneath the stove was burning low. Pots and pans stood upon the oven top. A kettle hissed as though in its last extremity. James lifted a pan lid to find a blackened sticky mess sizzling at the bottom. The kettle gave up the struggle and expired with a gasp and a death rattle of pops and crackles.

The galley was hot and the smell of burning flesh rose like a sacrifice. He stepped back on to deck just as the starboard door beneath the poop opened and a wild-eyed apparition appeared. It wore a frock coat and a floppy black hat. Crazed eyes stared out from behind a monstrous halo of red beard that swept down to its chest. The wide mouth slobbered.

"Abomination! Satan!" it thundered in good Yankee New England accents. "Beelzebub! Spawn of the devil! He called, Lord. He called upon thine afflicted one! Yeah, his voice was that of brazen trumpets and his words were tongues of fire! They that forsake the Lord shall bow down in worship before Baal and Ashtorath! Now, know ye all by these present that I, Thomas, Captain of thousands, Master of men, afflicted of the Lord of Hosts for the sin of corruption, the sin of the flesh, the sins of Babylon, do hereby declare to all men of good faith, that the Day of Judgment is nigh." The madman's voice rose to a howl and James saw that he carried a bible in one hand and an ancient brass-bound cap-and-ball pistol in the other. The pistol rose at the full length of the lunatic's arm until the muzzle seemed as wide as the mouth of a cannon.

"Get thee from my sight, Satan," screeched the maniac, and pulled the trigger.

There was a flash and a boom and a cloud of smoke and the pistol ball whined and whispered its tiny message in James's ear before thunking into the mast beside his head.

The smoke blew away and the insane eyes stared at James.

"Thy Will be done," said Captain Joseph Thomas, stepped to the taffrail and launched himself over the side. His head appeared once above the surface of the water. "Lucifer!" it howled. "Lucifer!"

James saw the boat rowing furiously

toward the spot where the madman disappeared, then turned and hurried below.

The saloon had been wrecked, furnishings torn and smashed to pieces. An axe was buried almost to the hilt in the dining table. The pantry shutters had been torn from their hinges and plates and crockery lay in shattered heaps on the deck.

At either side of the saloon were fore-and-aft alleyways which housed the staterooms. James heard a whimpering coming from behind a door. He tapped. The whimpering stopped. He tapped again. There was a sound of movement, a voice "shushed", then there was silence.

"It's all right," said James. "All clear. He's gone now."

The whimpering started again and was quickly stifled.

James scratched at his brain for fragments of Portuguese.

"Proteccao," he called through the door. "Sao e salvo. You can come out," he shouted. "There is nothing to fear."

A key turned slowly in the lock and the door opened a crack. A woman's face appeared.

"Socorro?" she asked. "Socorro?"

James stepped back and spread his arms like a magician demonstrating that there was nothing up his sleeves.

"Socorro," he repeated. "Safe and sound."

The door opened wider. The woman, he saw, was olive-skinned, plump, and about thirty years of age. Her hair hung down, she had large liquid eyes and a bruise upon one cheek. A trickle of blood had dried at the corner of her mouth. She was, he thought thankfully, more frightened than hurt. He peered past her into the room. Two children were huddled in the furthest corner, round-eyed and rigid with terror; a boy and girl of about the same age.

James smiled ingratiatingly at the woman. "Mae ?" he asked. "Mother ?" and pointed to the children: "Gémeos ? Twins ? Yours ? You, mother, children ? You Mrs. Tomas, maybe ?"

Her answer was to screech and tear her hair in a paroxysm of hysteria.

James held out his hands making pushing motions. "Wait," he said in alarm. "Wait. Me come back. Yes ?" and turned tail and scampered back to the deck above.

It was self-evident, he thought, lowering the companion ladder for the others; the Yankee Captain had gone off his head and run amok. Too much religion, no doubt. It was a common enough affliction and by no means the first time that in combination with the loneliness of command it had driven men mad.

"We could not save him. He drowned," said Braganza as he and Diaz came aboard.

James grunted and led them below.

The woman sat in the wreck of the saloon, her head buried in her arms and the two children clutching her skirts.

Braganza spoke to her softly and swiftly.

"She is the wife of the American Captain," he confirmed. "The man has been behaving strangely for some time. Paid off the crew, pulled up the gangway and claimed he was waiting for a visitation."

"Ask her," said James, "if she wants to sell the ship."

Braganza stared at him. "You cannot be serious! At such a time?"

"Why not?" said James calmly. "She is now the owner, and that is the purpose of our visit."

"I could not possibly take advantage of

the lady under such circumstances," said Braganza, angrily.

"I said nothing of taking advantage," said James, exasperated at the intrusion of sentiment into a perfectly clear-cut business deal. "You can accommodate both our consciences by paying a fair price. Remember, my friend, without the ship you will go to perdition as sure as her husband."

"I cannot. And no man of honour would expect me to."

"Sentiment," said James. "You may be prepared to pay a high price for the luxury, but I am not."

"Sentiment!" cried Braganza. "You call it sentiment?"

"Yes. And you are allowing it to cloud your judgment. All we require to know," he explained with as much patience as he could muster, "is whether the woman wants to sell. If she does not, there is no more to be said. If she does, we can settle the financial arrangements later when she is recovered. Confound it, man," he snapped, "We shall be doing her a favour. Do you think it a kindness to add financial worries to the rest of her misery? Once this matter becomes common knowledge she will be at the mercy of every usurer and shark on the waterfront. Ask her, dammit. Ask her a simple question. I think you will find," he added drily, "that it will have a more soothing effect than you imagine. I shall take a turn on deck while you think it over."

The purchase price of £9,500 was agreed upon two days later in the presence of the sorrowing widow, her attorney and Senhor Diaz. The lady, James noticed, seemed to have recovered sufficiently to fully comprehend the bargaining power of tragedy and drama, and was not so distressed that she could not itemise every piece of cutlery aboard ship.

James arranged for a Portuguese captain to return with the *Charlotte Rhodes*. Then he, Anne and Baines boarded the *Pampero*.

Baines surveyed the ship with pride.

"She's the sauciest vessel I ever did sail aboard," he said.

"You must drive her, Mr. Baines," said James. "Drive her hard. I want a fast passage."

"You shall have one, sir," said Baines.

"I'll lick 'em into shape never fear." He balefully eyed the Portuguese crew idling about the decks. "A new crew and heathens to a man, no doubt. But I'll haze 'em, sir. Before this day is out they'll be running up and down the rigging like organ-grinders' monkeys." He cupped his hands to his mouth: "Move, you dozy, sleepy-headed farmers! Move!"

One or two of the crew gazed at him blankly, grinned and shrugged their shoulders.

"Going to play that game, are they?" growled Baines. "No spikka da English, eh?" He picked up the speaking trumpet and bellowed: "Movam-se depressed, seus porcos, ou esfolos-os vivos! Movam-se ou espanco-os por um! Quero este convez tao branco como a face da minha mai!"

The hands stared in horror then scuttled about their work as though pursued by the Devil himself.

Baines replaced the trumpet and grinned at James who was staring at the linguist in surprise.

"I picked up the elements of the lingo while serving aboard a Portuguese whaler, sir."

"Hrrmph," said James. "Carry on, Mr. Baines. The deck is yours."

"Aye, aye, sir," responded Baines.

The last of the lightermen dropped over the side. The carpenter and his mate were busily battening down the hatches. On the fo'c'sle head the handspikes were shipped into the capstan pigeon holes, the crew breasted the bars and began their shuffling walk-and-heave around the trundlehead. The cable rattled link by link through the hawse pipe. A hundred and fifty feet above the deck the foretop men and maintop men, strung out along the yards, released the robands securing the sails to the backstays. On deck below, the heavy-gang hauled on the halyards; the yards rattled up and the topsails caught the wind, filled, and the ship started to slide through the water, easing the strain on the anchor cable. The men at the capstan bars tramped more quickly round the capstan. The anchor rose from the water, the ship leaned forward and reached for the open sea.

Baines, standing on the poop deck beside the helmsman, surreptitiously took a crumpled sheet of paper from his pocket.

His lips moved slowly. "The cat — sat — on — the — mat. The cat sat on the mat," he repeated in quiet triumph.

THE END

The story of the Onedin Line will be continued in another volume.

This book is published under the auspices of the

ULVERSCROFT FOUNDATION,

a registered charity, whose primary object is to assist those who experience difficulty in reading print of normal size.

In response to approaches from the medical world, the Foundation is also helping to purchase the latest, most sophisticated medical equipment desperately needed by major eye hospitals for the diagnosis and treatment of eye diseases.

If you would like to know more about the

ULVERSCROFT FOUNDATION,

and how you can help to further its work, please write for details to:

THE ULVERSCROFT FOUNDATION
The Green, Bradgate Road
Anstey
Leicestershire
England

FICTION TITLES IN THE ULVERSCROFT LARGE PRINT SERIES

Wyatt's Hurricane	*Desmond Bagley*
Landslide	*Desmond Bagley*
The Spoilers	*Desmond Bagley*
Green Hand	*Lillian Beckwith*
A Man of His Time	*Phyllis Bentley*
The Episode at Toledo	*Ann Bridge*
Letter from Peking	*Pearl S. Buck*
The New Year	*Pearl S. Buck*
Mandala	*Pearl S. Buck*
The Three Daughters of Madame Liang	*Pearl S. Buck*
The Melting Man	*Victor Canning*
The Green Fields of Eden	*Francis Clifford*
The Long Corridor	*Catherine Cookson*
The Unbaited Trap	*Catherine Cookson*
Hannah Massey	*Catherine Cookson*
Love and Mary Ann	*Catherine Cookson*
Fanny McBride	*Catherine Cookson*
Kate Hannigan	*Catherine Cookson*
The Menagerie	*Catherine Cookson*
The Nice Bloke	*Catherine Cookson*
A Song of Sixpence	*A. J. Cronin*
A Pocketful of Rye	*A. J. Cronin*
Shannon's Way	*A. J. Cronin*

The Green Years — *A. J. Cronin*
Flowers on the Grass — *Monica Dickens*
Mariana — *Monica Dickens*
Magnificent Obsession — *Lloyd C. Douglas*
My Friend My Father — *Jane Duncan*
The Bird in the Chimney — *Dorothy Eden*
Hornblower in the West Indies — *C. S. Forester*
The Ship — *C. S. Forester*
Flying Colours — *C. S. Forester*
The Gun — *C. S. Forester*
Blood Sport — *Dick Francis*
For Kicks — *Dick Francis*
Rat Race — *Dick Francis*
Bonecrack — *Dick Francis*
Flowers for Mrs. Harris and Mrs. Harris goes to New York — *Paul Gallico*
Love, Let Me Not Hunger — *Paul Gallico*
Edge of Glass — *Catherine Gaskin*
The Swan River Story — *Phyllis Hastings*
Sandals for My Feet — *Phyllis Hastings*
The Stars are My Children — *Phyllis Hastings*
Beauvallet — *Georgette Heyer*
The Convenient Marriage — *Georgette Heyer*
Faro's Daughter — *Georgette Heyer*
Charity Girl — *Georgette Heyer*

Devil's Cub	*Georgette Heyer*
The Corinthian	*Georgette Heyer*
The Toll-Gate	*Georgette Heyer*
Black Sheep	*Georgette Heyer*
The Talisman Ring	*Georgette Heyer*
Bride of Pendorric	*Victoria Holt*
Mistress of Mellyn	*Victoria Holt*
Menfreya	*Victoria Holt*
Kirkland Revels	*Victoria Holt*
The Shivering Sands	*Victoria Holt*
The Legend of the Seventh Virgin	*Victoria Holt*
The Shadow of the Lynx	*Victoria Holt*
Wreckers Must Breathe	*Hammond Innes*
The Strange Land	*Hammond Innes*
Maddon's Rock	*Hammond Innes*
The White South	*Hammond Innes*
Atlantic Fury	*Hammond Innes*
The Land God Gave to Cain	*Hammond Innes*
Levkas Man	*Hammond Innes*
The Strode Venturer	*Hammond Innes*
The Wreck of the Mary Deare	*Hammond Innes*
The Lonely Skier	*Hammond Innes*
Blue Ice	*Hammond Innes*
Golden Soak	*Hammond Innes*
The River of Diamonds	*Geoffrey Jenkins*

A Twist of Sand	*Geoffrey Jenkins*
Scend of the Sea	*Geoffrey Jenkins*
The Safe Bridge	*Frances Parkinson Keyes*
The Brittle Glass	*Norah Lofts*
Scent of Cloves	*Norah Lofts*
Decision at Delphi	*Helen MacInnes*
North from Rome	*Helen MacInnes*
Horizon	*Helen MacInnes*
The Golden Rendezvous	*Alistair MacLean*
Puppet on a Chain	*Alistair MacLean*
Caravan to Vaccares	*Alistair MacLean*
Night Without End	*Alistair MacLean*
The Satan Bug	*Alistair MacLean*
Where Eagles Dare	*Alistair MacLean*
When Eight Bells Toll	*Alistair MacLean*
Bear Island	*Alistair MacLean*
The Guns of Navarone	*Alistair MacLean*
The Painted Veil	*W. Somerset Maugham*
The Flight of the Falcon	*Daphne du Maurier*
Frenchman's Creek	*Daphne du Maurier*
The House on the Strand	*Daphne du Maurier*
Valley of the Vines	*Joy Packer*
Mission in Tunis	*Jacques Pendower*
The Barefoot Mailman	*Theodore Pratt*
Dragonwyck	*Anya Seton*
So Disdained	*Nevil Shute*

An Old Captivity	*Nevil Shute*
A Savage Place	*Frank G. Slaughter*
Cup of Gold	*John Steinbeck*
To a God Unknown	*John Steinbeck*
The Moon-Spinners	*Mary Stewart*
Airs Above the Ground	*Mary Stewart*
Madam, Will You Talk?	*Mary Stewart*
This Rough Magic	*Mary Stewart*
The Gabriel Hounds	*Mary Stewart*
Wildfire at Midnight	*Mary Stewart*
Thunder on the Right	*Mary Stewart*
Nine Coaches Waiting	*Mary Stewart*
A Many-Splendoured Thing	*Han Suyin*
The Big Story	*Morris West*
The Second Victory	*Morris West*
The Devil's Advocate	*Morris West*

NON-FICTION TITLES IN THE ULVERSCROFT LARGE PRINT SERIES

Nurse of the Islands	*B. J. Banfill*
A Rope – In Case	*Lillian Beckwith*
The Sea for Breakfast	*Lillian Beckwith*
Lightly Poached	*Lillian Beckwith*
The Small Woman	*Alan Burgess*
Adventures in Two Worlds	*A. J. Cronin*
Finding My Way	*Borghild Dahl*
Three Singles to Adventure	*Gerald Durrell*
I Bought a Mountain	*Thomas Firbank*
Trigger in Europe	*William Holt*
The Bears and I	*Robert Franklin Leslie*
Ring of Bright Water	*Gavin Maxwell*
Road from Singapore	*Diana Norman*
Drums Along the Amazon	*Victor G. C. Norwood*
Patients in My Care	*Bridget Ristori*
Place of Stones	*Ruth Janette Ruck*
Rex	*Joyce Stranger*
Antique Dealer	*R. P. Way*

THE SHADOWS OF THE CROWN TITLES IN THE ULVERSCROFT LARGE PRINT SERIES

The Tudor Rose — *Margaret Campbell Barnes*
The King's Pleasure — *Norah Lofts*
Brief Gaudy Hour — *Margaret Campbell Barnes*
Mistress Jane Seymour — *Frances B. Clark*
My Lady of Cleves — *Margaret Campbell Barnes*
Katheryn the Wanton Queen — *Maureen Peters*
The Sixth Wife — *Jean Plaidy*
The Last Tudor King — *Hester Chapman*
Young Bess — *Margaret Irwin*
Lady Jane Grey — *Hester Chapman*
Elizabeth, Captive Princess — *Margaret Irwin*
Elizabeth and the Prince of Spain — *Margaret Irwin*
Gay Lord Robert — *Jean Plaidy*
Here Was A Man — *Norah Lofts*
Mary Queen of Scotland: The Triumphant Year — *Jean Plaidy*
The Captive Queen of Scots — *Jean Plaidy*
The Murder in the Tower — *Jean Plaidy*
The Young & Lonely King — *Jane Lane*

King's Adversary *Monica Beardsworth*
A Call of Trumpets *Jane Lane*
The Trial of Charles I *C. V. Wedgwood*
Royal Flush *Margaret Irwin*
The Sceptre and the Rose *Doris Leslie*
Mary II: Queen of England *Hester Chapman*
That Enchantress *Doris Leslie*
The Princess of Celle *Jean Plaidy*
Caroline the Queen *Jean Plaidy*
The Third George *Jean Plaidy*
The Great Corinthian *Doris Leslie*
Victoria in the Wings *Jean Plaidy*
The Captive of Kensington Palace *Jean Plaidy*
The Queen and Lord 'M' *Jean Plaidy*
The Queen's Husband *Jean Plaidy*
The Widow of Windsor *Jean Plaidy*
Bertie and Alix *Graham & Heather Fisher*
The Duke of Windsor *Ursula Bloom*